# PACTUM

## Memoir of a Traitor

## AJ Roberts

Orange Hat Publishing
www.orangehatpublishing.com - Waukesha, WI

www.orangehatpublishing.com

To my friends and family,
past lovers and the lost, those
colleagues, confidantes, and patient
professionals who inspired these
characters . . .

. . . and the special few who helped
them build a home.

*Thank you.*

*July 4th 2018. Les Ambassadeurs, Hôtel de Crillon, Paris.*

*Nearly twenty years in the business was enough. I was tired. Too tired to even use the word accurately anymore, but ready to take my first cautious steps into the light. It would be nice to be Alex Hope again. I ran a finger around the rim of my glass deciding how best to dissect the situation. It would be sensible to start with the basics. Baby steps.*

*"People think the stock market is complicated, numbers whizzing around and supercomputers racing to find the next boom, but there is no sense in it. You'll have less hair than me by the time you realize some spotty teenager in Baltimore beat you to it by reprogramming his PlayStation and stealing daddy's credit card. The market, above all, is about people and the ways we play them against the trade."*

*"Playing people?" Hamilton interrupted, the impatience of his age shining through.*

*"Yes. Human beings are wonderfully predictable in their reactions. Trying to guess what any given individual will do next is almost impossible, free will being the bastard that it is, but if you give them something to respond to then 90% will react the same way. Nature takes over. Wildebeest running back from the river, leaving the weak and naïve to get slaughtered." He had his head down, scribbling every word in his dog-eared notepad. I leant across the table and prodded his water glass off balance to see his hand thrust out and catch it just in time. "You see, the second you saw that you reacted. The market is no different."*

"I don't understand, if people react the same way then who profits?"

"The people who see it first or, in my case, the people who know beforehand exactly when the glass is going to be pushed. Understand this, if a Middle Eastern country is invaded then oil prices rise. If a gas pipeline is severed due to political differences in Eastern Europe, then energy companies splutter with the rising cost of fuel. If cars get recalled, then equities in the manufacturer plummet. Liquidity problems at a bank will do the same. It's all a matter of the companies and their shareholders reacting to things outside of their control: scandal, opportunity, or disaster. Sometimes, you need only a rumour to topple an empire."

Hamilton put down the pad and rolled his eyes. "That's insider trading or…or…market manipulation. Even I know that's illegal in both our countries." I smiled and took a sip of my Montgomery.

"Not when I do it."

"Okay, then why now? Why me?" I took a long pause wondering if I should spin some great tale of morality or simply tell the truth. It had been a while. I answered.

"Him."

*March 1st, 1999. London.*

The radio squawked into life with more volume than was necessary for a Monday morning, with some teenage songstress bouncing round my ears asking to be hit one more time. I was feeling delicate, overcome with the sort of hangover that required a damp cloth to coax my eyes open. Sunday drinking seems like such an innocent idea at the time, but never in hindsight. Back then I had my own little patch of London alongside the Albert Bridge and that day, like many before, I girded up my pyjamas to venture outside: sitting on the balcony in my dressing gown, rubbing my head, and self-medicating with tobacco and ibuprofen.

"Silly, silly boy. How many times do you have to repeat this journey?" I asked, knowing full well the answer was always "once more." Gagging on a cigarette, I watched as a lonely tug pootled down the river like a weary traveller, his engine throbbing almost as loudly as my head. I sympathized with his struggle and staggered back inside to escape the ensuing drizzle. Strong coffee was required. I waited impatiently for the espresso machine to spit out my salvation, swaying back and forth and pleading for the sluggish fucker to hurry up. It always felt like such an effort for so little reward. Some colleagues still championed a powdering of the nose as a more efficient pick-me-up, but I couldn't stomach it in the morning. It had been my experience that cocaine needed something to balance it, usually a brunette or a Bordeaux, but management had recently deemed it unprofessional to seek either before lunch. Most now put their trust in the more time-consuming alternative.

Many deep breaths and two shots later I cocooned myself in a hot shower with the breakfast radio bleating from the next room as I steamed out the toxins. While the water beat down on my hastily thinning hair, washing away the malaise of the morning, I was slowly beginning to feel human. The radio was transformed. It grew from annoyance to cheerleader as I applied my façade for the working day to the beat of the 6:30 news jingle, each step as important as the headlines they accompanied. Honed over several years, it was a well-practiced routine and always performed in the same order, starting with a shave and finishing with eye drops. It was a matter of personal pride that no matter what I'd done the night before, I always arrived at the office looking my best. Luckily, that youthful dedication lasted just slightly longer than the exuberance that made it necessary. When final pre-flight checks were complete, I could raise a smile in the mirror, supported by a double Windsor knot, and cut with a freshly starched collar. A poster boy for the city ambitious.

It was a relatively short walk from the flat to the Sloane Square tube but seemed twice its usual length in darker months. Largely thanks to the wind fighting against me and the extra vigilance required to avoid the disastrous mating of puddles and tyres. People often write how you can feel the pulse of a city, or hear it breathing. If London were described in such ways, she would be an asthmatic suffering acute tachycardia: her heartbeat the clattering of railway tracks and her breathing the constant wheeze from the pitter-patter of rain and marching feet. Charlie, my close friend and colleague, was meeting me at Waterloo before riding the tube to Bank, something we would do most days depending on our schedules. It's quite fascinating for those who enjoy people watching, a strange combination of optimism and palpable misery. Little wonder that short line was known as "The Drain".

Charlie was his usual self. Floppy brown hair and cheeky smile, oozing self-confidence and somehow managing to make a wrinkled shirt and stained tie look fashionable. He greeted me with stories of his debauched weekend and continued as we followed the herd into the depths of the station. I was relieved when we finally reached the platform as some respite was in sight.

"…and that girl yesterday, from Geneva, your jaw would have hit the floor!"

"I know. I was there."

"Were you? Sorry my friend, I must have had more than I thought."

"I certainly had more than I intended."

Blissfully we were able to squeeze onto the next carriage, immediately adhering to the unwritten rule of the London underground: Nobody talks. Out of habit my eyes wandered the carriage to examine my stable mates for that morning. The competition is immediately obvious; younger people, questionably dressed and modelling hairstyles reminiscent of a glossy-paged magazine. Then you have the old boys, well past retirement age but still working because they gambled their pension on a "sure thing" or still had ex-wives to fund. Charlie and I sat neatly between those two groups, young blood but old money. The carriages on the tube jolt back and forth with changing speed and over time you develop an acute sense of balance. I marvelled at the seasoned professionals: coffee in one hand, paper in the other and swaying or bracing at just the right moment to maintain their composure. I hadn't reached that level by that time and resigned myself to maintaining three points of contact, keeping an arm free to stop my face smacking a window. After pulling into Bank we'd follow the herd up the stairs and escalators before emerging outside the Bank of England, spat out of its bowls like the thousands of others every day on a conveyor belt of white collar gamblers sure of starting a new streak. The city itself is delightfully grand and historic, a far cry from most casinos, but the stonework doesn't appreciate the rain. Its tone turns a miserable colour when wet, leaving us with a full greyscale cityscape; from tarmac roads to concrete pavements, up the Greystone buildings to an overcast sky. Enough to drop seasonal depression on the most cheerful of beginners.

With everyone jostling for space on the pavement, even the short walk down Old Broad Street to our office could be quite treacherous. It's not the weather that's the problem, it's the umbrellas. When people stop in the middle of the pavement a stray spine can easily take an eye out. Being a man of below average height, I was relatively secure under my own brolly unless someone even shorter crossed my path. Charlie wasn't so lucky. Not only was he well north of six foot (the perfect height to be skewered), but he never remembered his umbrella. On the plus side it was probably the closest he'd come to a shower in days.

The 35th floor of The Tower was home to SC Securities. An office blessed with a view from Lloyds to Aldgate, with the continuing squabble over St. Mary Axe playing out dead centre. It had been several years since the bombing and the future of the area remained a topic of heated debate. Charlie finished bringing me up to speed on his nocturnal antics with all the tact of a town crier just as we stepped off the lift and Bridget at reception handed me my morning paper. Charlie went to dry off and I made my way across the floor passed rows of Bloomberg boxes and bravado. It's hard to explain the feeling of a trading floor to those who have never experienced it, but after I begrudgingly accepted an internship in my penultimate year of university, I was hooked. You can feel the tension build the closer you get to the open, like waiting for kick-off at a cup final. Some small talk, plenty of back slapping, and most importantly, catching the word on the street: where did the DOW close, how's the NIKKEI been this morning, oil, gold, etcetera. Cash is changing hands between colleagues over the weekend's football results, and fresh wagers are being made for the week to come. When the city opened up during the Thatcher years the playground mentality came with it. Everyone has a name, it's visible on business cards, but most people don't use it. Instead you get stuck with a nickname that remains with you your entire career. It makes sense in some ways. If you're calling a market maker where there are three people name Richard, it's easier to ask for "Titch" than to use a full name. At the same time, I always felt sorry for one of our colleagues who went by the name "Tits". I'm sure I don't need to explain where it came from. It was still a male-dominated game, but there were those women who managed to rise above the testosterone and certainly gave as good as they got.

Having spent two summers making coffees and photocopying, Charlie and I had joined the bank full time after graduation. Six years later we were still relatively close to the bottom of the food chain, fighting to push our way ahead at every opportunity, or at least I was. Having his family name, Smyth-Cummin, above the front door left Charlie lackadaisical on occasion, especially on Mondays. We sat in a row quite far back from the door but close enough to Stephen Gatley's office, the head of trading, so he could keep an eye on us. Originally, we would spend a few hours a week with Stephen to go over our progress; there was always more to learn and people to meet, with more importance being attached to the latter. These days it was usually just a few minutes if he caught us in the lift. Stephen had been with SC for longer than anyone else in the city and was immensely proud of his humble beginnings in East London. He would tell fresh graduates that he grew up with an outhouse in his garden and, frankly, he was built like one: shoulders broad enough to fill the door frame and a chin like an anvil. He could be quite intimidating when he wanted to be, which was most of the time.

"Black and sweet for you, my friend," said a freshly dry Charlie, plonking our coffee cups down between us.

"Why don't you ever bring your brolly?" I asked for the umpteenth time.

"I like to start the day feeling mildly moist." I still hate that word. He insisted on using it as often as possible for that very reason.

"You're an idiot."

"Possibly, but that's why you love me. I make you feel special." He patted the top of my head, prompting my hand to strike upwards like I was fending off a fly. Irritating bugger.

I was logging in and glancing over my emails from Friday afternoon through the weekend when apart from trade confirmations and complaints from the back office, I spotted one from Charlie's father, David, current CEO and Chairman of SC securities. SC maintained its small head office in the St. James area of London, home to analysts and board members, but Old Broad Street was the major hub in the modern age. David's email was a blast to all employees detailing the immediate retirement of one of our research team in St. James. Nothing of great importance to us in the city, people come and go throughout the year for various reasons and its normal to only learn about it after the fact. I didn't even read to the end of the first line.

The screens began to flash and flicker as the volume on the floor notched up. The whole office rushed to life and people shouted across the floor with phones wedged against either ear. The game was on. It was like we had a seat at the world's largest roulette table and got to play with other people's money. It was a "win-win" back in those days, client wins then we win, client loses then we apologise and carry on regardless. I remember it was a great start to the week, the market was strong, and I don't think we closed out any positions for a loss that morning. During the lunchtime lull Stephen stepped out of his office and clapped his hands for attention.

"Drinks and nibbles for Jimmy's send-off across the street at the close."

I had no idea what he was talking about but was sure Charlie would. He was much closer to the senior figures. Not only had he been coming to SC since he was a small boy, but while I spent my days working for smaller clients Charlie would sometimes handle orders directly from his father. He was on the phone so I shrugged my shoulders at him, he tapped on my computer screen at the email blast I had ignored from that morning. I opened it again to pay it the attention it apparently deserved. After the initial line announcing the 'retirement' it gave a brief explanation:

"…after a short battle with illness, Mr. P. Jayms passed away on Friday…"

I still didn't know who it was referring to. Hardly surprising if he was based in St. James. The only one who ever came down to the city was Charlie's father for Wednesday meetings. Once Charlie was free, he helpfully intervened. "Jimmy" had been with the firm for thirty years, first in the exchange, then the city office before moving up to St. James. A number of the longer-term members of our office would have known him well. I thought I remembered meeting him once during my internship but couldn't be certain. No matter, I thought, would raise a glass to him anyway. The office started to thin towards the close, more and more migrating across the street as soon as they could, eager to take advantage of an open bar. Charlie was obviously among them, but I stayed behind until the market closed and I had taken care of my paperwork.

I had been expecting a sombre mood when I joined everyone else at Corney & Barrow, but was wrong. I couldn't decide if this was because people were celebrating a life or celebrating his death, one usually preferable to the other. I mingled and chatted with colleagues to try to ascertain which it was. Those who had spent time with him in the city office had fond memories of the man, but nobody had seen him since the move. I continued to work the room before eventually catching up with Charlie, who was leaning over the bar, desperate to fill as many glasses as he could before Stephen called time.

"Nice of you to show up."

"We all have a job to do. You know I don't like to play at the start of the week."

"Yes, but WE still came over earlier than you did. Busy polishing Stephen's apple were you, or was it his plumbs?"

"Hardly, he came over before me."

Charlie was the one who had the height, jawline, and smile to grab the attention of barmaids with ease. It made him very useful at social events. I knew as long as I stayed within chatting distance, he would make sure my glass was full. I didn't understand the makeshift wake we were having for someone who seemed to have distanced himself from everyone in our office. Charlie gave me a simple and somewhat insulting answer: "Officers don't mix with regulars." It was rich coming from him, since he had only spent one week in the army cadets at school before quitting over a refusal to sleep under a poncho. As was always the case at a company-funded reception, someone had already had too much: Stuart, Stephen's right hand man. He didn't really mix with most of the floor but spent his time in Stephens office planning some of our largest transactions. They had always worked together and meshed well, despite being total opposites. Stuart was a family man who quietly did his job, while Stephen (at twice his size and twice the personality) was married to his work. Usually so calm and collected, Stuart was instead tripping over his feet to get to the bar. Falling into the back of me he physically hauled himself up on my coattails.

"This is a fucking joke, absolute fucking joke," he slurred into my ear.

"They're doing their best, I don't think they expected it to be this busy on a Monday."

He smiled at me with glazed almost teary eyes, slapping his hand onto my shoulder.

"You have no idea, do you? Not a fucking clue. You just skip along your gilded pavements thinking the world is your oyster." I humoured him with a few 'okays' and friendly agreements, hoping he would take his brand of crazy somewhere else, but he continued "Jimmy was one of the good guys, you know?"

"Yes, lovely chap. He'll be sorely missed."

"By who? By fucking who?!" His raised voice brought Charlie to the rescue, who pointed a drink in his direction.

"Here you go Stu, one more for the road." Stuart looked at the glass then back at Charlie with a grimace on his face. Rather than take the glass he slapped it out of Charlie's hand and it shattered across the floor. Neither of them said anything. Just when it looked like the standoff would be broken with a scuffle, Stephen came from behind and put his arm securely around Stuart.

"Come on then mate, think it's time you found a taxi."

Stuart kept his eyes fixed on Charlie as he was shepherded away. He shrugged off Stephen's attempts at help and staggered out into the street.

"We've all got to let our hair down sometimes, boys," quipped Stephen in defence of his colleague. I hadn't planned on staying much longer considering the delicacy with which I had started the day. Charlie had gone to powder his nose, so I gathered my things and finished my drink. When he came back still sniffing and wiping his top lip, he tried persuading me to stay.

"Bertie is going to stop by for a jar, you should stick around."

"Not tonight, I'll catch up with him another time."

"Suit yourself, my friend."

As I walked back towards the station, a crowd was swarming

on the corner. Typical of any large city, if there's an accident of some sort it takes one person to call 999 and thirty more to stand and watch. I crossed the street to avoid the fuss and thought nothing more of it. I should have paid closer attention.

\* \* \* \* \*

"We need to ramp it up, things are moving quicker than planned and we're two men down."

"I agree, we have the one primed but the second needs work."

Charlie looked the worse for wear the following morning. Dressed in exactly the same clothes as the night before, smelling like the dawn floor of a nightclub, and staggering in just before the carnage was unleashed for the open. He grabbed the emergency air freshener from his desk and gave himself a quick spritz, more for the benefit of his neighbours than himself. It would do enough to mask his odour in the short term. I fetched the coffee that morning, feeling duty-bound to return the favour he afforded me the previous day, and hoped it would nurture him into some sort of professional before the phones started ringing. Just then, Stephen marched out of his office and boomed like an open-collared cockney silverback, "Gentlemen and ladies! Welcome to Tuesday! The word for today is 'oil'. The order from the top is to bring in the black, BUY BUY BUY!" He was waving towards himself with his hands in a nostalgic gesture to the days of open outcry. SC had a reputation for being able to catch a falling knife, buying just at the bottom, so on the rare occasion Stephen stepped out with a specific instruction we all paid attention. I was reaching for my phone when he turned his attention to Charlie and me.

"You two. My office."

It reminded me of being called out by a teacher at school, where the immediate reaction is to think, *what have I done wrong?* Stephen was the only man who could get away without wearing a tie in the office, but he was still enough of a traditionalist to insist everyone wore a jacket when they weren't sat at a desk. So, we got our jackets and gave each other a nervous glance before stepping inside. Stephen closed the door behind us and perched on the edge of his desk, peering beyond our shoulders through the glass before deciding to lower the blinds for extra privacy.

"What's my job, boys?"

I sat in silence, wondering if it was a trick question. Charlie was the first to pipe up, "Head of trading?"

"No shit Sherlock, but what does that entail?"

Charlie sat there with the same confused look on his face that I had seen countless times at school. Shuffling in my seat, I did my best to salvage the situation.

"To oversee and manage the floor while maintaining your own book?"

"Close enough…I started in this business when you two were still figuring out the best way to wipe your arse, or in your case who was going to do it for you," he snipped, targeting his bile at Charlie. "I have spent my entire career here and seen a lot of changes, not only in house but with the industry as a whole, and always come out stronger. Not only am I fucking good at what I do, but I make this whole floor look far better than they actually are." He stopped, expecting either applause or argument, but we knew better than to open our mouths any more than necessary. "Anyway, I have been told that you two are going to take some of the pressure off me so I can focus on babysitting that lot out there." He jabbed his finger towards the door, plainly displeased with the idea. "Stu is going to be taking some time away, so I'm going to need both of you to step up. Your regular accounts will be split between Tits and Biggy and you will only work the orders I give you. Stick to the limits. Don't try and be clever and most importantly, don't fuck it up. Got it?" We both nodded in agreement. "Right, you heard me this morning; we're going for oil. You two are going to focus on BP and Shell. Charlie you've already been working this so can stick with your RDSB, limit 1100, you know the score. Alex you're on BP, limit 450. I want you to fill this in tranches of 100,000 pieces and spread them over these fifty accounts. Iceberg it." He handed me a file and continued his instruction. "Our goal is to open as large a position as possible, without moving the market or giving away our game plan. Play smart and spread the love around. I'm happy for you to pick up calls but steer clear of bonds, I don't trust your maths. I'll see your trades every morning and will tell you when to stop, if I don't tell you to stop, just keeping buying. Any questions?"

Charlie stepped up. "How do you want us to handle moving out our old accounts?"

"Already been taken care of, and before you ask, no, this won't fuck your bonus. Do this right and you'll be laughing. Anything else?"

Stephen opened the door and Charlie left first. Before I got out of the door I thought of one question I did want to ask. "Sorry Stephen, but with us dealing on fifty accounts, can I ask how many clients are we actually talking about here?"

"Does it matter? Your orders will only come from me." I didn't want to push the subject, but as I made my way back to my desk his voice followed me. "Alex...one. Just one."

With that, his door closed, and we had a job to do. We were buying 100,000 shares at a time, with the only limit being how high our price could go. We couldn't just jump in and buy them all at once, since that would get a bad price and possibly move the market, so we would "iceberg" the order per his instructions: like an iceberg hides most of its mass under the water line, we would only be showing our "peak" ten thousand or so shares on the book at a time. I immediately started checking the pricing and graphs for BP. We made no comment on Stuart's absence, totally focussed on our own situations. It may seem selfish to the unfamiliar, but the city is a fickle place where only the strongest survive. Burnout is common, and Stuart was a textbook case.

The volumes were decent and the opening price from that morning was comfortably within my limit, progress was quick, and you can achieve much more when not worrying about multiple clients or stocks. I was so absorbed in the task that I didn't even notice Charlie leaving for lunch, but he gave me nudge on his return.

"You haven't moved since I left."

"Huh, what? No, I've got a lot to do."

"No, WE don't. We just keep going until we're told to stop. This isn't sports day, it's not possible to finish first."

"You deal with it your way, I'll deal with it mine. Would you mind grabbing me a sandwich when you go for lunch?"

"I've already been! Take your eyes off the screen for a second and you might've noticed. Here, I got you some chocolate instead."

"Cheers." I finally turned away from my computer. "How was Bertie last night? Heavy one?" I asked before tucking into the Mars bar.

"He's always the heavy one, my friend. On good form though. We're working on a little side project together." Bertie Kirkman worked in wealth management, with a waistline to match. Charlie and he would pair up now and again for mutual benefit, passing clients back and forth or filling in the other's shortcomings. Charlie may not be the sharpest knife in the drawer, but he was great with people. His success at university was largely down to trading favours with Bertie or myself in exchange for academic help. While I had learned from Charlie's example and built up my social side, Bertie remained quite firmly at the other end of the spectrum.

I had almost finished my first 30 tranches by the end of that second day, putting 60,000 or so shares in each account, averaging the price at 441. As time went on, I pushed harder and came dangerously close to moving the market. Desperate to impress management I still knew I'd have to step back, much to my frustration. Hampered by the constraints of both Stephen and the market, the stresses started taking their toll.

\* \* \* \* \*

"He won't be back."

"It's for the best. Be sure to send flowers."

A few repetitive but focussed weeks later I was stood outside a pub in Leadenhall enjoying some well-earned drinks. Baggy-eyed and running on a diet of coffee and...well...other things, I would have been better off in bed, but my friends had other plans. Charlie and Bertie had finally coaxed me out to the pub, unhappy with how antisocial I'd become since the new project. We were joined by another friend from university, Rupert Folks. We all worked in the city in some capacity, and Rupert was at a large accounting firm with a strong grip on a future in mergers and acquisitions (affectionately referred to as "Murders and Executions"). Charlie and Rupert were telling tales and I was trying my best to mentally drag myself away from my desk. Between the faux machismo and one-word compliments of the conversation I had time to appreciate the splendour of my surroundings, the beauty of the gilded arches and grand lighting. I'd rarely paid them any mind before. Not a bad place to pass the time, but I was still running the orders in my head. The weeks had brought reasonable success but it was starting to absorb my every waking moment, as the price of BP was creeping northward and it was becoming harder to fill my orders within the limits. I wasn't doing a bad job by any means, just not hitting my own personal targets. The market is a living entity that is outside of a regular trader's control. Under normal circumstances, when she moves you have two choices: hold on tight and ride it out or get off while you still can. These weren't normal circumstances. My only goal was to tighten my foothold. Looking back on the situation I concede that I was also chasing that rush I felt on the first day, and, like any addiction, I needed to up my dosage. Nonetheless, I had to think outside the box if I wanted to kick on. Lost in this train of thought, I felt a hand slap my left buttock. I spun around and came face to shoulder with Charlie.

"Think less. Do more. Drink up," and with that, a pound coin plopped into my drink. At risk of seeming unpatriotic I raised my pint as quickly as possible, that beautiful gilded ceiling now being viewed through the bottom of a glass. Catching Her Majesty in my teeth, I was handed a fresh beer by the devil on my left shoulder.

"That'll help blow out the cobwebs. You're coming out tonight, right?"

"No, no, no. I can't play on school nights at the moment."

"You used to! You haven't been out with us for weeks, have you got a woman tied up at home or something?"

"No, just trying to keep a clear head..." This had the potential to go back and forth for hours. Arguing with Charlie was like negotiating with a terrier to release a tennis ball. "...I will stick around for a couple, but that's it." I think I was trying to convince myself as much as I was trying to appease the others. Charlie gave me a grin and clinked our glasses together, while I leant across him to drop the Queen into the welcoming embrace of Bertie's bitter. It's only fair to pass her around.

Time hastened and beer flowed and with each passing hour

we were collectively able to reconcile the great problems of the day: how to improve the national team at every mainstream sport, how could we survive the continuing Labour government, did FHM get the right choice for top ten sexiest women, and how many different ways could we insult Rupert. He was the only one who wasn't trading the market and that made him the ideal butt for our jokes. There was blood in the water and no chance of me heading home at the time I originally intended, but this transpired to be to my benefit. We spluttered through the night in an ageing black cab, complete with a driver who knew the longest route west to take full advantage of our more than usually forgiving demeanour. Stumbling out of the taxi and into a bar like Bambi on a pub crawl, I was pleased we were switching to cocktails. I can't stand the feeling of a bloated beer belly but it remains popular and visible in large sections of society.

We commandeered a table close to the bar with an opportunist's view of the dance floor. Various nubile young things popped and shimmied with fluid motions and alluring glances, mesmerizing my companions while I attempted to figure out if I had been given a drink or a dessert. The amount of fruit stacked high around the rim would provide enough vitamin C for an ancient ocean crossing, but required facial gymnastics to sip. Rupert and Charlie were actively scouring the Kings Road's talent for the evening and while Bertie plonked himself at my side. I was still trying to decipher my drink.

"Mind if I pick your brains?"

"Not at all, I've picked yours before."

"What do you think of Charlie's project?"

"The oil play? Well its very similar to mine, just different stock. Nothing too taxing really, but a little tricky."

Bertie shook his head. "No, the other project."

"What other project?"

"Never mind, it's not important."

"Oh, come on now. You can't leave it at that." I hate not knowing things and Bertie knew it was like a red rag to a bull. "Spill the beans."

"It's nothing major, he's asked me to open up a corporate account on my side. Just strikes me as a rather odd, he has never handed off an account of that size before. I just wondered if everything was okay at SC?" Bertie couldn't see it, but behind him Charlie's attention had switched from the girls on the floor to our conversation.

"Not that I'm aware of. I shouldn't worry about it." I caught Charlie's eye and Bertie, noticing my changing attention, immediately switched subjects.

"I'll go and grab us some more drinks while the bar is quiet." I shrugged it off as a friendly competition and refocussed my efforts on the fruit salad atop my glass. While I was pulling a smirk not dissimilar to an anteater attacking a termite mound, a triumvirate of girls approached our table, all clad in knee-high boots that were a sign of prostitution in the eighties but had become the height of fashion in the late nineties. Two sat between Charlie and I with the other hovering between Charlie and Rupert.

"Hi, I'm Tracy, you alright then?" she said in a thick cockney accent. To me it was like someone dragging their nails down a chalk board. I gave her the customary glance up and down to see if she had the talents to obscure her accent. She wasn't entirely unpleasant to look at, embodying that classic mismatch: body from Baywatch, face from crime watch. That's not to say I condone such opinions, but it was the humour we grew up with. I remained as polite and accommodating as possible.

"Alex," I said, shaking her hand. "Yes, I'm fine, thank you. Would you like some mango or, I think this is guava?"

"No thanks, I don't do that sort of thing," she said replacing 'th' with 'f' at every possibility.

"You don't 'do' fruit?" I replied, gesturing to my glass.

"Oh, I'm sorry, I thought you meant something else." She grabbed a few sticks of mango and gnawed one in a manner she thought would look seductive. It wasn't. I knew this would become tiresome very quickly but on the plus side, at least I now had a much easier time gaining access to my drink. Bertie came back from the bar with a fresh round and perched himself at my other side.

"What's this corporate account he's sent over?"

"It's a prop account for SC, he wants to use our US presence to hold dollar and trade in New York." Before I had a moment to process and respond to Bertie, Tracy slid her hand onto my thigh in a painfully obvious way. She didn't appreciate losing my attention.

"You make a lot of money then?" She was going from bad to worse, but rather than answering or pointing out how rude the question was, I flipped it back to a topic she would probably be more comfortable with.

"Those boots are quite striking, they suit you well."

"Aw, thanks. Yeah, I got them at Selfridges in the sales," she replied while extending a pleasantly lengthy leg to show off her prize.

The penny dropped. How could I have been so stupid? Bertie's comment and Tracy's innocent name drop gave me an epiphany. I leant forward and clasped my hands on her cheeks, before planting a smacker of a thank you on her lips, buried as they were under what felt like half an inch of lipstick.

"Listen to me carefully because I doubt you have heard this before: you are an absolute bloody genius!" She sat dumbfounded as I grabbed my coat and made for the exit. Bertie was delighted that although our conversation was cut short, he had been promoted from casual observer to potential suitor. My knowledge of his university conquests told me he was a firm believer that you don't look at the mantelpiece when stoking the fire and he hoped she'd followed an inverse philosophy. I grabbed the first taxi that drove past and went straight home bouncing in my seat with excitement.

The night watchman rarely saw me return home that late in such a good mood if alone, but there was good cause for my cheerfulness: Selfridges was the first British company to issue an ADR, American Depositary Receipt, back in the late 1920's. It enabled Americans to invest in British companies and the ADR would trade in New York, essentially mirroring the activity in London or vice versa; you can argue whether the tail wags the dog but whatever the cause, they follow the same path. BP had an ADR listed on NYSE and if I could get approval to start buying up overseas then I could double my rate of acquisition while staying under the radar. Stephen would need to set new limits and tranche size (ADRs and ordinaries never trade 1:1) but I was sure he would support the idea. After all, it posed no extra risk to the firm.

I fired up my PC and started digging, gathering all the information I could to pitch Stephen in the morning. Noting volumes, pricing and potential arbitrage opportunities, I pushed on into the early hours until I couldn't keep my eyes open. The beep and cackle of the modem reconnecting woke me the following morning, and as I staggered to the bathroom the radio jumped into life. The familiar routine started all over again but this time with a spring in my step that was alien to the soft pounding in my head.

\* \* \* \* \*

"It's happening, just like you said."

"Good. Remember what we discussed."

"Why can't you just leave it alone?" Charlie pleaded, exhausted from my barrage of data and excitement. He didn't enjoy playing the listener, much more at home on the other side of the conversation. "We're given a very specific job. We do that job according to our instructions: Keep our head down. Get paid. Grow old. Die happy. That's the way this game works."

"So why shouldn't I do the job better, get paid more and live happy?"

"You know what I mean, don't want to upset the apple cart." Charlie often felt the need to have the last word. Seeing that morning was my first near hangover in almost a month he took it upon himself to get the coffees, if only to avoid any further snippets from my late night analytics. The mood in the office was starting its build up to bonus day, a few weeks off. It had been a good year and the whispers of extravagance were telling me that car dealers and watchmakers could expect a bumper month. Stephen's door was closed, and he was pacing back and forth barking at his speakerphone. Charlie the barista joined me and offered a suggestion in contrast to his earlier scepticism.

"Would you like me to come with? Safety in numbers, you know."

"That's probably a good idea, if he hates it at least I can deflect the meeting onto a simple update of orders. How's yours coming along?"

"Fine, ticking along nicely as always."

Stephen was off the phone, allowing me a small window of opportunity before the market opened. I gave Charlie a tap on the shoulder and we headed into battle, fingers crossed, and jackets on.

Stephen gave me a suspicious look as I finished presenting my suggestion.

"Are you trying to tell me how to do my job?"

"Not at all. I'm trying to think of ways I can better do my own."

"Ha!" His scowl shifted into a wry smile. "The boss always pegged you as the brains of the outfit. Let's do it. I'll send an email across to the back office so they know what to expect, they won't thank you for it." I breathed a sigh of relief and fought the urge to punch the air in triumph. "Right, get going, bell's about to ring." Stephen opened the door and signalled us back to the floor. Charlie, not wanting to be outdone, came forward with his own fresh suggestion as we were leaving.

"I'm thinking about taking out some CFDs to help our position in Shell…" Before he could finish Stephen shot him down, "Don't be an idiot, might as well tell everyone our play. If I were you, I would be more worried about Alex building a position that's already thirty percent deeper than yours, and you had a head start!"

Charlie should have known that a Contract For Difference wouldn't fly. You're basically betting the brokerage a certain number of pounds per penny that the stock will go up or down. You never own it, but everyone hears about it. Very high risk.

He hardly said a word all morning, trapped somewhere between jealousy and embarrassment. I didn't know the full details of his side project with Bertie but offered what I thought would be some helpful advice.

"Not trying to tell you what to do here, but maybe put a pause on other projects until we've finished these orders."

"What other projects?"

"Whatever it is you're cooking up with Bertie. Just pump the brakes for a few weeks."

"What do you know about it?" he snapped.

"Nothing, but when you and he join forces its usually something." Charlie calmed down before responding.

"Well, it's no big secret if I'm honest. I have a client who wants to deal with US equities and I haven't the time to be handling it right now. Bertie has plenty of time, so I can hand it over to him and he gives me a little kickback. Very simple really."

"I was hoping for something more exciting than that. Bertie was awfully sheepish."

"You know how it is, Stephen doesn't like us referring things outside of the group when he thinks he can handle it in-house." He was right, referrals within the trading group were the preferred option in any situation but Charlie wasn't the only trader who offered up business to friends. It didn't mesh with what Bertie had told me though, not a prop account at all. A prop account is one trading for the bank rather than a customer, but I gave Charlie the benefit of the doubt. It was possible that a SC branded account could be representing a specific client as a nominee and I simply misunderstood the situation. Possible, but not probable.

Charlie was still rather sulky as we approached lunch time, but I had an idea to cheer him up: sandwiches. Charlie was rarely found in the office during lunch, but after Stephen's comment I doubted he would be bouncing out the door. There was a wonderful little sandwich shop in the arcade by Liverpool Street, and it had become a personal favourite of ours. Since starting our work with Stephen I'd taken far fewer liquid or club lunches, maximising my time at the desk, and had become something of a sandwich aficionado. Sort of. I would spend five minutes studying the menu and order the same thing every time, a strange habit I have replicated at several restaurants over the years. Their BLT was very good: thickly sliced brown bread, nicely crisped bacon, generous slices of beef tomato, flavourful lettuce (far better than the watery iceberg popular everywhere else), homemade mayonnaise, and a sprinkling of flaked sea salt. I picked up two sandwiches, some crisps, and two bottles of Perrier before heading back to the office, hoping to find Charlie in a better mood than when I left.

Approaching the office and hastily pumping up my nicotine levels, I spotted a familiar vehicle nestled on the down ramp for the car park under The Tower. It was a Wednesday. The drivers would hold a position there rather than risk a ticket on the street, or fully committing to the car park below. The old Bentley has been a regular sight at school sporting events or dramatic productions, and I must admit I had quite the experience in the backseat with Charlie's sister a few years previous. Luis was a loyal chauffeur and, thankfully, a master of discretion. Amelia, Charlie's sister, on the contrary was as brash and boastful as her brother, regularly commenting on my motoring skills. I resented the public discussion of such matters but thinking back to that intoxicating combination of alabaster flesh on rouge leather (not to mention getting one over on my friend) it was well worth the fallout. She was spending a fair chunk of her twenties working her way up the social ladder and studying art in Florence, one on her back and the other in her books.

As I crossed the trading floor I could see Charlie and his father chatting away by our desk. I got closer and Charlie raised a hand to gesture in my direction, prompting his father to turn and greet me "Ah, there he is!" he exclaimed, thrusting his hand out for a hearty shake. David was an endlessly likeable character; he was the father other boys would often envy at school, especially those who grew up without one. My father had passed away before I was in long trousers so my memories of him were little more than stories told by drunken relatives who painted a frustrating picture, or people like mother who only offered highlights. David mentioned him very rarely, as with them both being in finance their paths had crossed once or twice so he could offer safe assumptions of support in that arena. "He would have been proud" was his favourite. The grey hair David had when we first met was now a bright white, and I was at least two feet taller for that matter, but despite his retirement being overdue he maintained an amazing zest for life. Typical for his type, his trousers were closer to his nipples than his waist and his double-breasted jacket was made for the narrower frame of his younger years. It would never be buttoned again. We were a similar height these days and I would sometimes chuckle when he looked up at Charlie. I never knew Charlie's mother, but she was probably built like an Amazon. In the realm of single parenting it must have been far harder on Charlie than me. He could remember the loss.

"Good to see you, David, how are you?"

"Good, good. I was just telling Charlie that you need to stop by HQ in a few weeks, meet the team up there. We've enjoyed your efforts on BP, keep it up!" He leant closer, adding,

"Try and drag this grumpy bugger up a notch, will you?" Intentionally quiet enough to sound private, but loud enough to make sure Charlie heard every word. I'm sure he meant it to be motivational, but I don't think Charlie was in the mood to take it. David moved on, stopping every few desks to offer a pat on the back to some of the veterans. It reminded me of a politician working a room, a niggling feeling that if he met some of them in the street he wouldn't have a clue who they were.

Lunch seemed to thaw Charlie's mood slightly, and he dropped a sizable dollop of mayonnaise on his tie with little care as he dug in.

"I'm going to hit up the Shell ADRs out in the colonies."

"You looked into it?"

"Of course I did. It's a decent idea, I just wish I'd thought of it."

"You just sat next to the wrong girl." Charlie gave me a nearly blank stare. I say nearly blank because he had tomato juices rolling down his chin which detracted from the moment. "Eliza Doolittle from last night. Her fuck me boots were from Selfridges," I continued. He wiped away the tomato juice and escalated his expression from blank to bewilderment. "Do you ever pay attention? Our first securities course after university, they told us the story of Selfridges when explaining ADRs."

"I pay attention to things that matter, you remember the things that don't."

"When's my birthday?"

"Not a bloody idea my friend, now pass the crisps."

The regular chipper Charlie was back.

\* \* \* \* \*

"Are you sure he will work with us?"

"I can keep him in line."

The week that followed was one of the most tiring of my then-young life. Working orders like that over both exchanges meant constant vigilance, patience, and the willingness to work from the London open until the close in New York, yet essentially playing the same game on repeat. I was desperate for Stephen to order a ceasefire, especially for Bonus Day (B-Day), so I could turn my compulsive competitiveness into carefree satisfaction. Very little work is done on B-day, but you could be sure every bar within the city had the champagne on ice. Forget the Christmas party, B-Day was the time for real presence and bigger presents: loud, proud, but totally confidential. We looked forward to passing go and collecting our £200 but Charlie and I weren't quite sure what to expect this time round. Despite dreams of extravagant rewards, I wondered how much our recent efforts for Stephen would either diminish or inflate our bonuses, if at all. The excitement that had been building in the office over the previous weeks had reached its peak and crashed into silent, analytical competition. Everyone was trying to decipher the expressions of their colleagues and figure out whose was bigger. The way to play the game is to look dissatisfied when you are given your letter in Stephen's office, but smug and flush when facing your colleagues; that way your boss thinks he isn't paying you enough but everyone else thinks you're the trader with the magic touch. We watched them file in and out of the office as the day passed, still working our own orders but not with the same focus. We gave the actors a score out of ten for their performance between ourselves. Tits was the only one to score a perfect ten and deserved a round of applause, which we duly offered. Finally, Stephen leant out of his door and beckoned us to come forward. "Both of you."

This wasn't a good start; bonus meetings are always one-on-one. We donned our jackets and walked towards his office totally lacking in confidence, but that didn't stop the rest of the floor eyeballing our every step. Stephen closed the door and sat at his desk, allowing the silence to stretch out and test our nerve.

"You're done." Stephen must have noted the look of abject horror across my face and quickly added, "The oil spree. We are happy with our positions, so finish what you're working today and draw a line under it." He opened his bottom left draw and removed two envelopes. One marked Hope, for me, the other Smyth-Cummin, and handed them to us one at a time. "Things are different this time, but the same rules apply. Even more so. You do not discuss the contents of these with anybody, including each other. Usually you open the envelope before leaving my office, but as you're in here together, I would wait until you get home. All good?" We were grinning and nodding like a pair of simpletons with a doughnut. "Right, get going… but make sure you look miserable. The rest of them will riot if they think we gave you a decent spot. Enjoy the day and get home safe. Good job."

I offered an Oscar-worthy performance of heartbreaking loss as I made my way back to the desk. Charlie took it a step further, whimpering as he pulled out his chair. I tucked the envelope in my pocket and took stock of where I stood with the market for what remained of the day. A few thousand still working in London from my most recent tranche and slightly less still open in New York. A few points sacrificed but I was able to finish up early, fill my tickets, and drop them in the settlement tray. Music was playing on the floor and the more senior traders were already leaving, palming off their work to those further down the totem pole. By the time I had cleared my things and turned off my box, there were one or two secretaries essentially running the entire trading floor, and even Stephen had gone to join the carnival.

The bars across the city were heaving, with revelry spilling out into the streets despite the chill in the air. One square mile of London congratulated itself on another good year and handed out billions of pounds as a reward. If there existed a modern Sodom and Gomorrah in England's green and pleasant land, then the square mile and Canary Wharf were it. Women pretending to be younger than their years, and those feeling older than they were, filed out of Liverpool Street station desperate to bag a banker on bonus day and avoiding frostbite only by chance. By the time the sun came up, most wouldn't have made it home, many would be in someone else's home, and some would have first-hand experience of what it's like to have coke snorted from various creases and crevices about their person. I shouldn't make it sound so sordid. Under agreeable circumstances, between consensual parties, and amongst the morally flexible, one might even label it empowering. Like Coyote Ugly with less denim, but more ugly.

Across the street, Stephen was at the bar ordering four cases of champagne on behalf of the company to add to the numerous bottles already on ice at the tables. Some were pulling cigars from their pockets while others were pouring shots of single malt to pass round. The smoke was thick enough that the doors were kept open despite the weather, helping to dilute the combination of tobacco and aftershave.

The envelope from Stephen was weighing heavily in my pocket, and I could see Charlie felt the same way. It was the first time in all the years I had known him that he seemed more eager to get home than to get another drink. He must've been incorrigible as a small child, anxious to open gifts as soon as possible. Not to pretend that I was any different, but at least the years had taught me some patience. Charlie skulked off to the men's toilet in the corner of the bar, emerging several minutes later with a disgruntled look on his face and zeroing in on a tray of charged flutes. Instead of powdering his nose he must have opened his envelope and his reaction didn't bode well for me. An evening with an angry Charlie never ended well for either of us. Seeing his reaction left me deflated and unenthused about the evening; perhaps it was better to just go home and get it over with.

Sitting on the tube a short time later I felt bad for my friend, as he obviously didn't get the news he was hoping for. Although I was missing one of the biggest nights of the year, and was anxious about my own letter, I was looking forward to getting home. After such a busy time, it was nice to head back and switch off. It was still light as I entered the flat and my answering machine was flashing with more than one message from my mother, all asking if I received her previous message. She had a nasty habit of pestering me about work. She said she cared, I said she was nosey, just wanting gossip to fill the gaps between soap operas. One day I would give her my mobile number, but at the time I was happy to continue denying its existence. I poured myself drink and slouched onto the sofa, taking several sips before lowering my tumbler to the coffee table. I was about to face the music and open the letter when my mobile rang. It was Bertie.

"I'm not out tonight mate, give Charlie a buzz."

"No, no. I'm not going out tonight in the city either. I just wanted to run some things past you."

"Is this about your and Charlie's thing? Look, if you're not happy with it then just tell him. He won't mind."

"He's been going long on ADR's in New York, enough of a position for me to wonder whether you guys are on the inside."

"Not at all Bertie, we're long on oil everywhere. I've been going long in BP, Charlies been doing the same in Shell."

"Then why is he buying BP with me?" I paused for a moment, it didn't fit with our assignments, but I wasn't going to rile Bertie up any more than he already was. In all likelihood Stephen wanted to go even deeper on my side, but it sowed doubt in my mind.

"We just wanted to get as much exposure as possible, you know how it is. We take our orders from up high. I can assure you there's nothing fishy going on."

"Right, okay. Just struck me as strange, it's a big position."

"We're feeling bullish. Feel free to stop by if you fancy a quiet night."

"Afraid I can't, I have a date tonight."

"Yeah right, you can just say you want to."

"I'm serious!"

"Well best of luck, we can catch up next week."

Having calmed Bertie's nerves, I retrieved the letter from my jacket pocket and peeled open the envelope. There was part of me still expecting a golden ticket, but I felt like I had underperformed following Bertie's revelation. I prepared myself for nothing more than token gesture as a reminder to do better in future. Instead, it contained a simple cream-coloured card, with a handwritten note in green ink: "Processing."

\* \* \* \* \*

"Forward on 1. Brake 2. Forward 3."

"Confirmed."

It was radio silence from Charlie all weekend. In fairness, I made no attempt to contact him either, feeling rather miffed that he appeared to be picking up my slack without giving me a heads up. Part of me expected we would meet that morning at Waterloo. No. Not something I'd worry about under normal circumstances. My concern grew when I reached the office and noted his desk had been cleared. Some suspicious glances were being directed my way by others confused at Charlie's sudden absence. Between the change in personnel and the closing of my oil binge I wasn't sure what to do with myself aside from fingering through my copy of the Financial Times. His absence was eating at me. "Where are you?" I jabbed out in a text message, but it refused to send. I tried to call and heard the robotic voice of denial, "The number you have dialled is not recognized." Surely if there was anything to worry about then I would have heard about it from mutual friends? I'd have thought he would let me know himself if something drastic was going to change. Stephen shattered my self-pity by summoning me to his office.

"How you doing?" he asked in a caring manner that I had never heard from him before.

"Feeling cheap and disposable if I'm being honest."

"Don't. Your spot is coming, don't worry. We just need to work through some things first."

"Well apart from that I'm just fine." Stephen could tell I was frustrated, but he wasn't there as my therapist.

"That's a lie, but if that's the line you want to take then that's up to you. I have a new job for you this week." His soft expression quickly dropped in exchange for his more familiar business attitude. "I have a potential client, big client that's approached us about handling the liquidation of some holdings. The boss has asked us to look at it, wants our opinion on whether or not this is something we can handle." He handed me an unassuming cream folder. It had some numbers written across the front, but not like the client codes we see on our usual accounts. I started to flick through the contents to get a better grip on what I was getting myself into. There was a photograph of very plain older gentleman and some letters of enquiry, describing himself rather ubiquitously as a consultant. He was looking to liquidate some holdings in Gazprom, the Russian gas giant that although privatized was still run like a government ministry. His assets were significant when considering the price where the depositary was trading at in London, but he held domestic stock which could make things more difficult. It was a strange situation for a British national to be in possession of that class of share. During the mid-late nineties all sorts of relatives and friends would find themselves gifted shares in similar companies by twisted executives, but not overseas citizens.

"Potentially lucrative, but also tricky considering the line of stock."

"Very, but there are a few options we could look at. We have some friends in the Channel Islands who deal specifically with Russian domestic via HSBC. We would like you to arrange a meeting and get a feel for him, see if we should be taking this on or not."

"Okay, could be interesting." The older oligarchs were starting to come under pressure from the new President so it wasn't too surprising to see them dump stock before they found themselves at the bottom of the Moskva River wearing concrete slippers. Back at my desk I assessed if it was the kind of trade we could handle on our own. The value was enough that I would move heaven and earth to make it happen if we could. I would have preferred to discuss it with our back-office team, but the settlement manager was still reeling over my ADR binge and wouldn't welcome the idea of stepping outside of his comfort zone again. We really needed to commute the Russian ordinaries into the London line if we were going to make the deal work. Not as easy as it sounds. I plucked the man's business card from the inside cover of the folder and dialled. The phone was answered very politely by a lady who informed me Mr. Lovegood was unavailable at present and offered to take a message. However, after explaining the reason for my call she was happy to make an appointment for the following day at eleven. I gave Stephen's office door a little tap and leant in to advise him of the arrangement. He was pleased that I hadn't wasted any time in organising the meeting but was eager for me to return the client file to his possession. I fetched it briskly and handed it back. Stephen grabbed a blank file from his desk, scrawled the prospective clients name on the cover and transferred the business card and two letters into the new file, leaving everything else behind.

"This is what you can take with you. Maybe print some charts and trade volumes for the different lines, give him an idea of the challenges we are up against. It's a great way to justify our take." That it was. Doesn't matter if you're a lawyer, banker, or estate agent. The fees are largely dependent on how you justify them, and thick folders were one of the easiest ways to do that. I spent the remainder of the day making sure the file was plumped up with what looked like several days' preparation. The unrest in Russia with a new President and increasing conflict within the satellite states were the basis for my argument to sell the stock quickly. The Rouble was already bouncing up and down like a yo-yo. I opened the communications with the Channel Islands to confirm they were able to handle the volume, but they could offer no guarantee on price. Wanting to get a fresh set of eyes on the problem, I knew exactly where to turn.

Bertie's office wasn't far from mine so it was easy to grab a quiet drink, on the rare occasions we were spared the influence of our more boisterous friends. It was far more relaxed and the best time to catch up on old school chat in the mile. It's worth keeping track of where old school friends land, the city may be open but ties still bind. This time there was one specific topic of conversation when it came to old friends, Charlie. Bertie hadn't heard anything from him since the previous week, but Rupert had mentioned that he was involved in a family matter.

"Look on the bright side, mate, if there's a family problem then Amelia might be in town."

"Give it a rest, will you? That joke is well past its sell-by date."

"Well you never know, mate, you're both single." Bertie winked. I rolled my eyes.

"If she's single why aren't you chasing that tail?"

"Because I am no longer single. Yes, this man is now spoken for!"

"Well fuck me sideways. Who's the lucky man?" I said sarcastically.

"Fucker. Funnily enough I've been seeing Tracy that you were talking to the other night."

"Seriously? Is that who you were meeting last week?" He grinned and nodded, feeling rather pleased with himself. "Good for you, I'm sure should the time come to meet your parents they will be equally surprised."

"I'll pretend I didn't hear that…so Amelia then?"

"Not interested," I said bluntly and gave Bertie the briefest of synopses regarding my meeting the following day. If we could work a deal then I may be able to offer him a slice of the action. He would, of course, show his gratitude for any referral of that calibre, crossing my palm with silver like some pinstriped gypsy soothsayer. The mere possibility was enough for him to pick up the tab that day, probably written off as expenses.

"That's a big chunk, Alex, it could take some time to clear out."

"I'm hoping you could spill some out via your firm."

"Possibly. Who do you deal with for Russian Domestic?"

"Friends of ours shuffle it through Honkers and Shankers off shore. You?"

"Some grubby communist in Panama that you don't want to know."

"As long as he can dump the stock I really don't care. We could drop the shares into that prop account Charlie set up, make things a bit quicker."

"Don't bank on it, looks like that account won't be with us for long. The request came through from SC today to transfer the stock and close the account."

"From Stephen?"

"From the signatories."

"Who are?"

"Alex, you know I can't…"
"Sorry, of course. Never mind, we can set up new ones easily.
I'll check with Stephen after the meeting tomorrow."

\* \* \* \* \*

"They'll give him a push,
but I think he can handle it."

"Like you did?"

I took my time the following morning, making sure I was looking my best and totally up to speed on the variables: currency fluctuations between Sterling and the Rouble, and pricing for all concerned. We were experiencing one of London's rare sunny days during the transition from spring to summer, with the cold still biting in the shade but the sun baking the bold and the rain living only in memory until tomorrow. The meeting was being held at Mr. Lovegood's office, also based in the city, but an area I was not familiar with. I had to cut through Broadgate to the other side of Liverpool Street. An area that stepped back in time. Less fancy bars, restaurants and office buildings, more cafés and corner shops and the faint hope that the Broadgate complex would expand the mile further. Lovegood's premises on Worship Street were far from impressive, with flaking paint on the exterior and not even a brass plaque or bank of doorbells to signal who was inside. I walked back and forth along the street a few times to make sure I was in the right place.

Hoping for the best, I banged on the door with the ancient painted metal knocker, which frustratingly left flakes of black paint on my hand. The pessimist in me wasn't expecting an answer but the door was opened in short order by a strikingly pretty young lady, the kind executives would pay a higher than market rate for just to see a saucy smile when they arrived at the office. She gave me a warm welcome and took my coat. The decor was a contrast to the bedraggled exterior, looking like an ultra-modern and efficient office. An abundance of white walls and inoffensive blue carpeting guided me up the stairs passed the locked doors of anonymous occupants. Reaching the third floor I realized how lazy I had become after years of mollycoddling with lifts at work and home. My wheezing did little to impress the shapely hips I had followed up the stairs, but she showed me into Lovegood's office and remarked that I should make myself at home. It was a large office, but it wasn't clear if it was to be divided or kept "as is" to compensate for something else. There were a few cabinets dotted around the periphery, with a long boardroom-style table and a more private desk facing the street. I set up shop at the long table and organized by papers into their appropriate sections while I waited. I remember thinking that he must have moved recently because there were pictures resting against the walls rather than hanging from them. A planned office more than a practicing one.

I heard the opening and closing of a nearby door before Lovegood entered the room. He showed no sign of urgency as he came to meet me, as if I was disturbing his day rather than responding to his own enquiry. However, as he stretched out his hand to shake mine his eyes lit up and he grabbed my elbow with his other hand to offer the firmest of greetings. I introduced myself, explaining my experience and handing over one of my cards. He tucked it in his pocket and sat next to me.

"Very kind of you to come and meet me at such short notice, I appreciate that level of client service."

"Well, we like to think that when it comes to high net worth clients such as yourself, we have the knowledge, experience, and standing to warrant the highest level of service. I've taken a look at your current holdings and they are certainly a volume we are comfortable with. We have several clients will a similarly sized portfolio, between 300 and 400 bar sterling…"

"Like who?"

"Uh…um…I'm sorry, but you must understand I am not at liberty to discuss our clients with others. A level of discretion which I'm sure you can appreciate."

"Oh, come on now. How do you think I first heard about your firm? Everybody talks, Alex, like gossip in the changing rooms at school. Everyone wants to know who has the biggest 'investment'."

"If others choose to do so, then that is their choice. I do not." It's always easier to nip uncomfortable requests in the bud.

"Well that explains the lack of a wedding ring, I suppose," he said, nudging my shoulder like we were old chums at a party. I smiled rather than pander to his efforts and continued to forge ahead with my pre-planned material. Lovegood stood up. I paused. "Please continue," he insisted as he ambled over to a cabinet at the far side of the table. While I continued my pitch, to which he showed lessening interest, he bent to the lower level of the cabinet and retrieved a decanter with two tumblers. Before I had a chance to object, he had flicked the stopper from the decanter with his thumb and poured two generous whiskeys, sliding the larger of the two across the table towards me.

"How long have you been with the firm?" He asked, standing over me like an examiner walking the lines of desks at school.

"Gosh, if you include my summer work at university, then I will be finishing my eighth I suppose."

"Do you enjoy the city life?"

"Yes, it certainly has it perks."

"That it does. Good. Now, what can you tell me about David Smyth-Cummin?"

I took a steadying gulp of what transpired to be awful whiskey and tried to hide my displeasure while Lovegood was staring at me. Seemingly impatient for my response, I would again cut that topic of conversation and steer us back on topic. Or try.

"Very good at what he does, he's guided the company well. Now, we have one possible route to flush your shares into a fund we are close to in Guernsey…"

"Children? Wife?"

"Neither…" I said with a hollow chuckle, waving my previously noticed bare ring finger "…we could deposit your shares with their local nominee…"

"Not you! David!" The conversation had turned from its already unorthodox foundation into something entirely more uncomfortable. It was not what I had expected, or experienced in other client meetings.

"Sir, I'm sorry but that is not something I believe is appropriate for discussion." I replied in my most polite and diffusing manner.

"I think if you want my business then you should consider answering my innocent queries rather than avoiding them," he responded agitatedly. I was starting to feel slightly giddy. I'd had less than one drink, but it felt like five.

"Perhaps we have our wires crossed a bit here, Mr. Lovegood. I think I should head back to the office and reschedule for another time perhaps. I'm feeling a bit under the weather." I fumbled my papers hurriedly back into my case with my rushed excuse to leave but Lovegood insisted.

"I think you need to answer my damn questions!" He kicked the legs of the chair out from underneath me, sending me to floor clutching my yet-to-be closed briefcase. He was much quicker than you would expect from a man of his age and within seconds was directly above me. Lovegood raised his foot and pressed it against my case, forcing me flat on my back with his full weight on my chest. "You need to tell me everything you know about David Smyth-Cummin and his family!"

Adrenaline pumped through me more than any drug had prompted in the past, clearing my head and making my heart beat so hard I could hear it hitting the side of my case. I swung my right leg in panic and connected with Lovegood's one steady foot, sending him staggering back and grasping at a chair but failing to prevent his own fall. I sprung up and ran to the door. My head may have been cleared by the fight or flight reaction, but my limbs weren't getting all the messages. I flung open the door, smacking it against the interior wall with a mighty bang, and made for the stairs as quickly as my drunk legs could carry me. The neighbouring door opened hastily and the woman who greeted my just a short time before ran onto the landing. She broadened her stance and planted her feet to block my path. I was not familiar with any violence outside of school shenanigans but gratefully familiar with rugby. Shoulder down and charge. She held on to me as we collided and tumbled down the stairs behind her, breaking my fall and knocking herself out cold on the floor. I instinctively apologised as I clambered up but had to keep going and tripped over the final few steps spilling my papers all over the hallway. I didn't care about them anymore. I just wanted to get out.

Stumbling out into the street, I turned for home but hadn't even reached the end of Worship Street when I found I could run no longer. My legs were failing. The sculpture at the centre of the Broadgate circle was in sight but I was soon on my knees. Nobody stopped to help, either ignoring me or laughing. People assumed I had overindulged at an early lunch or a corporate fun day. I fumbled in my pockets for my phone but couldn't find it. Barely teetering on the cusp on consciousness I heard a faint but familiar voice; it was Bertie.

"Alex, what the fuck are you playing at?" I couldn't even get my lips to form words anymore, instead groaning an indecipherable plea.

"I thought you were supposed to be meeting a client? Jesus, man!"

Bertie managed to commandeer another passer-by and they pulled me upright. Hanging between the pair of them, my arms draped over their shoulders and my feet dragging along the pavement as they carried me forward, my eyes caught the rusted footing of the Broadgate sculpture before they flickered to a close.

\* \* \* \* \*

"Are you both in?"

It was dark. The office was eerily quiet, the bouncing company logo on the trading floor screensavers the only movement visible through bleary eyes. I was slumped in a corner of the conference room, my shoulders wedged between one solid wall and another of glass. A mild glow from the kitchen clawed out to illuminate the floor. I gingerly got to my feet and stretched out the tension in my neck and back. There was a thoughtful glass of water and some sorely needed Alka-Seltzer on the table. As I tore them open and dropped them into the glass, I noticed light coming from Stephen's office at the other end of the floor. He was stood with David discussing something when he spotted me out of the corner of his eye. David nodded in my direction and the two of them walked over. I was expecting them to deliver the mother of all disciplinary lectures for what they would perceive as a drunken employee. Instead, they were totally relaxed.

"How you feeling, kid?" asked Stephen sympathetically.

"I've been better."

"Are you hurt?" added David.

"I don't think so."

"Good. Good." He turned and retired to one corner of the room while Stephen pulled out two chairs for us to sit on.

"Okay Alex, I want you to tell me exactly what happened."

I talked him through how things had played out that morning, explaining that I hadn't even finished one drink and how Lovegood had been asking peculiar questions.

"You were in a bit of a state when we got you, lucky your friend from Monnow Wealth found you when he did. Took him and I almost half an hour to drag your arse back here."

"Bertie's a good friend."

"I'm sure he is. What else do you remember from this morning?"

I wiped the sleep from my eyes. "I've told you what happened, I don't know what more I can add."

"Do you think he was who he said he was?"

"Lovegood? I don't think so."

"Lovegood, his office, his staff, the premise of the meeting, everything."

I told him how tatty and anonymous the building had been from the outside, how the interior had been sparse in comparison to our own office and gave the impression of being a work in progress.

"The people, Alex, tell us about the people," piped up David from the far corner.

"The lady that let me in seemed nice at first, but she definitely didn't want me to leave. Wasn't afraid to get physical either, put her body on the line." David came towards me from his corner.

"How about Lovegood? Why don't you think he was who he said?"

"I don't know; it just didn't feel right in my gut. He was asking a lot of questions about you and our clients."

"Your gut is a great indicator. I think of it as your subconscious reacting to things you are yet to notice, but I'm old-fashioned like that…" He stood behind me and placed his hands on my shoulders. "…I want you to relax and think back to this morning. Try to reconcile everything about the meeting that didn't add up."

"David, the guy was a nutter…"

"Just close your eyes and try to pick out what didn't make sense."

I appeased him and tried to replay the meeting in my head.

"Well?" asked Stephen.

"He was asking the wrong questions…he didn't care what his shares were worth…"

"Good, what else?" said David softly.

"Umm…the scotch was cheap and the tumblers weren't crystal."

"How do you know?" interjected Stephen.

"Taste and feeling the glass on my lips. This is stupid…"

"Very good, more. What more can you tell me about him?" came further instruction from behind me.

"He was wearing a new suit, shirt and shoes. The wrong ones at that."

"Why were they wrong?" queried Stephen from across the table. With my patience running thin on our group therapy session, I just let it all out at once.

"His shirt had a chest pocket and button cuffs, his suit still had the pockets stitched closed and his shoes had a rubber sole…with the price sticker still stuck to the bloody heel. He was dressed like a fucking estate agent!"

The hands lifted off my shoulders. Stephen was smiling at me, either in pride or amusement at my pomposity. David reached inside his jacket pocket and pulled out an envelope, which he dropped on the table before leaving.

"Good work."

Stephen offered his congratulations and followed David out. I tore the envelope open expecting to finally get my bonus but instead was left disappointed, yet again. Like before there was a simple card with a green scrawl that read, "36a St. James. 7am." I got up, followed the other two out and, behaving quite out of character, boldly shouted after them. "Am I even getting a bonus this year?"

"Go home, Alex, I'll see you in the morning," responded David. I just flung my arms in the air in frustration and tossed the note into the nearest bin.

It was almost ten by the time I reached my flat, just in time for the evening news and a spiteful nightcap. My trousers were ruined in the knees with no chance of repair, just another annoyance in a day filled with them. The answering machine was flashing at me, no doubt another effort from my mother to discuss the shocking village gossip of a missing cat or a pensioners' affair. I really hadn't the patience to handle it that night, or her badgering about work, but it would only get worse. I reminded myself what good whiskey tasted like and picked up the phone.

"Hello Mum…no of course I'm not avoiding you…she said that in church? That's terrible."

⋆ ⋆ ⋆ ⋆ ⋆

"Stage 1 complete."

"Stage 2 approved."

I was still frustrated the following morning, enough to turn off the radio before reaching the shower, but admit I was curious about finally seeing the head office. Coffee, cigarettes, butterflies in the belly and a sprinkling of pride as I turned off Piccadilly. The rain just started as I walked past Bianco's, a club next door, and reached the head office. 36a was the upper floor of number 36 and the door was separate to the gallery occupying the primary floors. A very unassuming black door with a polished brass number above the letter box. No name plate and, more awkwardly, no doorbell. Without request, a buzzing sound came from the door and it popped open to let me in. I was stood in a hallway, barely wide enough for two individuals to stand side by side, and roughly forty feet long. The tiled floor clashed with the colourful walls, a popular choice in the seventies, but also reminded me of the famous corridor in Charlie and the Chocolate Factory. In the near corner was an umbrella stand holding one lonely damp umbrella, and facing me from the opposite end of the corridor was a mirrored lift door. The only other feature of the area was a simple side table with a telephone. The phone started to ring and being the only occupant, I assumed it was meant for me.

"Good morning, can I help you?" came a soft female voice.

"I believe so, Mr. Hope here for a 7 o'clock."

"Thank you." The phone went dead and the lift doors opened with a chime. There were no buttons to press on the inside but when the doors opened again I was met with more usual surroundings. The room was classically decorated with large windows, skylights drumming with the rain, and a white marble floor. It was bright, but still had a warm feel to it, like a Georgian country house. Immediately opposite the lift was a dark wooden desk, attended by a petite but stern-looking older woman; she reminded me of a matron I had at school. In front of her she had several telephones of different colours and an ageing switchboard. Directly behind her a large rug lay in front of the windows with a chesterfield set. David was nestled in the corner of the sofa with a copy of the FT and a cup of tea. Peering over his paper, he waved a hello.

"Morning, glad to see you found the place. Pull up a pew."

I removed my overcoat and perched on the edge of the sofa feeling slightly apprehensive and gripping my overcoat on my lap like a security blanket.

"Well rested?"

"Uh yes, thank you. Very quiet night," I said meekly. Matron approached us without instruction.

"Joan, would you mind taking this Mr. Hope's unnecessary items and rustling up some coffee for the other side. The young ones seem to prefer that to tea these days," instructed David politely.

"Yes Pater," she replied in the same soft voice I had heard earlier, very different from what I had imagined from her grizzled exterior. She took my coat and stood waiting. "Telephone, sir." My perplexed expression prompted David to intervene.

"No phones beyond the front desk I'm afraid, you can collect it on the way out. Standard procedure, Chinese walls and such."

"I don't have a phone anymore, lost it during the commotion yesterday."

"Ah, right. Nasty business that, yes. No matter, we've got a new phone organized for you." Once Joan scurried away through one of the few doors in the room, David finished his tea and hopped up, leaving the cup and saucer on the table.

"Your generation are so attached to coffee. I can't stand it myself. Too much of a lingering aftertaste for one to drink regularly. Shall we?" He led me through a large oak double door, adjacent to the one Joan had used. We were stood in a large circular room, the marble floor from the reception continued but everything else changed. The walls were clad in wood panelling that matched the door we passed through and several other doors dotted around the room, although none bore any distinguishing features. There was no natural light flushing in, unlike the reception, which made the towering ceiling feel quite ominous. The lights around the outside were classically cloaked in green glass shades, preventing almost any light from rising. Interspersed between the lights hung beautifully vivid oil paintings in a feeble attempt to liven up the place.

In the centre of the room was the most striking feature: a giant brass structure, similar in appearance to a Victorian birdcage with a chandelier dangling from its highest point. I walked around its exterior admiring its assembly and musing over its purpose, while David stood smiling by the door. It was a full thirty feet high, and slightly greater in diameter. Inside the cage was an octagonal table inlaid with various veneers making the shape of a compass, but rather than having the traditional lettering for north, south, east, or west, it bore the letter "P" in the centre directly beneath the chandelier. Grand chairs with ornate engraving, scrolled arms and studded leather cushions sat at the four points. My concentration was broken as David unlocked the cage with a clang, the hinges squeaking like an old gate as it opened.

"Come inside, Joan will have your coffee here momentarily."

As I came around David sat at the head of the table, having pulled back the chair to his left hand side suggesting where I should sit. Joan appeared from one of the doors with a tray carrying my coffee, bringing it to the edge of the cage and standing patiently. I politely relieved her of my cup and was reaching for some sugar when David somewhat impatiently interrupted.

"I believe you will find it sweet enough, Alex. That will be all, Joan, lockdown please."

"Yes, Pater."

Joan closed the door of the cage and slammed the bolt home before leaving through the double doors, the loud bang of a heavy lock making it clear she would not be joining us again.

"Careful. Don't touch the bars." He put his hand under the table and flicked a switch. A crack came from his end of the table and a low humming noise spread around the cage, the bars behaving like giant tuning forks.

"Ah, much better. Now come sit down my boy, we have a lot to talk about. To start with I would like to point out that this conversation stays firmly between the two of us. This isn't the sort of thing you discuss with friends or family, no matter how close..." He pulled a scrunched-up piece of paper from his pocket. "...and it isn't the kind of appointment you toss in a random bin either." I was a bit embarrassed that he had seen me throw the note away the previous night, but the conversation was beginning to feel less formal. He sat back in his chair, crossing his legs and fiddling with the coins in his pocket. "Why don't you start? I'm sure you already want to ask something."

"What is this place?"

"Straight to the point I see. Well, this is Pactum, hence the P on the table, or affectionately 'the cage' for obvious reasons. It was designed by an old colleague in the nineteen forties, he is commemorated by that apple painting over there. All of the paintings are a memorial to a past member. That still life of a green inkwell embossed with a 'C' is for my grandfather. Anyway, the purpose of the cage was to prevent any prying ears from hearing our conversations. Totally useless by modern standards, but it's nice to fire the old girl up now and again. The desk has been around since 1914 when my grandfather commissioned it and founded the company, but the chairs were just something I spotted at an auction after I took over. The old ones were a little stiff."

I sipped my coffee, looking at the paintings around us and listening to the hum of the cage. David seemed totally unaware how bizarre he was sounding and how little sense it made to me.

"So those are the offices for the analysts?"

"Ah, yes, and no. Those are offices, that's the door for the loo. Kitchen is that way, I think, but that's usually Joan's domain. We are not analysts in the traditional sense. We do a specific job, for a specific client. We exercise discretion, cautiousness and certainly analyse everything we do very, very carefully...I suppose in that sense we're better than analysts." David thought his dig at analysts was very funny, but it didn't really register with me in the moment. Things weren't adding up for me. David seemed to be enjoying himself, whether he was hoping for me to figure things out on my own or just relishing my rare moment of speechlessness.

"I know you're a bit of a history buff, Alex, so let me tell you ours. My grandfather founded a little group called the SSB in 1909, a small part of the Admiralty which served little purpose until the great war came along, and subsequently split between domestic and international. My grandfather was the first head of the international arm, currently referred to as the Secret Intelligence Service or SIS. When the Great War charged across our horizon, it became immediately obvious that he simply didn't have the budget to fund the efforts of his service. He arranged that the budget could be advanced, invested and managed for future years to bolster the coffers, and it immediately yielded rewards. At first he was investing in small enterprise, imports and such. Very quickly, thanks to the increased staff he could now afford and in collaboration with old colleagues, twenty-two German spies were weaselled out in greater London. This gave credit to his funding ideal, and as such Pactum was born.

"Of course, there were failures as well as successes. Every new venture has teething problems. For example: Reilly was a great success and the first person to sit where you do now. On the other hand, the failures in Ireland also meant the person who would normally sit opposite you never enters the field. When my grandfather died in 1923 and my father took over his place at this table, he stepped things up. He showed great foresight regarding the whispers on the continent and built a great portfolio during the interwar period. Those efforts helped to fund the explosive works of the service and its sisters during the war: Bletchley Park, SOE and similar projects all paid for by enterprise rather than taxation."

It was a fascinating revelation, not one that changed history but instead lifted the curtain on an aspect that had never crossed my mind. You could tell how proud David was, not just of the originality and financial successes, but the tangible difference his family had made to Britain and the world. It didn't matter that nobody else knew about it. He knew, and that's all he needed. He went on, "As you can imagine, the silent war that followed was even more costly. The service grew in size, and so we as a firm had to meet those capital requirements. We started investing more in the financial markets, as the insight of the service and our own research made the stock market a natural home. We no longer hold any private interests or property, too much traceability and management involved. My father was the last one to have us holding physical assets, and I like to think my biggest contribution to Pactum has been to focus purely on the financial markets. It funded the public face of the bank, paid for that green and cream monolith at Vauxhall Cross and enables us to maintain our place in the world. Had it not been for our efforts, the service would be nothing more than a subsidiary of US intelligence by now."

I finally coughed up the question. "So, you're a spy?"

"God no. I'm not cut out for all the cloak and dagger stuff at my age. I sit at the head of this table, using the name Pater, 'Father', like my predecessors, but the head of the service and the head of Pactum have been separate since my grandfather. The head of the service sits opposite me under the moniker of Patruus (Uncle), known as P in the service, who you will see later this week. We have full access to the service's intelligence, and that gives us insight into the macro-economic and political shifts long before the market has a chance to react. For example, you have been trading oil these past few weeks, but do you know why?"

"To be honest, I simply did what I was told and assumed our analysts had good reason to be bullish."

"But now you know that we don't have any analysts here, so?"

"Because we know something nobody else does?"

David leaned back in his chair, satisfied that the message was getting through. "Correct, if vague. In the next two weeks the Lockerbie Bombing suspects will be delivered to Holland. A military base to be precise, temporarily acting as part of Scotland. When that happens, the sanctions against North Africa's largest oil producer will be lifted. That is an example of the information we get from the service, although we had heard whispers from our own sources. However, we also know arrangements are being made for BP or Shell to be granted exploratory rights in Libya. That is the information we gather by ourselves, the business side. After all, we are not civil servants, we're bankers."

"David, that's insider trading, it's illegal."

He paused and considered his answer carefully. "Yes. When you look at it alongside the book, it is. After all, the most valuable commodity in the world is information. When it comes to the market, he who knows first makes the most profit. With that being said, every single action we take here must be morally defensible. We may work outside the rules of the exchange, but we hold ourselves to a far higher standard. We work in the shadows, but always we work in the best interests of the British people, not ourselves or anyone else. If the service had to pull more and more money from the government, then the tax increase would affect the entire population. It could take badly needed funds from services that are already struggling, such as the health service. Instead, we use the markets and make our own profits. Nobody 'loses' per se, but if there was a group that did it would be high net worth individuals and international financial institutions. The difference it makes to them is barely noticeable, yet it makes a positive impact on the country as a whole. Would you rather the terminally ill have to wait for medication, or the elderly go without their winter fuel allowance? Of course not."

"It is still illegal, David. Isn't there a chance we could get into trouble?"

"No, not within our own borders. The government is aware of how the service is funded and how damaging it would be for them to foot the bill themselves. They turn a blind eye. I would like to think it's because they respect our privacy and appreciate our work, but the pessimist in me knows it's for deniability. What Mother doesn't know, doesn't hurt Mother."

"I understand. And where do you see me fitting into all of this?"

"Well my boy, I have a question for you: do you fish?"

* * * * *

"Is he a threat?"

"To him or us?"

"One and the same in this business."

*"You're telling me the British intelligence service has been playing the stock market?"* Hamilton had the same confused expression I wore when David first explained it to me.

*"Yes, for decades."* I ordered another bottle of wine and prepared for the questions to roll on. He had been respectfully tight-lipped so

*far, likely waiting for something worthy of a headline.*

*"…and nobody said anything about it or figured it out?"*

*"Why would they? The public only care about their own pockets, the government only cares what the public thinks. You must remember the service didn't officially exist until the 1990s, and when it became official the numbers quoted in the budget where simply plucked from thin air. Nobody had anything to check it against. It takes billions to run an operation like that, and who would question a bank for having assets in the billions?"*

*"Nobody, especially with the new liquidity rules."* Hamilton raised his eyebrows as he said it. His generation were familiar with how the world changed after the credit crunch. The newspapers had turned everyone into a pseudo regulator in public opinion.

*"They weren't so much of a worry back in those days."*

*"and what was your role in the intelligence agency?"*

*"In Pactum you mean?"* Hamilton nodded. *"As I was saying…"*

If I had to compile a list of questions I'd expected to be asked that morning, my interest in fishing would not have made the top fifty.

"Not recently."

"That's a shame, it's good for teaching a young man patience. Where you are sitting now has always been occupied by a man referred to as Piscator, The Fisherman. He is the person that brings in our supper. Puts a fishy on our dishy, if you remember that song…" I was sure that song was a shanty from the 1950's but I wasn't going to point out to David how long ago that was. "His role is to follow leads, work our network and bring us the information the service cannot. He is a professional and as such moves freely amongst the individuals holding the information we need. He can judge characters or situations, exercises discretion at all times and always goes that one step further to get what we need. I asked you here, because I believe you are the right person to occupy that chair. We have 'lines in the water' if you excuse the analogy, and I trust you to take on the responsibility of managing this part of our work, to make it your own and add to its past successes."

I had known David long enough to feel I could be totally

honest with my concerns, even though the continuing buzz from the cage wouldn't allow me to forget the seriousness of the situation.

"I'm incredibly flattered that you'd think of me for such an important role, but I'm not some sort of spook. I'm just a trader."

"I understand that, Alex. You must try to think of this position as an extension of that. You will be trading information. You will be the force behind some of the biggest investment decisions the firm makes. You will still be an employee of the bank and receive remuneration appropriate to your position, yet whatever turns the market or economy takes, you will have absolute job security. We may be dealing in a murkier world than others, but we are still business people. For example, we underwrite public offerings for the government, BT is a classic example. The IPO was handled by us and was totally above board. The government offered it to us so that any fees that would normally benefit the private sector helped fill the public purse."

How could I refuse when he put it like that? I couldn't see any downside but rolled my fingers across the table in front of me, as if I had to actively consider my choice. "I suppose I should start calling you Pater."

"Excellent! Only in this building mind you, everywhere else I'm still David. Now, we have a lot to get done this morning, so we best get cracking." He flicked the switch under the table and the cage wound down, the humming noise deepening in pitch before disappearing all together. David reached through the bars and slid the bolt back to open the door. I followed him outside where he introduced me to my new office, the blank door directly behind my spot in the cage. It was larger than I expected. The cold marble floor switched to thick maroon carpet, and instead of sparse decoration the walls were covered with classic prints of the English countryside and, of course, fishing. I imagined this had been David's choice of décor as it reminded me of his study in the country. A nice stout traditional desk sat in the middle of the room with a few chairs, topped by an outdated Acorn computer and an even more ancient telephone, complete with rotating dial. Given her antiquated tastes, my mother would have approved.

"This will need some updating, and of course you will have the funds to do so. Any trades you wish to make on the market will be done via Stephen, and for the short term will come with my oversight. The cabinets along the back wall contain all our asset files. I firmly believe that physical files are still the best option for us. Don't trust the computers." He walked round the desk and opened up the first cabinet. "We have them organized by sector, then by company name and asset name. Makes things easier to find when working a particular angle. You will have some time to look over these and get to grips with the set up later on. I keep my own files on individuals I work myself, but they will be handed over to you in time." David turned from the cabinets to again face me and began gesturing with his hands like an air stewardess before take-off "My office is to the right, to the left we have the facilities. Any questions?"

"Yes, David. There are the two of us, then P…"

"Patruus."

"I'm sorry, Patruus, but that leaves one seat open at the table."

"Oh! I almost forgot!" he exclaimed, excitedly rushing past me. I followed. "Yes, opposite Piscator sits Procurator, The Manager. He is a liaison between Pactum and 'friendly' groups, be that in government or elsewhere. More often than not these days it's the Americans. After all they are our closest ally and, at times, whiniest neighbours." We rounded the cage to the opposite wall "Hopefully he's in because I have a meeting at 9 o'clock, and you two will want to talk." David gave the door a gentle tap then swung it open. Sat with his feet on the table, flicking through a magazine, was that ever-familiar dishevelled figure. That's where he'd been hiding.

"I'll leave you boys to it."

"You sneaky, slimy, smug-faced bastard!"

"Come now, my friend, be honest. You'd rather it be me than anyone else, wouldn't you? Don't be so dramatic."

"Not a word from you. Nothing. You could've at least given me some warning. There were times this morning when I was wondering whether I was being inducted into some sort of cult!"

"Oh, sit down and stop whinging, this isn't the kind of thing I can bring up in the pub, is it? What if you turned it down? I'd be compromised." I admit that a large portion of my frustration was because this was the first time in our long friendship that Charlie had, in my perception, outsmarted me. I also couldn't escape the fact his office was much nicer than mine. Lucky bugger had a television…and more computer screens.

"How long have you been in on this?"

"I've known about it for a while. The work we've been doing over the last few years has been slowly gearing towards this, I just had a better idea of where it was heading. Those business trips I would take with the old man and any trading I did for him were always Pactum-related."

My recent work with Stephen had clear connotations with my new role but while I sat there listening to Charlie, I started to think back over the years I had known the family. I felt cheated in a way, like I'd been cultivated over time.

"Did Pater get you set up?"

"No. Gave me a run-down of the organisation and basic job description. Not much of an on-boarding."

"Okay, Joan must be dropping it off. Have you seen the market yet this morning?"

"No, I came straight here."

"We are already seeing a nice uptick in our efforts, couple of points but it's starting well."

"Lovely."

"Why are you being such a sourpuss? We've been trading for the last few years, living and dying according to numbers on a screen. You come here this morning and get the news any banker in his right mind would sell his left nut for."

"That the rules don't apply to some people? How is that supposed to make me feel better?"

Charlie sighed in exasperation at the moral dilemma that escaped him. "No. You have just been given the tools to never lose. We know exactly what card the dealer is going to flip next, and we use these skills to save lives."

"Don't you think part of the excitement in the market is that risk of not knowing for certain what's going to happen next?"

"No, the excitement in the market is how much money you can make in as little time as possible. If you wanted a job for excitement, you should've been a soldier or fireman. You got into this game for the same reason as everybody else, to make money."

"Easy for you to say, I was coming here hoping for a decent bonus." As if by appointment, a delicate tap at the door announced Joan's arrival. She quietly placed a box on Charlie's desk, not wanting to interrupt, and left as silently as she arrived.

"You got a bonus, my friend, trust me. We both did." Charlie opened the box and started to split the papers between us.

"Start working your way through these, make it all official." Charlie handed me one pile at a time for me to peruse and sign. The first was the Official Secrets Act, no surprise there. A relatively boring one-page document that carried a lot of weight. As rudimentary as it may sound, I did feel some pride signing it. It reasserted the patriotic argument David and Charlie had repeated several times, and I suppose it made it feel real. There was a standard employment contract, basically identical with the one I signed when I first joined the bank, complete with a confidentiality agreement which seemed rather hollow considering the document that preceded it.

"Finally let's get you signing these, so we can put a smile back on that face."

"What's this?"

"These are the authorization forms for your new company account. Your standard salary will still be deposited in your old account, but all expenses, bonuses and perks will go through this one. We can drop the papers by the when we're done." Charlie delved into the box a final time and pulled out a new Nokia box. "Poor old Joan used to sit downstairs like a gatekeeper, but the old man took my advice on replacing the door locks and moving her up here. Bless her, it was cruel to keep her in that chilly corridor during winter. These days we all carry our phones everywhere, so in the back of our phones we have a chip that pops the front door and calls the lift. Quite nifty really. Your new number and charger are in the box, you'll want to practice with it for a bit. Get the emails set up and such."

"It's a bloody brick!"

"Hey, this is cutting edge. How many phones do you know which allow you to send emails and check market data?"

"At this size I might as well use carrier pigeons." We finished putting the papers in the respective envelopes for filing away, leaving them at the front desk when I picked up my coat and returned to ground level. We still had the envelope for the bank and set out on the short taxi ride to The Strand. Cocooned in the back of the cab, I broached the question that had been festering with me since I walked into Charlie's office.

"So, am I your friend because you wanted me for the job or... am I getting the job because I'm your friend?"

"You've ended up here because you are clever, hardworking, blah, blah, but above that you are my oldest friend. I, and more importantly my father, trust you."

"Thank you, that means a lot."

"Do you want a hug too?" he said, deferring to sarcasm before the conversation became too sentimental.


\* \* \* \* \*


"Acquired."

"Any resistance?"

"Some but less than expected."

We pulled up outside Croups bank on The Strand. Croups had the distinguished moniker of being the Queen's bank of choice, as well as the choice for anyone with enough liquid capital to open an account there. They still had the staff in morning suits but managed to walk that fine line between modernity and tradition, in addition to the line between prestige and infamy. We spent mere moments at the front desk before an excitable personal banker arrived to tend to our every whim, guiding us to his desk while approaching a curtsy with every other step. He quickly flicked through the papers, only caring to make sure the signatures were present on the appropriate pages. He made a few jabs at his keyboard then with two clicks of his mouse his printer whirred to life. Just one page printed out, which he neatly folded and delicately sealed for modesty.

"Mr. Hope you will receive your chequebook and card within the next week, while I've taken this opportunity to print your current balance for your records. Is there anything else I can help you with today?" I declined any further service and after accepting the numerous compliments sent my way, we headed back to our waiting carriage.

"Are you going to open it?" I was sure Charlie had a pretty

clear idea of what was inside, and was more curious about my reaction. I popped the seal and unfolded the paper, very different from the inky printed bonus cheques I was used to getting. I freely admit that the balance was wholly grotesque to those who have experienced even a remotely hard day's work. Enough to keep me comfortable for quite some time.

"Club lunch on you today, my friend."

"Bollocks, I got you a sandwich the other week!" It was lucky we weren't back at The Tower as I would have failed miserably in masking my excitement. I had to give credit to Charlie when it was due, for he had indeed put a smile back on my face. After his "club lunch" comment I was expecting us to be heading east. We had spent many lunch times at The London Club next door to our old office. Instead we pulled back up on St. James, almost exactly where we were picked up a short time earlier. I knew both Charlie and David were members at Bianco's, which made sense as it was right next door. The oldest club in London was originally an oyster bar, centuries before it had the reputation of being the ultimate members' club. Not for the facilities, but for its wine cellar and list of illustrious past and present members. They had a clever habit of purchasing fine wines when first available, hiding them away in the cellar until the time was right (could be years or decades) to crack it open and sell it back to the members at zero profit. You could enjoy some of the finest wines in the country for the price of a regular bottle anywhere else. As we climbed the few exterior steps and entered the building, we were met by a portly gentleman in what I can best describe as a mahogany phone box. He was charged with guarding the interior from undesirables like left-leaning politicians or women. He gave Charlie a familiar nod as we passed and made our way to the bar, ordering up a brace of gin and tonics to start with. Heading towards the back of the ground floor we took up positions by the snooker table. Some low and simple black leather furniture nestled around a television alongside some convenient tables to hold our drinks. I imagine in the early years they had staff to hold the drinks for each man while he tried his hand at billiards, or whatever the game of choice was at the time. Charlie had an unfair advantage, not only because he was familiar with the table, but his height gave him at least twenty percent more reach for a long shot. I learned a long time ago to only play for money when the table was more appropriately sized.

"Bit more relaxed than the mile, isn't it?" I chirped after potting a red in the lower left pocket and positioning myself perfectly on black.

"At times, but we are always working. Especially you. At least I can turn my phone off and go home at night, as the old man tones things down you'll be expected to attend every event possible, building the network…putting 'more lines in the water'."

"I didn't know David was planning to step back. When's that going to happen?"

"Not for a long time yet, he doesn't want to drop you in the deep end. Then I'll switch to his spot and we'll bring in someone new to cover my duties."

"Should we even be talking about this here?"

"This is one of the few places we can talk about it. The ears in these walls are so firmly shut, that nobody noticed Kim Philby and his crew taking lunch here back in the day. Pater conducts almost all his meetings on that sofa or at lunch."

"Who are you lining up to take your spot when David goes out to pasture?"

"Can't say, but we have someone in mind. I'll get you involved when the time is right." Another few stiff gins passed our lips before we finished the game, a comfortable win for Charlie, despite my strong start. For lunch we had a choice between two dining rooms: one with the long members' table, reminiscent of the dining hall at school, and the other which had more of a restaurant set up. We chose the latter towards the front of the building and grabbed a table for two by the window. The lunch was fantastic and the decanted claret (a nice 1972) even better. Sitting back in our chairs, our belts suitably strained, we opted to keep it light and stick to cheese for dessert. I, for one, needed the fat in my stomach to help with the amount of alcohol already dancing its way round my system.

"What's the plan for the rest of the day?"

"Well, Pater just told me to get paperwork done. All that's left is to get you squared away here, we've made provisions to work around the usual hurdles." We went back downstairs where our gatekeeper had put aside a very large book. Charlie flicked through the pages pointing out notable current or previous members. Pater's page was filled with endorsements, Charlie's less so. He finally came to another page full of signatures, I recognized Pater's scrawl immediately. There was no name listed at the top of the page, just a logo. A simple fish drawn in pen, like the Icthus sign you see bandied about on bumper stickers for the pious. Charlie pulled a pen from his jacket pocket and proceeded to write today's date under the logo and the word "Quiz?"

"Okay, I just need you to respond and put your initials next to it." When we were very young, we used to use these words in school, a silly game to make light of learning a dead language. Charlie was asking 'who' and I just needed to respond 'I'. I was about to bypass a thirty-year waiting list with a schoolboy joke.

"Ego. A. H."

When Charlie had shown me the pages in the book I noticed another page with the fish symbol and flicked back to find it. I recognised Pater's signature as before none of the others. It was dated seven years ago with the initials P.J.

"Charlie, who is this?"

"Your predecessor, by the looks of it."

"When did he leave? This was signed just before we started full time."

"Look at the initials again. That's Peter Jayms, remember? Officers don't mix with regulars." I had asked the question of *why me?* but that page had answered the question of *why now?* I felt I should have made more of an effort at his send-off than I did. Charlie took control of the book again and turned the pages back to my own. The gentleman from the pillbox came to verify our new addition, shook my hand and returned the book to the archive. It was a shame, as I would have liked to investigate it further. I wondered how secret our organisation could be when I had already been endorsed by so many people. It reminded me of what Charlie had said earlier about trust within the walls of the club.

We returned to the office next door, Charlie having me go first to make sure the door popped as intended. Walking back to the cage, we saw that David's office door was open and he was enjoying yet another cup of tea while going over our positions. Shouting across the floor, Charlie asked, "How's the market?"

"She's doing well, flirting with many and sleeping with a few. You boys get yourselves sorted out?"

"Yup."

"Right, well you can both head out. I think our new Piscator has enough to get his head around on his first day. Enjoy yourselves and blow off some steam, tomorrow we get to work properly. Lights out early, boys." Charlie didn't need a second invitation; this was our belated bonus day. We headed back to the city, since I wanted to pick up some personal items from the old office and Charlie wanted to flash the cash in every bar that would accept us. We parted ways outside The Tower and Charlie went straight to the bar, expecting me to join him in a few minutes. Exiting the lift I received nothing from Bridget but an unwelcoming glance and when I stepped out onto the trading floor I felt the daggers of a hundred angry eyes. Not a single 'hello'. My desk had already been cleared.

"Alex." Stephen called over. "I've sent your stuff up to HQ."

"Oh, thanks. Why is everyone looking at me like I just killed their cat? What did I do?"

"Truthfully? Nothing. You don't need to worry about it. As far as they are concerned you have been promoted and that has created a lot of bad feeling. You're not high on the list of experience or production, so the consensus is it's because of your relationship with the family."

"Well, they're not wrong are they?" I couldn't pretend that this new opportunity came from merit of any sort that would measure against my colleagues.

"Don't put yourself down. You may not have a professional qualification for the role, but you have the attributes and abilities to thrive in it. This wasn't a decision made lightly. For the others, there are still people with chips on their shoulder. You and I know what's happening, but as far as that lot out there are concerned, you were born with a silver spoon up your arse, while they were born with a shovel."

"Couldn't we explain it in a way that didn't turn the office against me?"

"With the work you're doing now the last thing you want is

some colleague rocking up and making a mess of things. It's for the best kid, it really is. I'll still be on the end of a phone for you." Stephen was trying to make light of the situation and I probably shouldn't have taken things to heart. I had always done my best to maintain good relationships at work. Finance can be a small world. I remembered something my late grandfather told when I was younger: 'Remember those you meet on your way up the ladder, they are sure to remember you on your way down.' Those words resonated with me as I made what I assumed would be my final walk down the floor. No good luck messages but at least one or two of my former co-workers gave me a wave. I attempted to wish Tits the best and offer to answer any questions she might have on the clients she was handed. She just turned her back towards me and carried on talking to Biggy. I pushed it to the back of my mind and crossed the street to where Charlie was holding court at the bar with a gaggle of young ladies, lining the drinks up and priming each shot with a three second countdown.

"Another glass! Another glass!" he crowed. "There's my brother from another mother!" I needed the first drink to better my mood. The ones that followed weren't as needed, but were equally as welcome.

\* \* \* \* \*

"He won't work."

"Shame, I like that one."

"I'll take care of it,
keep in mind the bigger picture."

I had often weighed regret against experience. There's a list. Number one was the yard stick against which all else was measured: being fellated by a feminist at a political rally. Her hateful stare had long been cemented in my memory. Number two was trying jellied eels, something which bore more than a passing resemblance to experience number one, and number three was about to make her mesmerizing debut though she would only stay on the list temporarily.

The next morning broke with a familiar feeling, a bastard behind the eyes and little recollection of the night before. I felt something sweaty on top of my leg and rolled over to see I wasn't alone. She smiled and nuzzled her face into the pillow. It's a good thing she didn't open her eyes; I was looking at her like a man who discovered dog shit on the sole of his shoe. I gently slid my leg free and weighed my options. I had made the walk of shame many times but was unfamiliar with the etiquette to eject unwanted company from my own home. Should I have called a taxi? Slapped her arse and thrown her clothes at her? If she used my toothbrush I would vomit.

There was a glass of water on my bedside table and I could smell coffee brewing in the kitchen. I assumed Charlie had stayed in the spare room and woke up before me. I peeled myself from the sheets and wrapped my dressing gown around me to cover my modesty, knocking back the water with the intent of heading outside for some fresh air, and not so fresh air, to clear my head. Opening the bedroom door, I could see the television was showing the news, but of greater concern was the man sat on my sofa with the morning paper and another larger individual standing in my kitchen. I closed the door behind me to avoid creating too much of a scene and rubbed my eyes.

"Good morning, Alex. Pleasant evening?"

He folded the paper back on itself me to reveal his face, but I already knew the voice. Lovegood. I went for my mobile on the kitchen counter but the other man grabbed my wrist before I even got close and twisted it up behind my back.

"I don't know what the hell this is all about," I answered politely, "but I'm sure we can figure out the problem ourselves without things getting out of hand."

"I agree. You see, I just wanted to return the items you left at my office the other day. Terribly careless of you to forget them, but luckily your address was inside."

I was marched over to the sofa and pushed down next Lovegood. The burly man released my wrist and fetched some coffee and juice from the kitchen. Putting them on the table, he then exiled himself to the balcony, leaving me and his employer to talk alone. After my previous encounter, there was no way I was going to drink anything they put in front of me.

"Who's that?" he asked, gesturing to the bedroom.

"Look, what is it you want? I mean who the hell do you think you are, just turning up at my home like this?"

"Like I said, Alex, I didn't have much choice. You left in such a rush the other day, really quite rude. We still have much more to discuss…and now it's your turn to answer my question." I flushed the colour of beetroot. I had no idea who my roommate was from last night, although my ignorance was probably in her best interest.

"I'm not really sure."

"Do you think that's wise, bringing strange people into your home?"

"Probably not, but you brought a stranger into my home so can hardly preach on the subject."

"What do you know about her? Judging by the handwritten notes in your briefcase, you certainly do your research. Does she have an accent? What does she do? Where is she from? What did you talk about? Did you say anything you shouldn't? Do you need to pay her before she leaves…?"

"I…I don't know."

"How was she?"

"I'm not sure what you're implying."

"You had a young woman in your bed when we arrived this morning. What do you think I'm asking?"

*Dirty old bugger,* I thought, but I wanted to keep humouring him since I'd already experienced his reaction to avoidance. "To be honest, I slept so soundly that all I can really say for sure is that she was comfortable to sleep next to."

"Nikki, you can come out now." Lovegood shouted.

The bedroom door opened and Nikki joined our conversation. In the clearer light of day and with a top to bottom view, I was feeling rather proud of myself. Carrying her shoes in her hand she sidled up alongside me and gave me a slow kiss on the cheek. I was half tempted to ask her to stay a while.

"How did Mr. Hope get along?"

"I would have said pretty good, but I'll just leave it as

'comfortable'," she said, spitting out the word while making quotation marks with her fingers.

"Who is he and what does he do?"

"His names Alex, he works in banking. Equity trader in the city. Fits the type too." Neither of which were delivered as a compliment.

"Still playing his cover, even with you. Thank you, that is all."

Despite the snide remarks all I could think was that as much as I hated to see her go, it was very pleasant watching her leave.

"You seem you have gotten off lightly."

"I'll take that as a compliment."

"You shouldn't. She may not know who you are, but I do and we have unfinished business. Get dressed, we're leaving."

"I don't intend to do anything of the sort."

"Whether you want to or not, we are leaving. I suggest you take my kind offer to put some clothes on before we do."

"Where are we going?" I asked, not believing for one second I would get a straight answer.

"My office. Oh, and Alex, never describe a woman as comfortable. Shoes or a mattress, yes, but never a woman."

I retired back to my bedroom, quickly throwing on yesterday's suit. When I emerged again several more men had arrived. One was stood on my sofa fiddling with a light fixture, others were attempting similar handiwork in the kitchen. Before I could question their efforts, I was hit from the side by a pair of huge arms grabbing around my torso and a black bag was pulled over my head. I kicked out in despair, striking the edge of my coffee table; I heard cups fall to the floor and the crack of glass against my foot. Lovegood's voice cut through the chaos.

"Don't make it any harder for yourself. Remember that."

Plastic ties zipped tight to my wrists with their edges cutting into the tendons behind my thumbs. I jerked my head backwards, cracking the back of my skull against the nose of my assailant who let loose with a barrage of abuse and a right punch to my kidney. It felt good to get at least one hit on the opposition. They took me down the back stairs, locking their arms under my own and dragging me along while I tripped over each step. It was uncomfortable on the shoulders but truly painful on my hands, those plastic cuffs cutting deeper with every lurch. I was finally tossed into a vehicle, a van I believe. I could feel the ribs of the vehicle floor against my cheek. We began to move and I was doing my best to decipher where we were heading. I could tell when we left my building we were heading east and was trying to feel for the tell-tale left turn and arching roadway that would indicate we went north of the river. The roundabouts made it difficult to be sure of direction but I was quietly confident I hadn't felt either. If we were going to Lovegood's office, we weren't going to the one I had visited previously. My captors didn't say a word the entire journey but before too long we took a sharp left onto a distinct downslope.

The rear doors opened behind me and I was dragged out backwards into a building, briefly hearing the city before it drifted away, replaced with the echoes of pounding feet against a concrete floor. I was dropped onto an uncomfortable metal chair with my arms hooked over the backrest, then they latched a set of handcuffs to the plastic ties on my wrists and secured them against the seat. The room was noticeably colder than outside and, judging by the noise, a decent size. Still nobody was talking but after a loud bang, I assumed from a slamming door, I was left in silent darkness. I was playing out potential scenarios in my head and how I could somehow get a message out. After what felt like a few hours, a man entered. He asked my name and job, to which I answered truthfully.

"Alex Hope. Equity trader." He asked me where my office was, and who I reported to, I replied with just the address of the office in the city.

"You're lying. How about I leave you to think about that for a while?"

I pleaded that there must have been some sort of misunderstanding, but he didn't respond, walking away and leaving me alone with my thoughts. I shouted out requests for water and a phone call, but I received no response. Time kept creeping forward. I regularly reiterated my requests and my insistence that an error had been made. I needed to use the toilet, so yelled louder and louder, hoping for some humanity. Still nothing. I held out for as long as I could but to my shame it became unbearable. They seized the opportunity to make me even more uncomfortable, lowering the temperature in the room. I shivered uncontrollably as the nervous sweat and stale urine chilled by back and thighs. I was still shivering when the man eventually returned. "Let's see if you're feeling more helpful now. Maybe I could get you some dry clothes and a cup of tea? I'm nice like that. How about we start out small. Who is your boss?" I didn't respond, my embarrassment mating with natural stubbornness and growing anger at my faceless antagonist. Instead of repeating the question, he started pounding at my abdomen with his fists. The first hit came from nowhere, winding me and leaving me gasping for air. While my head was down to catch my breath, he continued to punch at my ribs until one on my left finally cracked and I yelped in pain.

"Still got a voice in there somewhere then, haven't we, Alex? It is Alex isn't it, my memory isn't too good." I wouldn't even answer those questions anymore, focusing my mind as hard as I could on convincing my body it was anywhere else. "Maybe you're losing your hearing." He left the room again when a deafening noise surrounded me from all sides, cutting between sirens, static and the sound of screaming. Now and then it would stop; sometimes for a few seconds, other times for a few minutes before blaring back at me. It prevented me from sleeping, despite my exhaustion, and was causing me to see things I knew were not there. At first, they were dancing lights like you see after rubbing your eyes too strongly. Soon they became confusing, like the black veil over my eyes was melting against my chin. I began rocking back and forth on the chair, humming hymn tunes I remembered from school as a distraction. The moments of physical torment became welcome relief from the sensory attack and allowed me to regather my thoughts. On one occasion I heard a popping noise and had the smell of red wine wafted under my nose. He lifted my cover just enough to put a glass to my lips and allow me a sip. It wasn't much, but it was heaven in that moment. I could hear the squeaking as the cork was twisted from the corkscrew and thrown at me, bouncing off my forehead while he laughed. Suddenly he stabbed the corkscrew into my knee and I screamed like never before. He shouted back over my screaming:

"You are going to tell me everything you know! The only question is how much longer you're going to try and fight that! Who do you work for?!" I shook my head back and forth violently to show my defiance. I was still swaying my head and gritting my teeth in pain when the sirens started up again. Before he left me, he turned the corkscrew a few times for good measure, only stopping when we could both feel the tip scratching against the joint.

My sadistic interrogator no longer stopped the noise when he entered, instead relishing how I would jump when I was finally become aware of his presence. I couldn't hear his steps nor did he utter a word, I would just be struck from nowhere. Rather than focus on my face he enjoyed playing around my knee or tugging on the corkscrew. When the noise eventually stopped again, I was too exhausted to even lift my head. "Where are your friends?" He ripped open my shirt and pulled out a staple gun, holding it against my chest while he asked the questions. "Who do you work for?"

Every time he would squeeze the lever as slowly as he could, making sure I could hear the tension build in the spring before the snap. That squeaking of the spring was worse than the pain of the staple, allowing a small window when I knew I could make it stop. I heard the screeching of furniture against the floor. The whiteness from fluorescent lighting burst through the weave all around my eyes and I heard a familiar voice call to me. "Alex...Alex." The bag was lifted from my head. "You're done. It's okay, you're done. You've done very, very well."

"Fuck you! What the fuck?! I'm going to fucking kill you!" Despite my condition the chair was bouncing off the floor as I fought to get my hands on him.

"Calm down, Alex, I need you to calm down." Some men held me down while another tended to my knee, carefully twisting out the corkscrew. "Get the fuck away from me, Lovegood!" I yelled.

"You keep calling me 'Lovegood'," he replied, cracking a wry smile. "That's no way to address your Uncle."

"What do you fucking mean? I don't have a fuck..." He waited for me. It took a minute to connect the dots. "You're joking?" The people behind me cut my hands loose, but kept hold of me fearing I would react too instinctively.

"You'll have to forgive the amateur dramatics, occupational hazard for me. You can just call me 'P'." He stepped slightly to the side. I could see another man with a bag over his head and his hands tied behind his back, sat on a chair similar to mine like a mirror of the before and after.

"Who is that?"

"That's the man who's been playing with you for the last four days."

\* \* \* \* \*

"The package is ready."

"Four days?"

My faculties were so disorientated I wasn't sure how long it had truly been. The people behind me released my arms and I slowly came to my feet. I shuffled towards the man, replaying in my mind what he had put me through and imagining what I could pay him in return. He was more rotund than I had imagined, and better dressed. When I got within a meter, P placed a hand on my shoulder to stop me. He put a pistol in my right hand with the other, holding my fingers around the grip with his and whispering in my ear.

"Don't you think he deserves it? Nobody will ever know." My energy began to return. He didn't need to hold my hand against the pistol, it felt at home despite never being there before. My finger began to stroke the trigger. I bent down in front of the bagged man and waited. I could see his breathing hasten as his chest rose and fell, tensing up and expecting the inevitable. I reached out with my free hand and grabbed his testicles in my fist, squeezing as hard as I could while he screamed through muffled lips.

"What the fuck are you doing?" came a voice from behind me. I immediately spun and pointed the pistol at that man instead.

"If I only know my assailant by his voice, do you think I would pull the trigger without hearing him bloody talk?" He stared at me blank and emotionless. His was the voice I knew. I released the unfortunate man who had been set before me and walked towards my target. He didn't move. It dawned on me that the pistol was probably only loaded with blanks. They weren't going to lumber themselves with a body, or at least I hoped they wouldn't. I kept the pistol aimed squarely between his eyes, but once I was close enough I pulled my arm back and struck him across the face as hard as I could. He hit the deck like a lead weight but I wasn't finished. I kicked him in the jaw once, then twice and watched a tooth skid across the floor behind him. Before I could finish what I started, but too late to stifle my satisfaction, I was restrained again. During the ensuing struggle a shot rang out from the pistol, ricocheting around the room. I dropped the pistol in disbelief and was rushed into an adjacent room.

"Deep breaths. Nothing more, okay, nothing more," said P. I shook my arms when they finally released me. The room was so warm compared to the other. There was carpet, furniture and bland yet blissful comfort. A perfume I knew cut through my own stench when a woman entered the room with fresh clothes and shoes.

"I suppose you've been enjoying this?" Nikki smiled, cheekily biting her tongue, and left with the others as a short older gentleman arrived with a large medic bag. He examined my knee and my torso, cleaning the wounds and gauging the damage. I was given two injections, one a tetanus booster and the other a painkiller.

"The medicine will help," he said comfortingly, and handed me a supply of pills to take when the pain flared up. After he was finished, I had some alone time to clean myself up. The clothes were my own, no doubt retrieved from the flat during my absence, and there was a small bathroom I could use. Feeling clean clothes against my skin was something I had always taken for granted; never again. I was happy to place everything I had been wearing in a rubbish bag I found under the sink and tie it very tightly. I still looked a mess but smelt less so. When a knock came at the door, I put my back to the wall and recoiled away. An unfortunate reflex of the experience. P kept knocking quietly as he slowly opened the door, aware that he may be entering a hostile environment.

"How are you feeling?"

"How do you fucking think?"

"Tired, angry, confused… to name a few. Do you understand why this had to be done?"

"No."

"You needed to know what you could handle, and I needed to know how you would react. If we are sharing information with you, I have to know it will be safe. Lives can depend on it."

"I didn't say anything."

"I know, and that's something we have to work on. You can say something. It hides the truth and offers you the chance of reprieve. The less you say the more determined they are that you're hiding something."

"So, after everything I'm not exactly making this role my own."

"This wasn't just about tolerating pain and guarding information." P explained, keeping his debrief as calm as possible "It's about mental toughness, keeping control of yourself under unbelievable pressure. Some people can handle it, others can't. You only need look at your colleague, Stuart, to understand the stresses of our work. He never sat on Pactum like you or me but was just as involved as Stephen. He couldn't handle the weight of expectation and gravity of the decisions."

"I see. What makes you think I can do better?"

"Given the chance of revenge against someone you were told was responsible, you still appraised the situation and acted with forethought. You remained rational and in control of the facts. You did very well."

"Thank you." P nodded a few times, as if pondering whether he had anything else to add. When he turned to leave, I asked, "Would you have let me kill him?"

"Who?"

"The man in the chair, would you have let me kill him?"

"Yes. He was a threat."

"To whom."

"You."

"Who was he?"

"I told you: a threat. Now go home and rest, you've earned it."

"Wait, what now? Where the hell am I?"

"See, you have to listen. I told you where we were going. This is my office."

I was at Vauxhall Cross, only a few miles from my flat. I had to see the irony that while I had faced physical and mental abuse, democracy was being practiced just over a mile away at the Palace of Westminster. My return home was far more comfortable, on the supple leather seats of a standard-issue government Jaguar. I had rarely been so pleased to get home, and never felt the urge to deadlock the door once safely inside. The answering machine blinked at me and I could guess who they were from. I dialled. It was nice to hear Mother complain about the weather and the disagreements with her book club. She asked the usual questions about work before moving on to more traditional queries about when I was going to settle down. I gave the same answers I always had. It wasn't riveting conversation, but it was a great comfort. I wouldn't have spent so long on the phone if I knew what was to come next. It was mid-afternoon but I was ready for bed. Limping towards the bedroom and nudging open the door with my shoulder I was surprised to see someone else had the same idea, wearing nothing but a smile and laying on her side facing me.

"I thought you might want to remember it this time." She was right in her assumption and giggled as I dropped my jacket to the floor. She came across the room and we embraced passionately, allowing our hands to explore recently-forgotten territory. I don't know what function she served in the service, but even if it was only to look good then she deserved a promotion.

"You can do anything you want," she said, nibbling on my ear.

"Anything?" I confirmed.

"Yes," she said as she turned my back towards the bed. I was still struggling with my leg but was feeling quite motivated and relieved that my natural instincts were still working as intended.

"And what are you going to do?" I asked as she unbuttoned my shirt and kissed down my neck and battered chest.

"Whatever you want me to do," she replied looking up at me as she kissed lower. I held her chin between my thumb and forefinger, guiding her back up to my eye level.

"That's *very* good to hear. I need this suit taken to the cleaners at the corner and could murder a bacon sandwich." She laughed dismissively. "I'm serious. Do something useful or get the hell out. I may not remember how things went last time, but I can assure you it cannot have been worth it. I suppose I should thank you, I now know the difference between a honey hole and a honey trap."

She huffed and grabbed her clothes, calling me several accurate but unflattering names as I followed her to the door. After I closed it behind her and slid across the deadlock again, I glanced downward at the old chap. He couldn't even bring himself to look me in the eye. "Sorry mate, maybe next time." I hobbled back to bed and collapsed on top of the duvet. I had learnt just how underrated silence was, and I was drinking in every ounce of it.

\* \* \* \* \*

"I can't find the woman."

"She'll find him at some point but I'm not worried. We'll cross that bridge if we come to it."

14

I dropped in and out of sleep over the following days, only waking when the medication had worn off earlier than intended or a passing police car jolted me awake with its siren. The phone rang several times. I didn't answer. Twice I heard Charlie knocking at the door and calling for me, but even then I didn't leave my bedroom. You have to understand, it wasn't depression or self-pity, it was self-assurance. I needed to be alone in an environment where everything was under my control. As my head began to settle, the flashbacks thinned, and the passing traffic startled me less. When the morning approached for me to return to work, I gingerly pulled myself out of bed. How I wished the doctor had given me something stronger. It was earlier than normal, so all was quiet in the flat. I needed the extra time to get ready with every little movement bringing sharp reminders of my recent ordeal. Aside from the pain, my normal routine was broken: I didn't want the radio to play. I didn't want to make coffee. I just wanted to enjoy peace and comfort while I watched the city stir. My case still sat on the sofa where P had left it. It didn't appear to be damaged by its tumble at Worship Street, so I popped it open to check the contents. All the papers I had prepared for the meeting had been removed, having served their part in the roleplay. My personal items remained, just desk fodder really: pens, blank paper and business cards. My old phone was there but smashed beyond repair. I presumed it to be the one casualty of my flight down the stairs. Still, it was nice to have my case back. Just like an old tennis racket, you become used to the grip.

When the time came to leave for St James, I stood at the door in the foyer watching the rain beat against the glass. I swore quietly to myself and stepped out into the weather, umbrella at the ready. While I wrestled to pop it up another umbrella was held out over my head. I turned to thank whomever it was, only to see Luis; David's chauffeur. "Good morning Mr. Hope, Mr. Smyth-Cummin thought you may appreciate my help this morning."

"Oh Luis, you have no idea." He escorted me to the vehicle, holding open the rear door for me to fall into the back. It was warm, dry and personally nostalgic. Luis couldn't resist a joke.

"Don't get too comfortable this time, Mr. Hope." It was a much better way to commute and I could understand why it was popular for those who could afford it, but I did feel uneasy about the attention it prompted from the damp and windswept pedestrians. The journey took longer than it would've by tube, queuing up with all the other vehicles jostling for every inch of progress. When we reached St. James, Luis shielded me to the door which duly popped open as I neared. I emerged upstairs to find Joan standing a few yards from the lift.

"Good morning, Piscator."

"Good morning, Joan, please just call me Alex."

"I'm afraid I can't."

She took my coat and I continued to my office. Passing into the back rooms was a peculiar experience and I imagined it would take some time to acclimatise to the drama of it all. I could see the office doors open for Charlie and David and the sound of the morning call coming from David's office. I made my way past the cage and received a very pleasant surprise. As I opened my door, I saw that the office had been redecorated in my absence. The old-world furnishings were gone, now replaced by items I would have happily bought for my own home. The old Acorn computer had vanished. Now, a new unit sat in its place alongside my Bloomberg box that had made its way over from the city with my personal items. Instead of the antique prints on the walls there were modern photographs of London, a cubist expression of a fish and a framed rugby shirt from university. Charlie came up behind me while I stood at the door.

"The rugby shirt was my idea."

"It's a nice touch."

We went into the office and Charlie sat down while I took a closer look at the wall decorations.

"Pater thought you could do with some cheering up."

"Remind me to walk a thank-you note over to his office with any therapy bills that may come in the future." Charlie wasn't sure whether to laugh at the comment or not. "Did you know what was going to happen?"

"Not really. I didn't know the extent of things until the next day. I asked Pater when you would be back and he gave me a brief overview."

"Have you done it?"

"No, I don't need it on my side of the cage. Pretty sure Pater has though, I've seen the scars."

"I can't recommend it."

"Well between that and Bertie he wanted to do something nice for you."

"What about Bertie?"

Charlie shifted uncomfortably in his chair. "Didn't you check your messages? I called you about it. I even came to your flat, but I don't think you were back yet."

"No I didn't, what's going on?"

"Fuck. There's no easy way to say this, my friend…" He explained that while I was away, there had been a bombing in Soho, North London. Part of a wave around the capital. Nails wrapped around plastic explosives, a rudimentary but effective method of inflicting as much damage and mayhem as possible. The bombings had been targeted at the gay and liberal scene, as well as ethnic minorities. Hate crimes before there was even such a category in the public conscience. "He had been stood outside a pub when the bomb exploded in a car next to him. He didn't stand a chance."

"What was he doing up there anyway? Can't imagine Bertie in that neck of the woods, can you?"

"I don't know, Alex, everybody has secrets. Maybe that was Bertie's."

"We would have known by now, surely."

"Maybe he was struggling to come to terms with it in front of his friends and family. You know how old-fashioned his parents are."

"His parents, yes, but not his friends."

"Have you ever seen him with a girlfriend?"

"Well, he told me about…"

"But have you actually seen him with one?"

"I suppose not."

"Then is it really that far-fetched?"

"I really don't want to think about it right now."

"Of course my friend, I'm sorry. I've had it spinning around my head for a few days, I forgot it's still fresh for you. The funeral is tomorrow afternoon near his parents' place in country. I know Rupert is heading down tonight, got a room at the local pub, but I'm going to drive down in the morning if you need a lift. The old man suggested you and I stay at the house, make a weekend of it."

"We'll see how it goes. I'm still feeling pretty rough to be honest."

"You're not going to miss the funeral, are you?"

"Of course not, I just don't know if I can handle your driving at the moment." The dig at Charlie softened the mood slightly. I told Charlie how Bertie had helped to drag me to the office the other day and we laughed at the image of him and Stephen lugging me up Old Broad Street. We talked a lot about him that morning, jokes from university and tales from the city. I didn't mourn him though. I can't say if it was shock or emotional numbness lingering from the interrogation, or simple disbelief. Shortly after the morning call was over, Pater knocked on the door and poked his head around the corner.

"Pactum meeting in fifteen minutes, boys."

⋆ ⋆ ⋆ ⋆ ⋆

"Lima 8 7 1 November Papa Romeo."

"Lima 8 7 1 November Papa Romeo. Copy."

We took our seats just as P entered through the double doors and jogged across to his local office. David taunted him about potential tardiness before they joined us in the cage.

"Golly, the first meeting for this complete incarnation of Pactum. Bit off the cuff, but a big moment for you two and I know I speak for Patruus and myself when I say how excited we are to be working together and equally excited for the future of Pactum. It's in good hands."

"Hear, hear!" agreed P.

"Procurator, what news from our colonial cousins?"

"Little to report from London, Pater, they continue to take an active interest in the winding up of the Lockerbie affair but no word on their intentions going forward."

"Our sources on the ground have indicated that whether the US has an interest in Libya or not, Tripoli wouldn't welcome their efforts. The Mad Dog will never forget what happened," added P. The US bombings of Tripoli had inadvertently killed the ruler's adopted daughter, something which could yet prove beneficial to UK interests as it gave our firms preference over the Americans.

"Good, meanwhile our holdings in BP and Shell are

performing as expected. The market is starting to get wind of the possibilities and our gains stood at 15% as of yesterday's close. Piscator and I will be attending an event for UK Oil and Gas next week, after which we will have a clearer picture of future strategy. Move more of our eggs into the one basket," summarized Pater before moving on to the next topic. "It's time for us to close out our holding in Pfizer for now, the rush from Sildenafil peaked and I doubt we will get anything else from the situation. I'll get that order across to Stephen before New York opens." We ran over our current holdings, giving me my first full look at the state of the accounts. It wasn't so different to large cap funds I had seen a hundred times before, only more focussed. Rather than hedging risk over an entire sector, the investments were targeted at specific companies. The balance was handsome, showed solid year on year growth, but the compounded performance was held back by the constant need for the service to draw down capital. It was immediately obvious that David and P had different viewpoints. David saw it as something he had been entrusted with and referred to it as the endowment, while P called it The Fund. A fund he regularly pilfered. One holding really surprised me, Gazprom. I had assumed that the holding Stephen had shown me for the 'Lovegood' meeting was just part of the cover. The shares had already started to be sold via Guernsey, just as Stephen had suggested.

"Patruus, what are your plans for Piscator at present?" asked David.

"We will need to borrow him for a chunk of time: training, field craft, and the like but we can figure out a schedule which works best for all us."

"I'll spend some time with him over the weekend, see if we can get something in the diary while things remain relatively quiet. Until Tuesday then, Patruus. Enjoy your weekend."

P left as quickly as he arrived, leaving me to wonder why he bothered having an office here at all. Charlie had to prepare for a lunch meeting in Grosvenor Square and it would be just David and I left in St. James that afternoon. I started up my Bloomberg box to check the market but mostly because I was anxious to see what my profits were from the BP trades. A shallow act itself, but a habit I was unlikely to break. As a percentage, the gains since I last checked remained modest, but the Sterling amount was far from it. I was confused by the total shareholding, showing only the trades I had placed and nothing in relation to the orders which Charlie had pushed through at Bertie's firm. I searched through the system to try and find any records of the trades. Nothing. If nothing showed in the system, not even the transfers to or from Monnow Wealth, then perhaps something would be in the physical files.

My eyes were instinctively drawn to "F" for 'Finance', and I wondered who I might recognize from the library of information at my disposal. I browsed the personal files for every board member of the major investment and high-street banks active in the UK, not to mention CEOs of similar institutions overseas. The number of compromising positions they had been photographed in came as no surprise, but the more interesting aspect was the details of their personal holdings. Mostly layered under shell companies and convenient legal wrappings on numerous continents. The manner in which they would constrict their clients with regulation while blatantly flouting it themselves left a slightly sour taste in the mouth. Accounts in Panama, The British Virgin Islands and other Caribbean territories. Some had purposely taken citizenship in smaller Caribbean nations or South America with the sole purpose of avoiding UK or

US taxation policies. In their situation it's an easy calculation: donate half a million dollars to a state-sponsored charity, then be gifted citizenship and the low income and inheritance tax perks that accompany it. While my initial reaction was one of condemnation, there was a part of me that realized it was probably something I should investigate for my own benefit. After all, tax evasion may be frowned upon, but tax avoidance has always been a flourishing industry. As enlightening as the finance section was, when I reached the Monnow file, there was no record of any recent transaction with us. It didn't look as though pages were missing, there was simply nothing there.

I moved along the wall to the Oil and Gas section of the cabinets, seeking out the BP file. The file was thick and heavy, barely containing itself as I carried it over to my desk. The first page of the file was a full catalogue of the trades I had placed, both in the UK and the US and notes on our anticipated investment horizon. It extended further than I had originally thought on a capital gain play, looking forward a few years rather than a matter of months. Still there was no record of the other trades, instead a catalogue of historical transactions flowing back to the privatization between 1978 and 1987. No prizes for guessing who handled the majority of the public offerings. Much of the file was ancient history and I simply glanced over it until things became relevant again. I could see the handwriting change over the notes from the service and as my predecessors came and went. I came to the final portion of the file and recognized the hand of the man I succeeded. It was the same as the members' book at Bianco's. There were only a handful of pages, not much to show for the years he spent in the role. I thought perhaps he had been focussing his efforts elsewhere. This side of the first Iraq war, Oil had been experiencing organic growth rather than drastic bursts of activity like we were expecting from North Africa. I was nose deep in the files when David suggested I join him for lunch next door, a chance go debrief between the two of us.

He was very patient waiting for me to climb the outer steps and then the stairs. My leg had stiffened up while sitting at my desk and I was exhausted when we finally reached our table. We were inundated with well-wishers, all pardoning their interruption but eager to meet the new boy. With each visit I would stand to be introduced, hiding my wincing behind a smile. They were the men who had signed my page at Bianco's, all aware of Pactum in some capacity but knew nothing of its function. It was an institution, not something to be queried but appreciated in its anonymity. One or two faces were familiar; I must have met them at one of the Smyth-Cummins' parties. They certainly remembered me, welcoming me on a first-name basis. Those that really stick in my memory are people I recognized from the papers: Gerald Didcomb from the Royal Bank (who I had recently learned enjoyed the company of young Eastern European women when his wife was away) or Matthew Capstan from BP, who was very excited.

"Good to see the new boy settling in well, David, strapping young chap like that will breathe new life into your outfit."

"We certainly hope so."

"Splendid, look forward to seeing you both at the conference."

I had just sat down from what I hoped would be the final time when a siren parped from right outside our window, making me jump and knock over my glass of water. As it raced across the tablecloth and began to drip to the floor I fumbled with my napkin. Eyes were watching me from around the room, the odd snicker from usually quiet corners sounding like hysterics to my embarrassed ears. David leant over the table and mopped it up with his napkin.

"Don't worry about it, it's all fine. It takes a while to pull your head out of that place."

"How long did it take you?"

"The worst of it passed within a couple of days, but some things take much longer. Others you just learn to live with."

\* \* \* \* \*

"It's going to be him."

"Who else knows?"

"Only me."

"Then we can fix that."

The reason for the sirens soon became apparent, a ministerial escort. Hardly anybody looked up from their tables when the Foreign Secretary walked across the dining room. Those who did only did so in disapproval of his political leanings. I expected him to approach our table as the final introduction of the day, but he walked straight past us, without David offering him as much as a glance.

"No introduction to the Minister?" I queried.

"I don't know him, my boy. Even if I did it would be different to the others. Politicians generally don't mix well with Pactum; they never stick around long enough. They know what it is but have no idea who we are. Even those at the service only know who they need to, usually Patruus and Piscator. Some of the more senior figures know me from my fishing days but that's about it."

"David, do you mind me asking about some of our holdings?"

"Not at all. Ask away."

"I noticed the Gazprom domestic stock on the report."

"I thought you might recognize those."

"I'm curious. Why on earth would we buy the Russian line?

It makes no sense for us to hold those instead of London."

"You're absolutely right, but we didn't buy them. That is one of the only examples I know of where the service has injected value rather than withdrawn it."

"The service gave us the shares?"

"Yes. Patruus, brought them in a few months ago."

"Where did he get them?"

"God knows. Probably some Kazakh arms dealer or something. Don't you know never to look a gift horse in the mouth? It could be worth holding onto some of them if the Rouble stabilizes. What moves in oil will inevitably move in gas."

"Yes, of course." The conversation stuttered to a pause. When the silence was about to reach an awkward length, David brought up a new topic. Not a comfortable one, but one that needed to be addressed.

"I was very sorry to hear about your friend. Always sad when you lose someone from a close group like that. Sadly, there is no way to protect people from the actions of one damaged individual. I liked Bertie a lot, good chap."

"I don't think it's really sunk in yet."

"That's understandable. There is no harm in telling you this now, but I had hoped that he may be the next one to join our team."

"Really?"

"Yes. There will come a time when I have to hand the reins over and Charlie's said how well the three of you worked together."

"He would have been a fine choice, David. Charlie and I are heading to the funeral tomorrow which will be difficult for both of us."

"Especially for Charlie. He doesn't deal with these things very well. That is one of the reasons you are where you are."

"What do you mean?" He didn't reply immediately, waiting for the waiter to leave our plates and move a safe distance away. "Since the beginning, Pactum has had a Smyth-Cummin at the table. At times there are two, prepping the next generation for a fluid transition. Traditionally, in the case of my father or myself, we spend our time in finance before coming to Pactum and taking up the position of Piscator. That way we have our banking background along with the training and experience of the darker side before we eventually progress to the role of Pater. That was the plan for Charlie, but he isn't capable. I had hoped to have him follow my steps as Piscator and have you sat opposite him. Things didn't really go to plan when he was due to meet Patruus."

"Clash of personalities?"

"They get on very well, actually. The problem was he gave up everything before even reaching the office. Crumbled like a soggy biscuit as soon as they put a bag over his head. I was relieved to see you perform better, or we would have been left at a bit of a loose end."

"What would you have done if I had declined your offer or didn't pass P's testing?"

"In the past we have, when necessary, brought in more senior people to the role."

"Like Mr. Jayms?"

"Jimmy, that's correct. After I took over from my father I had a cousin from the foreign office take the Piscator seat, hoping he would hold it until Charlie was ready, but he expired too soon. Jim kept the seat warm as a favour to me until he sadly went the same way. That's the big problem with having older people in your position, they don't have time on their side. You and Charlie have decades in front of you."

Decades seemed like a long time to spend at the same company; the best bankers usually spend time at several firms, following fattened envelopes and flattery around the city. It became clear this wasn't the sort of firm you left until nature or fate made the decision for you. I was surprised to hear of Charlie's shortcomings, especially from his own father, but not surprised Charlie had chosen to keep it to himself. I didn't even want to share my experience with him and mine had been viewed as a success.

Lunch meandered on at a leisurely pace and David became more relaxed, and I grew more comfortable. Although we had known each other for years, it was always as Charlie's father. Now, I was starting to build what felt like my own friendship with him as a colleague and mentor. "Our job can be incredibly rewarding but at the same time terribly lonely. There are more people alive who have been to space than have seen the cage, but like any job there will be times when you need to talk to someone, get things off your chest. You have my number and my door is always open, whether at work or play. I wanted us to have this time today to assure you of that. It wouldn't be right to have this sort of chat over the weekend when Charlie is knocking around."

"I won't mention anything to Charlie, which reminds me I need to call him to sort out my lift for tomorrow."

"Don't feel like driving?"

"I just don't see the point of owning a car in London."

"Ha! Same excuse every young man makes when he can't afford the car he wants."

"There is some truth to that."

"There used to be, maybe that would be a good way to spend your afternoon," advised David as he stood and failed to button his jacket over his lunch tummy. "By the way, new boy always gets lunch the first time. Bill it to your account."

I pressed my nose and palms up against the glass of the dealership like a boy at a sweet shop window. It was still raining outside but she was gleaming under the spotlights of the concourse, flirting with me and begging to be taken home. The glistening navy paint flowed over every sleek panel, from her pert front end to her voluptuous hips. As she turned on the rotating display it was like watching a perfect pirouette, waiting for her to turn back towards and lock me in with her hypnotic Aryan stare. This precious moment was shattered by a rude little man flicking his hands at me beyond the pane. His attempts to shoo me down Kensington High Street left me half tempted to go elsewhere, but I was there for her, not him. When I instead walked into the dealership the same man seemed far more helpful, offering me his best apology in a very confused accent. He tried to offer me all sorts of drinks, brochures and keepsakes but I had one question for him.

"Do you work on commission?"

"Yes, why?"

I looked around the sales floor and spotted a young man playing with his pencils and stacking up business cards like a pyramid. "Excuse me young man. Young man! Can you help me with this?"

"The Turbo?" he asked as he looked up from behind his desktop construction.

"Yes. I'll take it."

\* \* \* \* \*

"The transfer to M is complete."

"Thank you. My cut?"

"Deposited as requested."

The traffic was thin in the morning. As we passed Chiswick towards the motorway, there was a cheeky whisper in my ear to tell me I was under starter's orders. We approached the national speed limit sign, I dropped two gears and rocketed down the road.

"You should call her Betsy!" yelled Charlie over the flat six roar.

"After the housemaster's Beagle?" I replied, notching through the gears and flying past more pedestrian vehicles.

"Yes, she's one noisy bitch! Ha!" Charlie wasn't a comfortable passenger but when I told him what I was driving he was happy to ride shotgun. He'd had a few nice cars in recent years, but the trees kept jumping out in front of him without warning, leading to a self-imposed sensible car period until the landscape learned to behave itself. After an hour or so heading west down the M4 we veered off to the ever-narrowing roads of the Cotswolds. The rear engine set-up of Stuttgart's finest hunkered Betsy down on her haunches and shot us from corner to curve…

*"You're a Porsche guy?" Interrupted Hamilton.*
*"I was. 993. Wonderful vehicle."*
*"996 for me."*

*"Ugly thing, but solid mechanics away from the IMS. Like a woman with land and a good personality but a face only a mother could love. I suppose in either case, you don't care once you're inside."*

*"I...I..."* Millennials always struggle to balance humour with morality, a silly problem in my opinion. If you can't learn to laugh in the rain, then there's a chance it will drown you in the end.

*"Never mind..."*

Neither of us had ever had so much fun going to a funeral. It might sound inappropriate, but I can assure you if it were the other way around, Bertie would have squeezed himself into the laughable back seat and goaded us to go faster. The drive was playing hell with my leg but worth every corner. We slowed it down as we came into the village and parked at The Saracen's Head, a pub where Rupert was staying opposite the church. We had arranged to congregate there and go across as a group. Although Charlie was normally a bit of a scruff, not quite "too posh to wash" but getting close, he made a special effort for matches, hatches and dispatches. Most of us invested in specific suits for the long term such as a good morning suit and evening dress. Another item from that category was the funeral suit, black or charcoal and a black tie. It was always sombre putting it on, especially for someone so close and young as Bertie. On the other hand, away from the depressing sight of black-clad mourners, today it managed to carry a side joke for our group of friends. The last time we were all in the same outfits, Bertie included, we were dressed as the Reservoir Dogs for a fancy-dress party. We had been to that very same pub and watched Bertie butcher the Backstreet Boys at karaoke for his birthday. Charlie, Rupert, and I joked whether any of their numbers may figure in the service. The mood quickly soured, though, when we saw people gather across the street and the hearse pull up. The sight of the coffin was enough to push Rupert over the edge, Charlie offering him a comforting rub on the back before we walked over to the church, which was touchingly full.

The service was pleasant, a good combination of poignant readings and rousing hymns. Mr. Kirkman, Bertie's father, gave a lovely eulogy. He managed to keep his upper lip stiff until his final line: "A life well lived is never too short." It pushed us all close to, if not across the line. You could tell that as much as he tried to believe those words, he felt both he and his son were robbed of a future. Personally, I believe we are programmed as humans to accept the natural order of things; we know that if things pan out properly then we will one day bury our parents. Watching someone bid farewell to their child flies in the face of that. It's not the way things are meant to be. Seeing Mr. Kirkman so emotional saddened me. He had always been such a stoic man. My intention had been to see him and Bertie's mother after the service to offer my sympathies, but I then wondered if it would do more harm than good. I could be too close a reminder of their loss.

The wake was back at the pub and relatively cheerful, everyone determined to live up the obituary cliché of celebrating a life. Stood alone at the corner of the bar, not knowing anyone else but still paying her final respects, was Tracy. I limped over to say hi, unsure if she would remember me. She certainly did. Rather than shying away or coming towards me after making eye contact, she just stared me down. I remarked how it was nice to see her again although under such difficult circumstances.

"You've got a nerve to come and talk to me." I knew I had been less than charming on our initial meeting and was surprised she even remembered it. I started to apologize but she cut me off mid-sentence by tipping her drink over my head, drawing gasps from the surrounding people.

"All you get is a gammy leg. He dies and all you get is a gammy blooming leg? It's not fair!"

Charlie rushed to my aid, standing between us and blocking any further outbursts. The bar man handed me a towel and I patted myself down. There was no way I could stick around after that so went to the car, embarrassed at the outburst inside and confused over her choice of words. I felt terrible about how I could be responsible for such a scene at my dear friend's wake. I stripped to the waist to throw on a polo shirt from my bag.

"I wouldn't worry about it too much my friend, everyone grieves differently…" I turned around upon hearing Charlie's voice and it immediately shut him up "…Jesus Christ…"

My left side was all black from bruising around my broken rib, fading into purples and reds at the edges. The rest of my chest was a mixture of yellows, splintered capillaries and more bruising. The staple holes left a variety of small scabs amongst the bruises, like someone had painted a poppy field on me. "That bad, is it?" I asked.

"No. No, its fine. I just wouldn't go sunbathing any time soon. Let's get you out of here."

"I was hoping you'd say that. You say goodbye to the Rupert?"

"Yes, said we would have to meet up back in London next week, do our own farewell for Bertie. You want me to drive?"

"God, no." It was only thirty-minutes to David's country house, ten minutes of which was on his own land. Enough time for Charlie to raise an ill-informed query.

"So, do you think Bertie was…you know…gay?"

"Would it matter to you if he was?"

"No, no of course not...but all those times we showered after rugby..." I burst into a fit of laughter as Charlie shuffled in his seat discussing the subject.

"You arrogant arse!"

"What?"

"You think that just because he was gay, he would automatically find you attractive?"

"Well, he's only human." Some great sweeping left and right handers broke the conversation as we listened to the whirring turbo and exhaust notes, windows down and foot to the floor. We only slowed down when the rear tyres stepped nervously to the outside during a boisterous exit. I reeled her back in a little, not wanting to follow Charlie's example of launching into a hedgerow.

"Do you think Tracy was under the impression I was there when he died, like I was the excuse for him going up that way?"

"That would make sense, my friend, you were the only one from our group she would probably remember, and you've got a few injuries. It's an understandable assumption."

"Possibly. On the subject of Bertie, I'm curious about the account you had with him."

"I told you I had a client who wanted to deal in US securities."

"Don't treat me like an idiot, Charlie. I know it's not for a client. Bertie told me it was a prop account for CS."

"I..."

"Furthermore, he also told me you had been going long on both our oil picks in New York."

"I don't know what to say."

"Just tell me what's going on, Charlie, we're on the same team here and it's not a very big one. We need to be on the same page."

Charlie hesitated before offering his answer. "The old man

was looking at Bertie for Pactum. He was the other recruit I was talking about in the club."

"Yes, David told me yesterday."

"Well, doesn't it make sense that he would therefore be given the same task as you and me? See how he did."

"Sorry, of course. I'm still not thinking straight."

"It's fine, don't worry about it."

"So why don't I see the trades reported in our files?"

"My God, Alex, just drop it! We're here to enjoy the weekend, so let's enjoy it." I didn't want to drop it, but we were already at the house. The estate encompassed a few thousand acres, mostly arable farm land let out to a miserable old farmer who had regularly chastised us when our youthful late-night revelry spilled into the fields. Apart from that, the few cottages remaining on the estate were occupied by locals and farm hands, although Charlie had talked about taking one over himself. The main house was the stereotypical Georgian style, Cotswold stone and columned grandeur. Not on the scale of the ancient aristocratic boltholes nearby, but still quite imposing. Unlike most of the large country houses, David had resisted the urge to open it to the public or close certain wings. The income from the bank was key to its maintenance, and he would often complain of the rules and regulations in place for listed properties that forced the costs up for any work that was needed. He still had a gardener and a housekeeper, but long gone were the days of employing a team of household staff. I jumped on the brakes at the final approach, terrified the gravelled final few yards might flick up and chip Betsy's skirt. David was sat at a rusted iron table, plonked at the edge of the gravel so as not to spoil the grass, enjoying some early wisps of summer with a familiar guest. It wasn't quite short sleeve weather but any slice of sunshine is enough to have the British reach for the Pimm's and a wide-rimmed cricket hat. He stood up and came to greet us as we rounded the flowerbed opposite the main door.

"German! Dearie, dearie me. Why on earth would you buy something German?" We still had the windows down and could hear his taunt before I even turned off the engine. After his comment I couldn't resist revving to the line before dismounting.

"Because she's fast, beautiful, and won't leave me at the side of the road."

"I knew a German girl exactly like that in the seventies, but she suffered the same problem as that car. No soul." He gave Charlie a brief hug, almost as an afterthought but still more than the business-like handshake he afforded him in the office. "You're lucky my father isn't alive. I turned up with a Beetle and he threatened to disown me if I didn't get rid of it the very same day. Come on inside, grab a glass." While David started towards the house, his other guest came towards me, her dress flicking side to side with each assured step.

"Long time no see."

"Amelia, how are you?"

"Good, I'm doing good. Are you going to take me for a ride?" she said with a gentle squeeze of my arm and peck on the cheek.

"I thought we already had that covered?"

"I'm right here!" shouted Charlie, still in earshot.

"Joking aside, it is good to see you." The way she hopped between flirtatiousness and sincerity still gave me shivers. She could play me like a hand of poker. We dumped my bag by the door and met David as he returned from the kitchen with our glasses, and a thoughtful bottle of water. I wasn't ready to stomach alcohol again by then. The men took up spots in the sun while Amelia went to fetch some sandwiches the housekeeper had prepped for our arrival. David quietly informed me that Amelia sat in the ignorant bliss category, knowing that we worked together but it was nothing other than what she described as "boring number stuff". It would make it tricky to talk shop over the weekend so the topic of conversation on her return was the woeful performance of David's beloved county cricket side.

"If you're not swinging the willow in a one-day game then you might as well sit at twelfth man. He's wasting another man's opportunity."

"Okay then, my boys, cucumber sandwiches for this afternoon. I thought it was appropriate being Bertie's day," interrupted Amelia, who held a deep-seated hatred of all things cricket. Too many long days forced to watch her brother on Saturday afternoons.

"No cucumbers!" shouted Charlie at me, to which I responded, "No, sir. Not even for ready money," putting us both into giggles as Amelia shook her head and David let it fly over his. In university we did a production of "The Importance of Being Earnest" with our college. Bertie was desperate to be involved but was simply terrible. We cast him as Bunbury, to his delight, until he finally read the script. It was a lovely afternoon under peculiar circumstance, even when the sun began to set and jumpers came out, we stayed outside until the wildlife began to chirrup the call for dinner.

✶✶✶✶✶

"This is different to Buynaksk and the others. Don't rush."

It wasn't a formal affair, the four of us sat around the kitchen table for sausages and salad, a tweaked family favourite. I'm sure the salad was Amelia's influence. When we were younger David used to avoid it like the plague, claiming himself to be above rabbit food. Amelia was the first to go upstairs, leaving the three of us to put in the late shift. With the coast clear it didn't take long for conversation to turn to work, but with their bellies of Pimm's and wine and port and scotch, it wasn't on a serious note.

"Dads, how old is Joan? She's been there for as long as I can remember." David chuckled to himself before admitting that he genuinely had no idea, she had been there longer than he had. We bounced round ideas of her being some sort of witch, duty-bound to Pactum after losing a wager on a long and lonely midnight road. We joked about all sorts of silliness, like using the cage as a giant barbecue or converting P's barely-used office into a bar. With the others three sheets to the wind I decided to play Mother and cleared away the items from the table, keeping the cheese and drinks out but doing my best to sort the rest. Charlie and David started getting quite heated about the direction Pactum was heading, David more UK-centric but Charlie far closer to the US side of things. Hardly surprising considering it was Charlie's job to liaise between the two.

"I'm sorry Dads, but we need to be working closer with the Americans. The market is bigger and the more information we have of theirs the better we are."

"Don't be silly, have you considered what they might expect in return? How about the FX risks we ride with trading overseas? One interest rate move in the wrong direction and we could lose millions."

"Millions would hardly kill us, would it? You're looking at a very slim chance of that happening without us knowing beforehand."

"Millions is a lot of money, especially when it's somebody else's."

"That didn't stop you buying Pfizer."

"Well…that was more about market penetration!" David thought the saucy joke was great, but Charlie didn't appreciate the timing. He was trying to be serious.

"What about the ADR's we've been using?" replied Charlie, feeling as though there was a double standard at play.

"Alex's idea with the ADRs is fine, it eliminates that risk."

"Then let's get Alex's opinion on it, shall we?"

They both turned to me like I was going to side with each of them. I tried to palm them off, saying it was outside of office hours and I was just there to wash dishes, but neither of them would accept it. I begrudgingly spoke out. "We couldn't eliminate the risk all together, but we could mitigate some of it by rolling FX futures. We may lose out on the potential upside of any shift, but it would help avoid any downturn. Having a US presence and dollar deposits would help, the settlement on holdings like Pfizer would be streamlined and we wouldn't be at the mercy of the exchange rate every time we wanted to make an investment."

"See! What did I tell you!" bellowed Charlie triumphantly.

"Alex may be right, but that doesn't mean I'm going to agree to it. We dabble in the colonies on occasion but I'm not comfortable with the idea of having a more permanent presence. We can bring it up in the cage next week, see what P thinks." David turned his attention to me "Nice work...again." Charlie took exception to his father's comment.

"Hey, hang on. That was my idea."

"It was, but you didn't know how to do it, did you? I have an idea I want to fly to the moon, but if I don't know how to build the bloody rocket, I'm not going, am I? This! This, is why I'm grateful, as you bloody should be, that you have a friend who can bail you out of situations like that!"

It was time for me to leave. I had no wish to be sandwiched between warring relations with fire in the blood and fuel in the belly. I quietly snuck out the door and grabbed my bag to head upstairs. There were plenty of rooms to choose from, but I had a favourite I would take whenever the option was available. It stood at the top of the landing immediately opposite the upstairs drawing room, giving the best view down the drive and over the rolling hills beyond. As I got to my room, I could hear the voices below getting louder and louder. Even with a bedroom door between us it was still going to keep me awake. The voices suddenly stopped. I ventured out to the landing to see if a truce had been reached. The kitchen door slammed, and they started up again, even louder than before with Charlie on the offensive. I noticed Amelia along the bannister, equally concerned with the racket downstairs.

"This could last for hours," she whispered.

"There is enough port on the table to keep them going until dawn."

"How about that drive?" I grinned at the suggestion. "I mean an actual drive. Christ, get your mind out of the gutter."

With no peace likely to come soon it didn't seem that terrible an idea, better than sitting on the stairs listening to them squabble like frightened children during a divorce. I grabbed my keys and we quietly slipped out of the front door. It was a cloudless night with a brisk chill in the air, the few minutes of driving it took to get the warm air flowing in the car was tortuous for Amelia, more used to warmer climes and with very little meat on her bones.

"God, I hate it when they fight like that. They can be so alike sometimes, and total opposites at others."

"I've not seen that side of them before."

"Get used to it, it's come out more and more with work. The more time they spend together the worse it gets."

"I don't spend that much time with your father to be truthful, just when he stops by the city."

"You've always been a terrible liar, Alex."

"What do you mean?"

"I can hear everything in the kitchen from my room." *Shit, shit, shit*, I thought.

"Relax, I've known since I was a girl. Mum told me Dad wasn't really what he seemed, he never locked his study and I got curious. I didn't blab then, and I don't intend to start now. Everyone has secrets, just some more than others."

"You know I can't talk about it."

"I know…" She put a hand on my shoulder and ran her fingers towards my neck. "…just don't take me for a fool and spin the same yarn as the others. If you need someone to talk to, I'm here."

"Thank you, I appreciate the offer…and what have you

been doing since I last saw you?" Distracted by her hand it was the best why I could think of to change the subject, but keep the conversation going. While my story had been quite boring until that point, what I could talk about anyway, Amelia was bursting with tales from her time in Italy. Some of it quite useful to know, such as to never visit Venice during the summer, as it's full of cruise ship tourists and the canals smell awful. While I had been pessimistic of her studies, she appeared very knowledgeable on the subject and passionate about her future in art. She had a bracelet with various charms dangling around it. I joked that each charm may correlate to a dalliance of sorts, a suggestion she snorted at with derision. It was hard to not think of our previous tryst; she was ageing very well. Maybe I should have gotten a car with a more comfortable back seat.

We pulled up to the house and saw the lights had already been turned off, signalling the end of the evening's debate and a safe time to return indoors. Amelia went in first, checking the coast was clear and guiding me up the stairs. It was pitch black, but she knew each step like the back of her hand. As we approached my room, with her walking in front of me and feeling emboldened by the late night drive, I placed my hands around her waist. She turned around slowly to face me before stopping me in my tracks with a firmly planted finger to my chest.

"Easy, tiger! Fooling around with my brother's friend is one thing, but someone that works with my Dad every day? That's a different story. Little 'rural soap opera' isn't it?"

"Ouch." It had been a while since I was halted so abruptly and honestly, especially by an old flame.

"Goodnight, Alex. Look on the bright side…" She held up her bracelet and picked out a charm in the shape of a car. "We'll always have the memories."

\*\*\*\*\*

"His Bosnian passport was cancelled but they still shuttle funds via the High Commission. We can go the same route if necessary."

I woke up early the next morning, early enough to see the sun shimmering off the dew-strewn lawn and puff a cigarette out the bedroom window. Mrs. Jones the housekeeper was already clanging pans around the kitchen preparing for Sunday lunch, and she faced quite the challenge feeding the family and invited guests. Limping downstairs in search of coffee, I found the kitchen a flurry of manic activity. I offered to help but was assured the best help I could do was leave her in peace. The last thing she needed was my lumpy gravy spoiling the spread.

I retreated to the safety of the drawing room with a sturdy mug of coffee and a stolen Sunday paper. David was the next up, probably nursing a heavy head but not showing it. He was in his Sunday best ready for that morning's service. I don't think he was necessarily a religious man, but as long as the family pew sat in the local church, he made sure it was used. He asked if I'd like to join him, but I politely declined. He knew I had spent enough time in the God Box for one weekend. It would also give me a chance to get showered before Charlie stole all the hot water. Charlie had an annoying habit of staying in there until the water ran cold, which had led to many arguments in the past. Lunch came around quite quickly and Charlie left it until the last possible moment to make an appearance, spending the morning sulking in his room while the rest of us went about our own business, David playing the country squire, Amelia engrossed in magazines, and me hobbling around like someone three times my age.

The lunch guests were generally unremarkable: the antiquated vicar who regularly reminded us that he and David were distantly related on his mother's side; the Hollands, old family friends who came to specifically catch up with their long absent goddaughter; and finally, we had Mr. and Mrs. Dawes, more specifically the Right Honourable Julian Dawes, a local member of Parliament for some thirty years and not-so-recently-deposed Secretary of State for Defence. Amelia was naturally sandwiched between the Hollands where she could field all queries ranging from courting to cookery, while Julian squeezed his bulbous frame between myself and David. That left poor Charlie tending to the flock of undesirables, the vicar and Mrs. Dawes, who continued their long-running fight over floral arrangements for the vicarage.

Julian was an interesting character, very strong views on the current government and how the champagne socialists were ruining the country for the rest of us. He had a keen eye to recover his recent position or something higher while there was still light in his eyes. I watched David closely, noting how he would navigate a conversation by saying as little as possible. He carefully considered his responses and only answered when directly required to do so.

"Alex has been with us for a while but has just joined my team. Treating him to a weekend away to show him it's not all work and no play. Clear some of that city dust out of his ears."

"Oh, is that right. Congratulations, young man, quite an accomplishment at your age."

"Thank you, we're very excited about where the bank sits in the current climate."

"Christ, you should be in politics, answering in soundbites like that," replied Julian with a chuckle. Between mouthfuls of roast beef and big-eared impressions of the Prime Minister, I wondered if I had in fact drawn the short straw being sat next to Julian. I was relieved for the intermission between courses, as it allowed me some peace and quiet behind a bolted bathroom door. When I was unhurriedly making my way back for pudding I was stopped by a "Pssst!" from the kitchen. I thought I was hearing something meant for someone else until the noise came again; I went to investigate. David was by the back door, kicking off his shoes in exchange for Wellington boots and stuffing his tie into a wax jacket pocket.

"Come on, we're getting out of here."

"What about lunch?"

"Do you really want to endure any more of it?"

"Not really, no."

"Well, come on then!"

I followed him outside where his old Land Rover was waiting, engine spluttering like it had consumption. He opened the back door for me and I hauled myself up on my good leg. A bottle of red was thrust into my face by Mr. Dawes from the front seat while David got behind the wheel. I had never been driven by David before, but I prayed he was better than Charlie.

"Hold tight to that Alex, it's thirsty work on the river. Next time you ask me down here to meet the new boy, Pater, I don't expect to be subjected to all that bollocks beforehand. How can you tolerate those people?"

"You always speak so highly of your constituents, Jules."

We tore up the gravel at the back of the house before the

stones quickly turned to dust and grass. I was bouncing around in the back seat holding the door handle for dear life as we romped over a few hills away from the house, rabbits and sheep darting out of our way until we reached the stony banks of the river. The old Land Rover gave a sigh of relief, as you would if woken up from a long slumber and forced to sprint across the countryside without warning. David pulled some rods down from the roof and began choosing flies from his bag. Julian on the other hand went for a picnic chair and wine glass.

Rather than set up camp on the river bank Julian took off his shoes and socks, rolled up his trouser legs and put his chair in the shallows. Letting his feet dabble in the gentle trickling waters while David donned his waders and headed to the deeper parts. There were no other waders, but there was another chair. My place was clear. Julian beckoned me and the wine bottle over.

"Good for the blood," said Julian as I sat alongside him, glass of claret balanced expertly on his belly.

"Bloody cold if you ask me."

"That's the idea." He reached down to his side and fondled a few stones from the river bed, selecting a few in his hand and offering them to me. "Put them on your leg, it'll help with the swelling."

"Thank you."

"It's not fun, is it?"

"What?"

"The interrogation. When it was my turn it was pretty easy going. Lots of shouting and slapping around but nothing more. David wasn't so lucky, still suffers from the nerve damage now. Hence you never see him drive on the road, he worries he can't feel the wheel well enough in his fingers."

"You were in Pactum?"

"No, no. I was in the service for the first part of my career and ended up as David's handler when he joined his father. Have you been given yours yet?"

"I don't think so, unless it's P."

"Weaselling little shit bag."

"Jules, be nice!" yelled David.

"Always! It won't be him. You'll be assigned someone to guide you at first. A trusted officer, mid-level but part of the inner circle."

"I thought Pactum didn't mix with politicians?"

"As a rule you don't do so professionally, it just so happened that I ended up on the other side during my career. It was a very successful time for both sides when I crossed over, I was able to get information to David from the military without having to use the service. It's important to keep that separation. Hence Pater and Patruus must remain different people. Don't want the tail to start wagging the dog."

Julian was very frank with his experience and advice. His biggest point was to always have the strength to walk away when I felt the time was right, be that with an asset or my own career. He chose politics and didn't regret the decision, only the election results.

"Have some money or gold hidden away somewhere that only you know about. When you need to go or just fancy going off-piste for a while to recharge, you will have the means to do so."

"When do you think David will walk away and focus on his fishing?"

"He hasn't caught a fish in years. He just comes here to think and have me poke fun at his silly rubber boots. Unfortunately for him, I don't think he will ever have the option to walk away."

It was so quiet by the river and charmingly uneventful. When we got back to the house it was less so. The Hollands had already gone home, and the vicar was asleep in the drawing room with no intention of leaving without prompting. Mrs. Dawes was standing on the doorstep with her arms crossed across her chest and a face like a gargoyle. Julian made his goodbyes very brief, wishing us luck but knowing he was the one needing it once Mrs. Dawes got him in the car. Charlie already had his bag packed and was eager to get going, choosing to ride back with me rather than head up with David later. I went upstairs and packed my things, catching Amelia on my way down. She wished me good luck with the drive back and thanked me for distracting her the night before. Holding my hand in hers she softly reminded me I could call on her if I needed someone to talk to. I made her promise to show me around if I found myself in Italy. It was clichéd, cookie-cutter conversation, but sincere. It had been good to see her.

As I got to the door I could see Charlie and David deep in conversation outside and decided to hang back. David had his hands on Charlie's shoulders forcing him to look in his eyes, like he was reassuring his son of something. They nodded a lot before Charlie got in the car, still holding his head down. As I went to follow him David took me to one side.

"Good chat with Jules?"

"Yes, nice to know who our friends are."

"Good, good. He's a nice chap, thought quite highly of you. We would like you to move ahead with the rest of the service training next week if you feel up to it?"

"Will it be like my last visit?"

"No, this is more like going back to school."

"I'll sharpen my pencil."

"Good man. See you at the office, drive safe."

Charlie was much quieter on the journey back, but as we passed the Reading services on the motorway he began to open up a bit more.

"I'm going to be honest with you, my friend."

"I thought you were."

"I am, of course, but about the trading Bertie was doing."

"Go on."

"Those trades were preparation for our push into the US. It's going to take some capital to get us set up and make the right connections."

"I take it you haven't told your father about this?"

"He wouldn't understand. I'm really trying to make extra effort with this, show him what I can achieve when he just trusts me to do my job."

"He trusts you, Charlie. He's a bit old-fashioned with some things."

"Just please keep it under your hat for now, I don't want anything to sour the old man's opinion before the meeting." Charlie asked nervously from the passenger seat.

"You can consider my lips sealed."

"Do you actually like my US idea?"

"Of course, it's a good idea. The small cap opportunities are strong out there and the large cap is on par with London, perhaps greater."

"We'll have to see what P thinks."

"Doesn't matter what P thinks, he wouldn't know a rights issue if it slapped him in the face. Do you want any help getting things going?"

"No thanks, my friend, I want to try to take this from start to finish myself."

"Fair enough." We passed the Lucozade sign by Chiswick before turning down towards Putney. Nothing more was said on the matter.

＊＊＊＊＊

"I will have a word. Keep him at
arm's length for a while, until we
know where he stands."

"When he gets back,
he will know where he stands."

Charlie was hard at work before I arrived, full steam ahead preparing for the Tuesday Pactum meeting. The only time he came anywhere near my door on Monday was to confirm that Gerald Didcomb from the Royal Bank was on the 'inside', eyeing him up as a useful route into America rather than striking a deal with an unfamiliar US institution. I had only met Gerald once, at the club during my lunch with David, but could confirm he was one of ours.

I was focusing my attentions on the Oil and Gas files in preparation for the conference. The list of attendees was longer than I expected, every facet of the companies having its own grossly exaggerated hierarchy from exploration to commodity trading. I was never going to remember all of them, so I tried to stick to Chairmen and CEOs, the calibre of people I had seen in the club. Nobody was supposed to remove files from Pactum, but I snuck a few photographs home with me that night for homework. David wouldn't mind. It was a very quiet start to the week and I enjoyed the leisurely night at home. Between studying pictures and flicking between news channels I was able to get some chores done, dropping items at the cleaners and picking up some staples for the fridge. It also allowed time to call home and appease the motherly inquisition for a week rather than have her pester my answering machine. Apparently, there was an uproar over the plans to build a bypass around the village. Mother was quite animated in her objections but delighted to hear I'd seen Amelia over the weekend. Delighted enough that she offered little lip service to the funeral or the loss of Bertie. I can't be too angry, she was always ambitious.

Charlie called me quite late wanting to run some of his pitch by me before the morning meeting. I had to give him credit for putting in the leg work to make his case. It wasn't like I was doing the work for him either, just reassuring him that he was on the right path. I was impressed and sure the others would be, especially David whose outburst on Saturday showed he thought Charlie a bit slow at times. Yet again he was at the office before me on Tuesday morning, I carefully returned the photographs back to their homes and went to see how he was feeling for his big performance.

"Ready?"

"As I'll ever be," he quipped, though appearing more confident than I had expected. He had a determination in his eyes which didn't align with his defeatist response. As our senior colleagues arrived in hurried tandem, I went to gather my papers.

"Break a leg!" I said to wish Charlie good luck.

When all four of us were sat around the table, David wasted no time in getting things started.

"Okay gentlemen, two topics of discussion today, perhaps best described as foreign and domestic, or ancient and modern. Either way, Procurator has been preparing for this and I will yield the floor to him."

Charlie handed out some printouts to each of us, showing

market data and the bullet points he was narrating.

"We have already seen from Piscator's efforts in the city that using the US exchanges to deepen our exposure to domestic stocks is a sound strategy, and I would like to take this even further. Between the UK and US, we can expose ourselves to the full spectrum of large cap in our hemisphere. Outside of Hong Kong and Japan there won't be a single company beyond our reach. We have never had the personnel to extend our sight into the east or the emerging markets, but we do have the assets and inclinations to increase our US exposure. We have traded in the US in the past, but not to its full potential. Historically the US markets have a habit of moving quicker that Europe, and more violently in the sectors where we remain light, such as technology or pharmaceuticals. As well as our traditional model, I would like to see us looking at small cap in the states. They are too small for us to take out our usual positions, but they are numerous enough that those small gains could add up nicely. Thanks to our friends overseas, I already have a list of companies suited to that model." He cleared his throat and glanced briefly toward me. "Piscator and I have discussed the risks associated with this plan and agree that the potential foreign exchange risk cannot be ignored, but can certainly be hedged against. Similarly, having a modest but approved US presence, a satellite office if you will, with the appropriate deposits would allow us to have greater control over our holdings and avoid having to trade and settle our transactions via specific London-friendly market makers and settlement houses. I believe our long-standing relationship with Royal Bank could be leveraged to get ourselves set up across the pond, while avoiding any unwanted press for the SC Securities name. The packs in front of you show comparisons between London and New York. The similarities will make us feel quite at home, while the differences will only work to our benefit. America is also much fonder of traded options than we are here, and the options exchange in Chicago would be another tool at our disposal, be it short or long." It was short and to the point, what the Americans would call an 'elevator pitch'. David was impressed, more than that he had slight look of pride edging across his wrinkled cheeks.

"Well done, Procurator, very well done. We don't tend to short stock in London, it leaves a nasty taste in the mouth to profit from the failings of a British company, but I may consider it when the ramifications aren't so close to home. Patruus, what are your thoughts on the matter?"

"I like it, really like it. I have been thinking a similar thing myself for some time, but lacked Procurator's market know-how to bring it forward. I would like to work closely with Procurator on this, the relationship with our allies will mesh well for this project."

"Good. Piscator, anything to add?"

"Great proposal, it has my support."

"Okay, so that is agreed. Procurator, this is your project. I have no objection to involving Gerry at Royal Bank. Between yourself and Patruus I am sure it will be a roaring success. Keep me updated and let me know when you need my input or sign off. While you two work on that, Piscator and I will be focusing on our oily efforts, our second point for today. We are joining Matthew Capstan at the London O&G conference tomorrow, after which we will hopefully be rebalancing our holdings into the specific firm due the Libyan rights. If we don't get some concrete direction, I would feel more comfortable pulling back and limiting our exposure. If so, that would also open up some funding for any new projects."

"Has a decision been made on Piscator's training schedule?" asked Patruus before the meeting closed.

"After the conference, he's all yours."

"Perfect, I'll get the ball rolling my end."

As we filed out of the cage I gave Charlie a congratulatory slap on the back. One other person came to offer his compliments, but it wasn't his father. P walked with Charlie all the way to his office, spending most of the morning speaking with him behind closed doors and then disappearing together at midday. Charlie's project had split Pactum temporarily in two, with each team having an old dog and some new tricks. David and I joined forces to focus on our prep for the conference, not that David needed any.

"I have hinted to Matthew that we could be willing to put forward some capital for exploration in the Libyan desert. Between you and I, we have no intention of doing any such thing, but I may entertain underwriting a new debt issue if they need it. He's more helpful when he thinks there's a carrot at the end of the stick."

"Aren't we all."

"Leave the nitty gritty to me, I want you there building your rapport and reputation. The more familiar you are to them the better it is for all of us. Joan has some new business cards for you. I thought 'Head of Business Development and Strategy' was the best title, manages to say a lot without meaning anything specific."

"I thought everyone was under the impression HQ was staffed by analysts?"

"If a CFA dragged you into a conversation it would only take a few minutes for you to be unravelled. As you get more comfortable, we'll bump you up to CIO. CIO's don't need a CFA level 3, just a good track record."

"Anything I specifically can or cannot talk about?"

"You cannot talk about anything you learned in this building. There are enough rumours on the street to discuss Libya but keep our legend in mind. We are there to consider doing something for them, not trying to get them to do something for us. As far as the other delegates are concerned, talk as little as possible or in generalities about the sector. You need to be listening to as many conversations as you can politely be included in."

"Just give me a kick if I'm doing something wrong."

"A kick? I won't be close enough to do that, my boy. What's the point of two of us going if we can't cover double the area? You'll be fine. Just treat it like a fundraising and enjoy yourself."

\* \* \* \* \*

"Just remember what side you're on."

"I'm not on anyone's side, I'm doing a job."

The conference was being held at The Savoy, a grande dame of the London Hotel scene in dire need of a facelift. Her reputation had kept her high on the list of desirable locations for many events but if I was organizing something myself, I would have gone for The Landmark. Aside from the American Bar, I held little love for The Savoy. The only hotel better known to foreign businessmen or dignitaries was The Ritz, another hotel needing more than a lick of paint. We could thank leather-bound pages and silver screen sirens for that.

David and I arrived together in his car, Luis feeling quite important under the famous entranceway but a little confused by the only road in London where he had to drive on the wrong side. We ambled through the lobby past tourists and staff, climbing the stairs to join a short queue outside the Lancaster Ballroom. Once the generic nametags and glasses of champagne were handed out to everyone, including lapsed Muslims, I glanced around the room. Tables filled every corner with a stage up front set for the speakers, they would be keeping their time short. Everyone knew the real reason for being there was business rather than education and the actual work was done between the speeches. The side wall hosted the predictable spread of assorted fodder, whimsically arranged on a theme: cakes like barrels and sugar work like oil platforms. A platoon of silent waiters meandered between the throng with their trays of offerings, the silence was partly to avoid interrupting the guests, but I assumed mostly because they were still spending their evenings with "English for Beginners." Scanning the room certain groups were obvious because of the clichés they embodied: the emerging markets like Brazil and Malaysia were jostling for a place close the big boys, the Americans had the loudest voices and the fullest plates, while the Arabs were holding court over a large section near the stage. The Russians sat plain-faced, making notes to remove anyone seen talking to the Americans from their Christmas card list.

Capstan brought quite a team with him from BP and David made sure we were introduced to all of them. David was focusing almost all his energy on Capstan, leaving me the rest of the room to play with and I knew exactly where I was heading. The Shell team were schmoozing West Africans, apologizing for any mishaps with car keys rather than clean ups. Amongst their team was a man a few years younger than me, but seemingly very uninterested in the day's events. While the others stood in conversation, he sat at the table dissecting his lunch. I put my business card on the table next to his operating area and made a bold but casual introduction.

"First time?"

"No, but I always hope it's be my last," he replied in a thick Dutch accent.

"Don't like meeting the competition?"

"The science side doesn't really compete, only against the elements. You?"

"We don't compete either."

He finally glanced over to my business card. "So, I'm the science and you're the money. Must be your first time."

"Why do you say that?"

"You're talking to the wrong person."

"Just prefer talking to someone my own age rather than a fossil."

"This is oil; fossils are what we do." He pulled out the chair next to him and handed me his own card: unpronounceable name inundated with vowels under the yellow and red logo. "So Mr. Hope, how can I help you?"

"Well, we're thinking of heading into North Africa, word is your chaps are going in the same direction."

"We thought about it, it was a natural expansion for us, but we couldn't even get our foot in the door. The government wouldn't talk to us."

"Bugger, well who are they talking to?"

"Some say the Italians, others say the British. My own opinion is the Russians. They have kept things open during the dark years and that must count for something. A friend of mine used to joke that for every gun they sent to Tripoli they would include twenty yards of piping for the oil fields."

"Is that why the Russians are like a spare wheel at these events?"

"The more time you spend at these things you'll realize not everything is as it seems. Everyone talks badly about the Russians in public but behind closed doors they all make deals with them. Whether we like it or not, they are a major player, especially with gas."

He asked me about the market, I think out of politeness rather than genuine intrigue. Scientists tend to distrust something which can only function on human emotion and the stock market reacts best to fear or avarice. I sat through two short presentations, one on the Niger delta and another on the Falkland Islands, the latter raising serious questions from several parties who aligned themselves with the Argentinians. I managed to get a moment with David while mingling around the room, passing on the message to close RDSB. It was the clarification he wanted so he disappeared briefly to relay the message to Stephen in the city.

I remember thinking, perhaps a little boldly for my initial outing, that if I wanted to get the inside track on Libya I had to find a way to talk to the Russians. Thankfully, they and I shared a habit which was slowly being squeezed out of hotels: smoking. Every few minutes one delegate or another from the Russian table was sneaking outside for a breather. One was doing so more than the others, spending the rest of his time gorging on cake, sweating and pulling on his perpetually tightening collar. Unlike his colleagues he wasn't wearing a name tag or engaging in small talk with other delegates. He was either very senior or very rude, possibly both. I followed him downstairs and asked him for a light, which he duly provided.

"Interesting day, isn't it?"

"Not really. Same shit…how you say…different day." He sucked on his cigarette with such force the embers burnt as brightly as a lightbulb.

"Making any new friends?"

"You ask a lot of questions."

"I'm sorry, it's my first time." I smiled and pulled out a card for him.

"I see. What are you people selling this time?"

"I'm not selling anything, Mr…?" I trailed off, hoping he might give me a name.

"What do you want, Mr. Hope?"

"We're bullish on North Africa but struggling to find someone solid to pair with."

"There is only one you can pair with."

"You?"

"Gaddafi."

"Aren't you already partnered with him?"

"The world is changing. New president in the Kremlin, new cooperation with the West. Our old friendships grow weak and that opens door for people like you. A word of advice, you can't work him like you did us with Volgodonsk or Moscow, he is an idealist. If you want to buy your way in, go with his children." He tucked my card into his pocket and stamped out his cigarette. "Good luck Mr. Hope, and happy fishing."

My heart was in my throat. Had I been made? My nerves found me smoking with the same force as the Russian. I finished my cigarette at speed and immediately lit another, making myself nauseous in the process. Reassuring myself that it was just paranoia, I continued to smile and shake hands at every opportunity over the afternoon but niggling at the back of my mind was a single heavy doubt. I had tried too hard and blown our cover. The Russian had implied not only knowledge of Pactum, but personal dealings with us. Once we were safely in David's car on our way back, I decided to come clean. To my surprise, and equal relief, he wasn't angry. In fact, he seemed almost as confused as I was.

"You are right to be concerned. Every businessman or politician worth knowing out east is ex-KGB or similar, it comes with the territory. As far as we know they don't know of Pactum, but they might know of the connection between SC and the service."

"Are you sure they don't know of Pactum? He mentioned something called Volgodonsk and Moscow. Does it mean anything to you?"

"Nothing aside from them being cities. I will speak to Patruus on secure this afternoon and see what he can tell us." David and I just made it back to the office in time to find Charlie tapping his watch on the pavement; we were meeting Rupert for drinks. David offered to take my case upstairs for me, as the only things I needed from it were my phone and keys. "Go and let off some steam, the stagnation over the last few weeks doesn't suit a man of your age. People in the city will start talking."

It seemed funny for my boss to encourage me to go out, even on a day with concern over my Russian encounter, but he had a point. Banking has always been part brains and part personality, if you're not making connections and cementing relationships then you won't last long. As Piscator this had become more important than ever. We took a taxi across town to meet in our usual haunt, Charlie seemed as excited as ever at the prospect of a night out with the boys, already sipping from a hipflask and doing his best to hand it off to me. I hadn't been out since being detained and no longer wanted to enter a situation where I wouldn't remain in total control of my senses.

*"Wow, even after that time?" interrupted Hamilton.*

*"Even now," I said, ironically sipping my drink.*

*"I've had some wild nights, but I bounce back pretty quick."*

*"I would hardly call a bonesmen's evening at Yale a point for comparison."*

*"How did you know I was...?"*

*"Knowing what little you do so far, you think I would arrange*

*this meeting without doing my research? Your family connections and alma mater are practically public knowledge, it wasn't a difficult assumption from there…" I rubbed my knees remembering what they had endured over the years. It's hard to sit without them cracking these days. "Rest assured, young man, what I've experienced from a physical and mental perspective is not something you can understand. Perhaps one day you will, but I hope for your sake that's not the case. Charlie and I were going to meet the others at Leadenhall…*

…a place which had garnered new significance as the place we met the last time we were together with Bertie. Rupert was already there and had drinks waiting for us, not the way I wanted to things to start or continue. I did my best to persuade Rupert I was on antibiotics and had to keep off alcohol, but Charlie shot me down immediately.

"Come on now. Don't give us some sob story of a sick note from the quack."

"I'm not having beer, then, I'll be feeling bloated the entire night."

The quickest way to end the discussion was to feign compliance and keep control of my own drink. I went to the bar and ordered myself a sparkling water, left the bottle behind and dressed up the glass with a slice of lime. Presto, a gin and tonic to the unobservant. We walked around a few more local bars where my generosity in getting the first round each time enabled me to repeat the gin trick. The only time I became unstuck was when we stopped for dinner at a French steak restaurant. With claret at the table there was nowhere for me to hide. Charlie was readily filling everyone's glasses at twenty-minute intervals and each time he passed my untouched glass he would drop his shoulders in disappointment. When we finished our meal and were settling the bill, my glass was still full.

"You better see that off before we leave," came the stern prodding from Charlie.

"I'm really not feeling up to it."

Rupert joined in the goading with "Get it down!", "See it off!", and other rugby club drinking taunts. With no other option left I knocked it back in one to cheers from the others. I felt sick to my stomach: the smell, the taste, even the edge of the glass took me back. I could almost feel the corkscrew again. As we hopped in the back of a taxi for our next stop I sat quietly in one corner. Charlie could see my angst and gave me a gentle rub on the arm in apology. I think he realized what had happened but could not understand the complexity of it. We were heading to The Ministry, a giant nightclub which had built a huge following over recent years. Rupert had a friend who worked in promotions, so we were on the guest list for the evening and skipped the long rain-soaked queue of merrymakers already lined up outside. The exterior of the building was a relic of 1970's urban planning, ugly yet functional, but the interior was like a twilight zone. After entering the main doors we walked down a dark corridor with twinkling pinprick lights. With every step the music got louder and as we neared the entrance to the club proper you could feel the bass vibrating in your chest. I couldn't handle it: I could feel my heart racing as my vision started to blur, and the walls looked like they were bending in front of me. I turned back and stumbled towards the outside. I could hear one of my friends calling after me, but I kept on going; I had to get away from the noise. I crashed through the doors and passed the bouncers before falling to my knees on the pavement. I gazed up at the sky and let the rain fall on my face.

"Well, I've seen you do worse," came a woman's voice from a nearby car. I couldn't help but smile at the absurdity of the situation while I got to my feet and walked down to the open car window.

"Wow, you just can't stay away from me, can you?" I asked Nikki through the window.

"Guess not."

"Don't tell me, you're the one I'm supposed to be training with?"

"A little birdy told me you might want to get started early."

"Is that right? Your boss definitely has a twisted sense of humour."

"That he does. You getting in or what?"

I walked around to the passenger side of the car and happily accepted the offer of escape. I shot Charlie a quick message, simply "Duty calls", as we pulled away.

"You'll want to stop by your place and grab a few things, we're going to be gone for a few weeks."

"Oh, a couple's getaway. You shouldn't have!" I said sarcastically "Did you choose Cornwall or the Lake District, dear?"

"Gosport, but don't bother packing for the seaside."

After stopping to grab my essentials we left the bright lights of London behind us. The first part of the journey was a little awkward because of our previous encounters. After stopping for petrol and a rubberized sandwich at the service station the tension began to thaw. Nothing like watching someone attempt to drive and handle an egg mayonnaise sandwich to remind you of their humanity.

"What do you know about me, about us?" I asked, hoping to gauge the relationships with the service beyond Patruus.

"Everything I need to."

"That could be nearly nothing or almost anything. I'm not trying to test you, just want to know where I stand."

"You are The Fisherman. The head of each station knows who you are plus a very small group of us in London."

"What do you know about *me*?"

"Only what you've told me. As far as we're concerned, you're basically an asset P runs on the side."

"I'm almost disappointed. I was expecting you to reel off my medical history or something."

"I know you snore when you drink, does that count?"

"I feel that I'm at a bit of disadvantage. You don't know much, but you know infinitely more about me than I do about you."

"I would argue that we are equal."

"How?"

"We both know only what we need to know."

\*\*\*\*\*

"I want you to shadow them and report back, understand?"

"Do we have ministerial approval yet?"

"I don't need approval! This is my team!"

We continued our journey. As we approached Southampton we first turned west towards Portsmouth, then onto the minor roads following signs for Gosport. To my civilian eyes it was a strange place for training but as we reached the outskirts the precise location came to the fore. Monkswood Fort was a relic from the Napoleonic War, originally designed to defend the harbour waters with booming heavy guns that sat silent until long after the fall of Napoleon. It was still in military hands, the only Army base in an area dominated by Naval establishments. Set up like a half star, it retained some of its history with a moat and outer ditch, although I was sure they served little purpose other than nostalgia. The security around the perimeter was incredibly high, with armed guards at an outer post who waved us on across the moat, past the helipad, and down the single road to the main entrance. The large gatehouse was the only way into the fort proper but as far as military bases go, it was certainly on the small side. It felt totally isolated. I could barely see the lights flickering in the distance and the only noise was the waves crashing below us.

We were met by three men with torches at the edge of the parade square. They had that military stance: rod-straight backs and rhythmed walk, but none were wearing an insignia or rank that I could see. They introduced themselves as Tom, Dick and Harry. I supposed if you are going to use a false name on your own turf then you might as well have some fun with it. They carried the confidence and swagger of people who knew they could tackle anything, but the stature, style, and tight-haired similarity to look totally average. Never the largest or loudest, nor the smallest or most different, but intentionally beige and easy to forget. They formed part of what's referred to as The Incident Team, an intimate group of special forces who are kept on permanent call by the Service. Tom was the only one I recognized. He was my tormentor from London.

"You know Tom, a good dentist could fix that smile of yours."

"Fuck off."

His friends thought it was funny, even if he didn't. Dick landed the job of showing me my lodgings, leading me across to a barrack building at the far edge of the square. The dark night and torchlight guide reminded me of going on a camping trip, but with the wind rushing off the sea I was relieved not to be sleeping under canvas. Once inside he took me straight upstairs. Rather than a private room it was a long, cold dormitory of twenty steel-framed beds. Hard linoleum floors and fluorescent lights lent the room an air of clinical functionality. One of the beds had sheets stacked neatly at its foot, with the usual itchy British Army blanket and an electric heater for added comfort. Dick handed me a stack of bland casual clothes from the wardrobe: military issue tracksuits, t-shirts and socks.

"You'll want to get that heater plugged in sharpish. Gets a bit nippy when there's only one of you."

"Any extra blankets?" He wasn't impressed at my request but

pointed me to a cupboard in the corridor which contained all the extra bedding.

The bathroom facilities were of a similar sparseness and scale to the dormitory, as was the mess on the ground floor. You could see the barracks were used to much larger groups. Plenty of room at the inn but I was the only guest. After making my bed and moving the heater as close as I safely could, I hunkered down to snatch a few hours' sleep. It wasn't as much as I would have liked. A horrendous bell started ringing at sunrise, followed by a miserable cold shower and the worst bowl of porridge I had ever eaten. I sat alone in the mess and poked at the breakfast suspiciously with my spoon.

"It's like wallpaper paste, isn't it?" came Harry from the doorway.

"I wouldn't know. I've never hung wallpaper."

"Probably never eaten a proper man's breakfast either, have you? This stuff'll keep you going all morning." Judging by his accent he was from the north of England. Without being certain if it was Lancashire or Yorkshire, I thought it sensible not to comment. Guessing the wrong one can cause as much upset as calling an Australian a Kiwi, or vice versa. Harry served himself a bowl and came to sit opposite me. Slinging a dollop of jam at his porridge, he pulled out a ratty bit of paper from his back pocket.

"Looks like we have you split between a few sets for the next couple weeks: languages, field craft and weapons. You'll be doing languages with Tom, weapons with me and Dick. Nikki will handle field craft. I'll take you over to the range after breakfast. Dick's going to meet us there and should have a schedule for you, so you know where to be and when."

"Lovely."

It was exciting of course, but so very different. The topics fed my illusions of espionage from the cinema and boyish books I'd enjoyed, but the glamour was clearly absent. The indoor range was only a short walk across the square and into the basement of the main gatehouse. Rather than a cubicle setup like you find at modern ranges, it was a World War relic with sandbags, mats on the floor for prone position rifle work and one single table behind the line of fire. When we walked in Dick was fastidiously preparing some small arms for my introduction.

"Done much shooting before?"

"Quite a bit. Mostly shotgun and rifle though."

"Hunting?"

"Well…yes…"

"Not what we're looking at lad, so let's start from the bottom." He walked the length of the table calling out that day's assortment like a football team.

"Glock 17: striker fire, 9 millimetre. Sig Sauer P226, single and double action, 9 millimetre again. Final pistol for today is the Beretta 92, same again. This is an older model with the magazine release on the bottom of the grip. The modern variants have the release in the same spot as the other two."

"So, which one is mine?"

Dick and Harry both chuckled at my ignorance, bursting my rather excited bubble.

"None of' 'em…" said Dick. "The boss just wants you to know how to use the weapons you are likely to come across, just in case."

"Just in case of what, exactly?"

"Just in case you need to use 'em."

The Glock and Beretta were familiar from television and film but the Sig was something new, although it reminded me of a British Army Browning I saw in cadets. I was treated like a total novice, which in fairness I was, with only a few rounds loaded into a magazine at a time. For someone more used to long guns, I found my target work disappointing. I had wide open groups and some rounds missed the paper altogether, but Dick and Harry assured me this was normal for newcomers. For the bench work I much preferred the Glock but when it came to hitting the target I was far better with the Sig. The Beretta stuck in my mind as the gun I didn't want to deal with. I didn't like the magazine release and the moment I felt the in my hand it brought back haunting memories from London. I suspected it was Tom's personal choice.

After a few hours at the range, enough for me to put most of my rounds on paper and learn the assembly of each firearm, it was soon time for linguistics, which would take up most of the daylight hours I was given. Dick gave me my schedule as I was leaving but it was more like a post-it note. It left me a few split hours during the day for myself and the evenings as well. I could safely assume the evenings would be spent studying but it was nice to have some time during the day to keep track of the market. The training would be for naught if I lost track of the market.

When I reached the classroom a few floors above the range, Tom and I were equally displeased at seeing each other.

"If it isn't posh boy pissy pants back for another lesson."

"…and will you look, Toothless Thomas is playing teacher."

It wasn't a good start.

The next four hours were spent with him dumped in a chair reading the Daily Star while I clicked through a CD-ROM teaching me how to greet a stranger in Russian. When my allotted time was done, he just stood up and left without a word. Once he was gone, Nikki arrived to see how my first day had been going and to joke whether Tom and I had "kissed and made up". I assured her that I didn't hold a strong grudge against the man for doing his job and that once he could appreciate my perspective, things would thaw. She sat next to me in the classroom and delivered the presentation I had been expecting from Dick rather than the scrawled note. She made some comparisons between what I would be doing and what an intelligence officer like herself had to do. I was barely scratching the surface, gaining some useful tools and insight but not the full arsenal. There simply wasn't the time or the need for me to reach her level. I had some language under my belt from school, half-decent French and Spanish, so they wanted to add Russian and German to that base. It was a good set for traditional concerns and they hoped I would continue to study in my own time. Like Harry had explained at the range, it was thought pertinent to give me some experience with weapons. It was also a good way for me to blow off steam while confined to such a strict schedule. I didn't understand why I hadn't seen field craft on my schedule from Dick, especially as it appeared to be the most important aspect of the training. I raised this with Nikki.

"We will be working on that all the time, especially in the evenings. You have some experience with it already from your trials in London, but we want to go far deeper, both in an offensive and defensive sense. Knowing how to illicit information from others, prevent them gaining too much from you and how to keep your mind focussed on the job at hand: removing your head from the situation in order to make informed decisions."

"If it's anything like London then count me out. I'm not having that bastard use me as a plaything again. Absolutely not."

"You're telling me you would rather find yourself in a

dark cell on the far side of Europe not knowing what awaits you or how to deal with it, than have experience of it in a safe environment?"

"I don't fucking care. It's not happening."

"It won't be like before, or anything physical, it's about mental strength and thinking when your body tells you not to. We don't want to 'break you,' we want to make you stronger, like exercising a muscle."

I thought about it long and hard. I didn't want to go back to London and disappoint David, but I also wasn't going to roll over and allow some cave dweller to toy with my senses.

"I want a safe word. A word that if I say it, it stops."

"Wow, that's just revealed more about your social life than I was expecting." She pulled out a scrap of paper and scribbled something down before tossing it over. As it fluttered to the table she continued, "That's your safe word. Now get yourself smartened up, we've got work to do." I picked up the piece of paper. She had written something in Mandarin knowing full well I would have no idea how to read it.

"Thanks, that's just wonderful. You might as well have written it in bloody Arabic!"

"I can if you like, but I doubt it would make a difference. Now, hurry up."

*****

"You need me more than I need you."

"I need you for now but you will always need me. Remember that."

155

We sat in a bar on the Solent brimming with university students and amorous yuppies who appeared as dim as the lighting. Nikki was casual in jeans. I was in a suit and tie.

"I feel like I'm having drinks with my father."

"Maybe if you'd been more candid about our plans I could've dressed more appropriately."

She stood up and pulled me towards her like a toddler with a smudge on his chin, took off my tie and undid my top two shirt buttons. She sat back and took a further look before stuffing the tie into my pocket and untucking my shirt on one side.

"Much better."

"I look like a car salesman." Charlie could play the dishevelled look; I just looked a mess.

"You look normal. This is Southampton, not St. Moritz. Wherever you are, dress to blend in."

I glanced around the bar and couldn't argue her point. I was sat with my back towards the crowd directly across from Nikki, so she started to test me.

"Where are the exits and how many men are stood at the bar?" I didn't know the answer to either. "You need to be aware of these things. Any time you enter a potentially hazardous area it must become second nature. What if there was a threat?"

I paused. "There is. Tom is stood in the far righthand corner of the bar, red football shirt."

Nikki seemed pleased that she wasn't dealing with a lost cause, but also because I had fallen perfectly into her trap.

"Nice catch. Shame you didn't see Dick and Harry at the table right behind you."

I turned around and they all gave me a wave before leaving by different exits. Nikki had made her point about removing emotion from the situation, my ongoing squabble with Tom had drawn me to him. We cruised round several bars running a simple drill: note exits, analyse occupants, and repeat. They were baby steps but every few days she would add an extra step to the routine. By the end of my first week it had become second nature to assess any room I entered. Now and again one of the boys would be planted and I took great pride in patting them on the shoulder as I passed or waving before they did. Similarly, that first week also saw me improve my pistol skills. By no means a sharpshooter but I could at least get shots on target and felt more at home with the workings of the firearms. We expanded my pistol selection to a Colt 1911 and a 40-calibre Glock 22. The Colt was a new style weapon to learn the workings on, but it also introduced me to .45 ACP. A much slower but larger projectile, it had more of a push recoil than the 9mm and was pleasant to shoot. The Glock 22 was not to my liking. Whether it was the polymer frame compared to the 1911 or the 40 S&W rounds, I found it very snappy and much more difficult to control. Dick insisted I spend time with it every day, and even as we progressed into rifles, I still had to work with that troublesome pistol.

The rifles took less time to hone the skills I had practiced on game in the past, though never in rapid fire or bursts. There were only two types of ammunition they thought prudent to bring to the table: 5.56 NATO and 7.62 x 39, better known as the standard chambering for the AK-47 as well as its numerous cousins. It was quite depressing really; the British SA80 was by far the worst weapon. Very comfortable ergonomics in the bullpup design but inferior in every other way to the Steyr Aug and Colt AR-15 A2. Of all of them though I was happiest with the Kalashnikov, for the same reason as the 1911; its calibre was just more pleasant to shoot. While other areas were showing progress and readiness for the next step, I was having trouble with my languages. Every day the stalemate between two stubborn men continued and Tom was the last person I was going to ask for help. I would rather stare dumfounded at the computer screen than admit defeat in front of him.

My evenings of field craft moved forward to the point where I was expected to gather information from strangers. Nikki chose them at random from whatever bar or pub we went to, spreading ourselves out over Southampton and Portsmouth on alternate evenings so not to rouse suspicion. The aim was to get strangers to divulge personal information without giving up information on myself. Breaking the ice and starting a conversation was the easy part, any young man has spent years practising it with varying results. The greater difficulty came when extracting the information. We started with simple things like birthdays, but it wasn't as simple as it sounds. The best method for me was flattering someone over their age and grossly underestimating it, slowly peeling out the information while faking disbelief. Rhetorical questions after more longwinded conversations held moderate success, "When did you say your birthday was again?" but on more than one occasion I was burned by their sobriety when they bluntly answered, "I didn't." One night it went totally wrong.

Nikki had challenged me to get the passport number from a young woman, not something most people carry with them, so I had to create a scenario that would make her want to fetch it for me. I had been using my real persona rather than a legend, but employed the excuse of being in the area to train for a yacht race open to amateurs. My method was to build the conversation over the evening to a point when I would invite her to sail to France over the weekend, thus I would need her passport number that night for the paperwork. Everything went according to plan but while I stood outside the bar waiting for Nikki to fetch her car the reality of the situation dove into view: all six foot four inches of him with shoulders like a tractor, a Portsmouth football shirt and bright white trainers.

"Oi! You the one trying to take my missus on a fucking boat?"

Before I could answer he punched me square in the gut, winding me terribly. He pushed me back against a wall, badgering me as to whether I felt like a big man or thought it was a good idea to try and steal his "bird". Another strike to the belly sent me to the floor. Laying curled up on the pavement I tried to reason with him, but he was having none of it and I could hardly catch my breath. He took a step back but only to kick me in the stomach, making it impossible for me to utter anything in my defence. He took two steps back the next time and realigned himself to strike me higher. He took his first step and I shut my eyes.

I was expecting the sharp snap of my nose breaking against his trainers, but he was the one to start whining. When I opened my eyes again his head was tilted back and a matte black knife blade was being held against his throat from behind, stroking up and down over his Adam's apple.

"Turn and face me," came the advice of the man behind him. When he turned, before any other words were said, an open hand shot out and struck my assailant in the throat, swiftly followed by the sole of a military issue boot kicking the side of his knee and sending it out at an awkward tangent. His bulk forced the leg to buckle under him with a sickening sound as the tendons snapped and he spluttered up a choked scream. With horror on his face and tears building in his eyes he crumpled next to me by the wall. An outstretched hand came my way and I was pulled to my feet. It was Tom.

"You alright?"

"I'll live."

"We look after our own in the field, let's get you back."

Tom wasn't the first person I would have imagined coming to my aid, but I was glad he did. At linguistics the next day the whole dynamic had changed, despite our misgivings towards one another, the previous evening had affirmed to us both one inescapable point: we were on the same team. Tom put it in his own words, saying, "You're a fucking arsehole… but you're my fucking arsehole." With our differences behind us we worked together and brought my languages up to the levels we had hoped for, perhaps higher. The final aspect of training was the one I was dreading but like the other areas it started off softly, stripping and assembling weaponry under duress.

I ran around and around the square to get my pulse up before having to dart down to the range, reassemble the weapon and fire a three-shot group on target. The mental strain was added with blaring noise and then sleep deprivation. Things were going well overall but the sirens and white noise tapes they had used in London would still cause me to flinch and pull my final shot left of the target as I snatched at the trigger in a rush to get things over with. With that being said, the most difficult mental stress didn't happen in the range. It came in a small room, no noisy distraction or racing pulse. No gun shots or running around.

Just Nikki and I with a few pages of photographs.

When I entered, slightly bewildered at the situation, she explained I would get to see an image for ten seconds and would then answer questions on what I had seen. I didn't think much of the challenge until she held up the first picture. There were bodies strewn across the floor, open wounds, fractured faces and twisted metal. Blood was spattered over the pavement, the people and flowing across the floor. On the right side of the picture was Bertie's body, shredded down his entire right side and barely keeping that leg attached. Of the ten seconds I had, I spent nine staring at his body in disbelief.

"How many bodies, Alex?" I turned my face away in disgust. I didn't have words to say, just hums and mumbles of refusal. "The young man screaming by the lamppost, what was on his t-shirt?"

"You monster. You indefensible...I need to leave."

I had been removed from the grief of Bertie's loss but my mind still fried at the time. It hit me like a brick wall in that moment, and apart from escaping the picture, I didn't want to break down in front of Nikki. When I pushed my chair back to leave, she leant across the table and cupped my cheeks in her hands, looking straight into my eyes and deeper than I expected or had welcomed by many before.

"I'm not happy about this either, but this is the quickest way to learn. There are two ways to deal with it: either you build a blind spot, pretending the distraction isn't there, or you put yourself above it."

"I can't pretend he isn't there."

"Then put yourself above it."

"What does that even mean?"

"Some chose to think of them as 'just' people."

I pushed her hands away from me. "Have you tried listening to yourself? That is the problem! They are people! People with families and friends…" I turned the picture back up and held it to her face pointing at Bertie, "…and he was one of mine!"

"I'm not saying you should do it that way, but you need to find a way that works for you. Whether that's putting yourself on a pedestal to look down on the situation or tricking yourself into thinking it's not real."

I stormed outside, my hands shaking so much that I struggled to light my cigarette. Harry was walking across the square when I slammed my lighter to the floor in frustration. He came over with a box of matches and some experienced advice. They all knew my schedule so he could guess what prompted my reaction.

"Do you remember the first time you shot a living thing?"

"Yes."

"What was it?"

"A pigeon. My air rifle was so feeble it took three shots to knock it off the roof."

"What did it look like?"

"Fat bugger, white flecks on his breast."

"Nice. Mine was an eighteen-year-old Argentinian boy." The statement put things in perspective and reminded me of my civilian sensitivities. "I stole his boots after. I still think about it. Wonder what he might have grown to be, how his parents felt, girlfriend, boyfriend, brothers or whatnot. But at the time, he was just like your pigeon and that's how I was able to pull the trigger. We all have our own way of handling it, there's no textbook on this shit, but when you've got a job to do you make it work. That make sense?"

"I see where you're coming from, yes, not that I've ever known a pigeon to fire back."

Harry grinned. "Good, now get back in there and do your job. You've only got another week and if you don't get this down we can't sign off on you."

I nodded, finished my cigarette quietly and leant one to Harry. When I slowly went inside, I thought back to my time in London, the way I had tried to block out the pain and noise. I had imagined I was somewhere else and sang hymns in my head, trying to remember the numbers from the hymn book at school. It worked for me then and when I had the pictures flashed at me the next time it was the method I reverted to. It wasn't perfect but with repetition I found the balance between the music and the job at hand. That night in barracks, alone in the dark, I grieved for Bertie. I needed to. I had held it in for too long.

*****

"Are they getting close?"

"Closer than you would like."

"You know what to do."

*"I'm sorry for your loss."*
*"No need. We all face death in our lives, and the older and more*

*aware we become of our own mortality, the more fate allows our load to increase. We accept it and appreciate the sickly inevitability of it all."*

*"Ain't that the truth," replied Hamilton, thinking it may offer some comfort. Flippant Americanisms rarely did that.*

*"You've got a long way to go, young man, before you can understand that, but I'm sure you'll be up to task when the time comes. In the meantime, silence is often the best option."*

*Hamilton didn't like to be called out, even as politely as that, so turned the conversation back to work. "Did you see anyone else at…" He flipped his notebook back a page. "…Monkswood?"*

*"No."*

*"That doesn't make sense, who made the food? Where did the guards sleep?"*

*"It wasn't any of my business. Would I recognize faces? Yes. Did I care who they were? No, and if I did, would I want their career or pension destroyed by the article we're putting together? No, and that is reason enough to keep them out of the light. I have met some good people during my career, and they will already face scrutiny when this gets out. I don't want to make that any worse for them. There are people who deserve everything that will come their way, and others that will hopefully skim under the radar to fade with grace between the lines of history. It's a luxury they've earned for service."*

*I was drifting off, remembering some of the good people I'd met, no matter how small, and the way I forgot so many under the clouds of circumstance. Hamilton didn't care for me reminiscing between my own ears; he only had a few days in Paris and wanted to hammer out the editorial as quick as possible. Ambition waits for no man.*

*"How much longer were you in training?"*

*"Not long…"*

My last day came around quicker than expected. I felt like I was only scratching the surface of what I needed to learn, but I must have reached the level they were aiming for. I came back to Barracks from my final language session with Tom to find my dinner suit hanging by my bed, recently fetched from London with a freshly-starched shirt. There was a generic hallmark graduation card with "Congratulations! See you in the officer's mess for dinner at 7. T, D & H." written inside. I was feeling quite excited as I pruned myself for sign-off supper with the team. I walked across to the officer's mess with a spring in my step under the summer sunshine. Skipping up the stairs to the colonial grandeur beyond, I was disappointed as soon as I opened the doors. Graduation dinner for a class of one was just that. Rather than seeing the team ready to celebrate, there was just one place set at the table and only the rumblings of the chef in the kitchen. I wasn't going to let it get me down and it had to be better than the slop I had been served over the previous weeks. My starter, a very mediocre prawn cocktail, was brought to the table by the chef, a large sweaty heap of a man. You may wonder how I could judge someone so harshly who had slaved in the kitchens for my benefit? Well, when he emerged from the kitchen with the food, he was wearing nothing but an apron to cover his modesty and a bow tie for decoration. He didn't act as if it was anything out of the ordinary, saying nothing as he shuffled across the room. I was speechless, losing my appetite while eyeing a suspiciously-proportioned prawn in my bowl. I could hear sniggering coming from the corridor. Sniggering that quickly changed to the sound of running feet when I went to investigate. I ran downstairs into the square and there was Nikki with the boys, all laughing like children who had put a whoopee cushion on a teacher's chair.

"Hey! Here comes the international man of misery!" yelled Dick.

"Bastards, the lot of you. Bastards."

"Lose the jacket and tie, Posh Spice, we're just going to the pub." Harry was right, it was just the pub, but it was a great night relaxing and enjoying a few games of pool and drinks. My time at the fort had moved me on from my ordeal in London and I too was able to enjoy the drinks without concern. I felt safe. Nikki remained pretty tight-lipped and naturally vigilant, but the boys let their hair down in true military fashion: beer, bluster and bullishness. Their stories from Hereford made my hair stand on end at times, while creasing me with laughter at others. It wasn't too far from my natural habitat and I made sure to get several extra rounds in. A nice way to thank them for their help and perhaps a farewell, as I thought it unlikely we would see each other again in the near future.

Nikki and I drove back to London the next morning, with only a slightly heavy head, and me trying to peel back her layers once again.

"Why spying? Of all the careers to choose, why the cloak and dagger stuff?"

"Why banking?"

"I asked first." Nikki sighed, but was willing to humour me. For now.

"It's exciting, interesting in its way, every day is different. Probably the same reason you took this offer. Now you."

"Same, but different. Bit of a family tradition on my side."

"Following your father? Sorry, it's in the file."

"No need to apologize, I was too young to remember. Everyone has their demons. Any family history on your side?"

"Of demons or the service?"

"Either."

"I wouldn't tell you if there was, and I couldn't tell you if I wanted to."

"Do you want to?"

She smirked and turned up the radio. I distinctly remember warming to her at the point, her guard had dropped only momentarily but enough to show a softer side. A human one. I liked that side of her very much.

When we got back to London, Nikki dropped me at the office rather than my flat. David had requested I come straight to HQ. Charlie and P were nowhere to be found, but David was pleased to see me and eager to enjoy the weather and catch up on the previous weeks. He wanted a report on training and the market, I wanted to pick up where we left off. Russia. He invited me to join him for a walk down from St. James's to Parliament Square, the summer sun being something to savour in England by all ages. We had grown closer over previous months; not to take anything away from his relationship with Charlie, but we shared an experience that Charlie did not. As we walked past the statues in the square and took a seat on the wall by the church, there was enough distance between us and the tourists to allow open conversation.

"Did you get any answers on the Russian front?"

"Nothing. P has assured me it was mere coincidence. I won't dismiss it out of hand as being nothing more, but I don't see any immediate concerns for you. You were right to bring it to me."

"That's a relief, but he seemed so confident in his comments."

"Russians are always confident, or drunk. Sometimes both. How are you feeling after your time at the fort?"

"How so?"

"Are *you* now feeling more confident, happy with what you've learned?"

"Yes, I suppose so. My officer seemed pleased with my progress, certainly enough to sign me off with P." David could see a change in me. I could feel it, even in conversation things that would have seemed fantastical months before just rolled off my tongue like stock quotes.

"Care to put yourself to the test against an old dog?" David must have missed the field work, as his eyes lit up at the chance of an exercise. It should've been easy for me. I'd been doing it so often at the fort it hardly seemed fair.

"If you think you can keep up."

"Well, I'll try my best. It's been a while you know. How about ten bob to the first man to get a drink at the members' bar?"

"At the club?"

"Not this time," he replied, pointing at the houses of parliament across the road. "…That members' bar, on the back terrace."

"You're pulling my leg?"

"Well if you don't think you have what it takes to beat and old timer like me…"

"Not at all, I would just feel bad taking your money." We shook on it and the race was on.

There are several entrances into the parliamentary estate. The public entrances have the highest security and would never get access to the members' bar. I needed to be taken there. I knew many of the young researchers used to eat lunch at the pubs on Whitehall, just outside the old Scotland Yard building. It was no longer a police station, repurposed as offices for the Members of Parliament many years before. I crossed over to Whitehall and aimed for The Red Lion. It was busy with the lunchtime crowd but I could easily spot the parliamentary workers, all wearing lanyards with ID tags hanging round their necks. I eyed up what was available, looking for a specific type of person. She had to be shy, understated, hair pulled back, and living in flat shoes but with enough mischief still hiding underneath. One girl caught my eye, quite short with glasses and unmanageable curly hair. Her glasses were thick enough to limit anyone's self-confidence but a tiny butterfly tattoo peeking out from the edge of her shoes showed her adventurous side. She was sat with some girlfriends drinking Pimm's on a pavement table and there was a spot or two still available on the bench. Furnishing myself with a fresh jug, I wandered over and asked if the seats were taken.

"No, please help yourself," she answered without paying me much attention. It was the start I expected. Sitting quietly for a while and playing with my phone I listened to their discussions on Wimbledon for that year; my target thought it could be time for a British winner. I thought it incredibly unlikely, we Brits pride ourselves on being gallant losers. However, for my purposes I was happy to chime in my support. Once the ice was broken it was easy to keep the conversation going, charming introductions and positive body language enough for her friends to quietly slip away, thinking it was one of the chance romantic encounters they read about in Cosmopolitan Magazine. Kismet for the easily duped.

"Do you work around here?" she asked.

"No, no. I work in the city. I'm just here meeting a friend for drinks, he works in Parliament."

"Oh, so do I! Where does he work?"

It was a safe bet, considering where we were sat, that she worked for some back-bench MP, so I described my friend as working in the Lords. As I suspected, she had never heard of my imaginary friend 'Dave'.

"He was supposed to meet me here half an hour ago, I better give him a call." I dialled my home number and acted out the disappointed conversation. "Oh, I thought we were meeting at the pub. Where are you? Ok, I'll head your way shortly. Met a lovely lady here so will just finish our drinks." I could see her blushing at the comment. Tucking my phone away, I turned back to my target. "I'm sorry about that, he's actually waiting for me on the terrace at the members' bar. Would it be forward of me to ask for your number before I go?"

She was very happy to oblige, so I had one more thing to ask.

"As I'm running late you couldn't take me across, could you? If I fight through the tourist lines, I will be lucky to get there before dinner."

She thought about it for a minute and I sowed some guilt for my benefit.

"I wouldn't want to put you at any trouble."

"Oh, no, not at all."

As easy as could be, like beating the blind at charades. She was able to wave me past the single officer guarding the nearby gate and escorted me down to the tunnel that ran underneath Portcullis House directly to the basement of the palace of

Westminster. Once we were close, she gave me final directions, and I thanked her profusely and promised to call her later to arrange dinner. Any remaining obstacles to the terrace were easily avoided via alternative entrances and confident walking. Ordering myself a gin from the bar, I stepped out onto the terrace to enjoy the warming embrace of victory.

Unfortunately, sat at a table under a red and white umbrella were David and Julian with several empty glasses in front of them.

"Ah, Alex. Glad you could join us. Took your time."

"I see, well, I didn't want to make you look bad in front of Julian."

Feeling slightly deflated I joined them both for a drink. Julian had to return to the affairs of state, before finding himself in too much of one. I pulled out my wallet and handed David his winnings.

"Come on then, old dog, how did you do it?"

"Ah, that would be telling."

"Think of it as extending my training."

"It's relatively simple, Alex. Why go through all the effort of building a legend, cultivating an asset, when you can achieve your goal by just being yourself? I suppose this is an area which only really applies to us, we live our legends, so our assets are real. I just called Julian and asked him if he fancied a drink. I can do the same with almost any work asset or personal friend. You should do the same." Despite all I had learned with the service, there would always be more to learn.

While we walked back to the office I told David of all the effort I went to on my chosen route, much to his amusement. He teased me about it, but I think it reminded him of his earlier days. When we got back to St. James he asked me to follow him to his office, closing the door behind us.

"We're really quite proud of you, all of us. It's not an easy job and the reports back from the fort were all very positive, 'flying colours' was the description I got from Patruus. Today was just a little reminder not to follow their book to the letter. We are a different animal."

"It was surprisingly fun when I got into the swing of things."

"It can be great fun, that's why so many of them never leave. I think even Jules misses it at times, not that he would admit it. I got you a small token of our appreciation. Charlie picked it out, said it's what you youngsters like these days." David pulled a small red box from his desk and handed it to me. Without being able to tell anyone of my time at the fort it was touching to have it recognised. It was a beautiful new Patek Phillippe Aquanaut in stainless steel with the rubber strap. I had been lusting after one for some time, loving the way it blended usability, style and elegance in a new direction for Patek at the time. The back is usually clear to show the movement within, but mine had a solid back engraved with the fish logo I had seen in the members' books.

"Thank you, David, it's stunning. I like the fish."

"My father used to say if you have a nice watch, wherever you are in the world you can always sell it for a ticket home. I've never done it myself hence I'm still wearing the one he gave me." He took his watch off, showing the same fish logo engraved into the gold. "Quite funny really, I told the engraver it was for my son's confirmation. Surprising parallels I think…" David paused for a moment of thought, but not for emotional reason. "…Alex, I know you have only just got back, but I'm afraid I have more to ask of you. We're still not getting far enough with this Libya business, no fresh news at all since you left. We are very exposed and it makes me nervous not having a concrete agreement in place for BP. We were up almost 40% but things have started to fall back. Patruus tells us two of the leaders' sons are in Paris for the next week. Capstan has a dinner in place to see if he can sway them. I want you there as a financial incentive."

"Will do, when shall we make the arrangements?"

"They've already been made. Patruus has approved your handler to go along under the cover of your secretary. A pair of experienced hands are always useful in the field. Not to mention, an attractive blonde is a great icebreaker. Joan will give you the details. You leave in the morning."

That afternoon I prepared for what was my first solo assignment, pulling the relevant files from the office and familiarising myself with the two sons I would soon be meeting. On the way home I followed Julian's advice and withdrew the majority of my remaining bonus from my account, locked it in an old case I had, and entrusted it to Derek, the simple yet amiable man who manned the front desk at my flat. He had been there as long as I had and maintained a good rapport with the tenants. It wasn't the first time asking him to hold a package for me, but it was certainly the most valuable one. When I opened the door at home, the accumulation of post from the previous weeks skidded across the wooden floor. It was almost eerie to spend a night at home again. I didn't miss the accommodation at the fort, but my flat certainly brought back memories and enough answerphone messages to make me wonder if mother had a stroke. She hadn't, and after I'd spun a tale of a business trip, she filled me in on the dull daily village life she loved so much. Some things (whatever turns our lives take) never change.

*****

"Is it live?"

"Yes, the data is coming through."

I met Nikki at Waterloo to catch the early Eurostar to Paris and felt a little nostalgic when I saw some of the old familiar faces still trudging down to catch the drain to bank. Nikki was fitting the secretary's role well, turning plenty of heads before we even got to the platform. Although I was unable to remove any files from my office, she had a travel pack from hers which we were able to discuss on the journey. More recent photographs and bios on the brothers, including their hobbies and vices. She would be reporting back to London every twenty-four hours, the top brass were still a little anxious for my first proper run.

"Nervous?"

"Not really, should I be?"

"No, this should all be very familiar for you."

"You?"

"I always get a little nervous, can't seem to get comfortable. Like my underwear is all twisted up." I laughed at her candid but accurate description.

"Haven't you learned to cope with it over the years?"

"In a way. I just don't wear any." I nearly choked on my coffee and couldn't think of how to respond to her comment, just gawked at her like a priest with a pole dancer. "Hey! Snap out of it. Mind on the job please."

"Sorry…yes…sorry."

I shuffled the papers hurriedly to detract from the awkwardness, but Nikki was unfazed, even enjoying my reaction. We spent most of the journey on prep, reversing our roles with me giving Nikki a crash course on international finance. Not enough for her to enter a negotiation, but enough to understand what was being said. As we pulled into the Gare du Nord, she switched bags with one of the train staff, a drop to dispose of the files and provide us with our emergency information and the most recent developments. Once we were in our taxi, she opened the package.

"They arrived three days ago, staying at the same hotel as us. They have been in touch with Capstan's people and we are meeting them for dinner tonight at 9 on a private boat on the river. Capstan's meeting us for drinks 7:30 at the hotel. Keep this with you. Bail-out info."

She handed me a small envelope then tore the note into several pieces and tossed it out the window, littering not being a major concern for her compared to being found with that piece of paper. We pulled up in front of the George V, a hotel I had stayed at before that was nicely sandwiched between the Arc de Triomphe and Eiffel Tower. It was a popular spot for Middle Eastern money men since it was bought out by Talal's Kingdom group a few years earlier. Joan had made the reservations for connecting rooms, useful for our purposes yet amusing for the mademoiselle at the front desk. She made her insinuations known not quite so subtly when advising us of the couples' massage sessions available at the spa.

After I settled in, I knocked the adjoining door. Nikki

shouted back that it was open and I let myself in. She was sat by the window looking out towards the Eiffel Tower, carrying that spellbound look in her eye that women get when they reach Paris.

"First time?" I asked

"Is it that obvious?"

"Nobody can take their eyes off the tower the first time, but it is a beautiful city."

"I nearly came a few times, but something always came up. The last overseas assignment I went on I was based in a Holiday Inn for two months. First assignment with you and it's the lap of luxury."

"Playing the part, I suppose."

It hadn't seen that reaction from her before, in awe at her surroundings and open about herself. I am sure I looked the same way when we first arrived at the fort, but that brief honest expression exacerbated what I'd seen in the car: someone less intimidating and more like a colleague than a mentor. I wasn't as fond of Paris; a few too many trips over the years had dulled its charm and while its landmarks faded into the background, I noticed more of the less appealing aspects of the city: tourists, traffic and dirty streets. At least the food remained fantastic.

"What is your cover for this?"

"Your secretary, PA, however you choose to describe it really."

"I meant your name."

"Nikki, obviously."

"You're using your real name?"

"Don't be silly."

"So Nikki is a cover name?"

"Of course, you're an asset. A very close one, but an asset all the same. Don't take it personally."

Perhaps I shouldn't have viewed her as a colleague after all. I may have been on the inside, but not as much as I thought. Still, no harm in a bit of fun. We were both well-versed in passive aggressive comments.

"Are you a Nikki or Nicole?"

"Does it make a difference?"

"Nicole is the type to read poetry and take walking holidays in the Lake District, but Nikki? She's the sex fiend I'd meet in a hotel lobby, masturbating to magazines." Bold move on my part, but she started it and I wondered if she'd catch the lyrics.

"If you think quoting Prince lyrics will make me like you, you're correct. But if you're suggesting a woman has to choose between those two personas, rather than being herself, then you'll wake up with a stiletto in your ear."

"Noted." Not exactly what I'd envisaged.

"You do learn quickly." She blew me the briefest of kisses across the room. "Now fuck off so I can get changed." Again, it was duly noted.

We met for drinks as planned and Capstan talked constantly for an hour about how much capital he expected me to bring to the conversation, interpreting me as a meal ticket rather than an ally. I wasn't going to reveal that we had little to no intention of financing his dream, so just nodded in acknowledgment and let him construe it in his own way. He was ringing his hands constantly like his career depended on the deal, which it didn't, and I was worried that he could spoil everything with his eagerness to please. At least he was staying at a different hotel. I shouldn't speak so harshly about someone who achieved great success in his chosen industry, but I mean it very seriously when I describe him as intolerable.

We shared a car to the Pont Alexandre III where a private boat was tendered for dinner. The brothers' security team approached as soon as we pulled up, not allowing us out of the car until they had checked our credentials. Once they were satisfied, we were shown down the footway to the vessel. Capstan was practically running. I took a more tempered pace, making mental notes of the security teams and the layout of the boat. When we reached the deck we were greeted by Hannibal, the older of the two brothers. He was a tall man of similar age to myself but with more oil in his hair than the Libyan desert. His younger brother Saadi was behind him and graciously introduced himself to the three of us, especially Nikki. It was an intimate event, only the three of us with the brothers and their security. The grand salon had been cleared apart from one table. The open space gave a relaxed impression but would also limit the chances for conversation to occur on the side. The boat was usually used as a tourist trap dinner cruiser on the Seine, but they had booked the entire vessel and brought in their preferred team from nearby L'Arpege to guarantee privacy and greatly improved catering. Capstan was gushing over his hosts, complimenting everything from the décor to their clothing, much to the annoyance of everyone else. When he eventually excused himself to use the facilities, I took what would be my only opportunity to talk privately and followed him below deck.

"You need to calm down."

"I don't need you telling me what to do, young man. I've been here before and know how these Arabs work."

"Well I can tell you that you are making everyone uncomfortable with your constant flattery."

"I need you to speak up, start putting some money on the table."

I squared up against him and stepped closer with each syllable, forcing him back to the edge of the sink.

"You need to learn your place. I am here as a favour to you, not the other way around. Don't make the mistake of thinking for one second that you're in charge. If you think we will invest our money with anyone showing the kind of desperation you are, then you are wrong. Shut up, sit down or swim back to shore. It's your choice."

"I will be speaking to David about this."

"I hope so. You'll be saving me a phone call."

When we came back to the table the mood was much improved, Nikki laughing at the awful jokes being sent her way. Saadi fancied himself as a football star in his national team, but I wouldn't want to judge how much of that was down to his position rather than his skill level. Before pudding was started, Saadi and I stood up and started kicking a bread roll around the deck, much to Capstan's frustration as his sat sulking over his zabaglione. When we docked again he made a hasty exit, distraught that I had made no talk of business the entire evening. I hadn't avoided the subject out of sheepishness, I simply didn't wish to discuss it while Capstan was there and was keen to build a rapport before making a move. With Capstan out of mind, Nikki brought an end to the football and kept Saadi occupied with playful conversation. I had time to talk with Hannibal man to man.

"We've had such a fun evening I would hate to spoil it by talking business, but we didn't come to Paris just to beat you at football."

"I understand. There are discussions with lots of parties for the drilling contracts in the desert, but no decisions have been made."

"I hope that we can help make those decisions easier."

"Maybe you can, maybe you can't but it helps to have backing for new projects like this. I know we have dealt with your bank before and that makes us comfortable, not so sure about BP."

"I'm sorry Matthew left so abruptly, Seasickness, I think, but rest assured we would not enter any agreement with a firm who couldn't meet our standards. We can discuss things more as time moves along, I'm sure we can work on a situation which would benefit all parties."

"I would like that. What are your plans for tomorrow?"

"Nothing I can't rearrange."

"Good. Why don't you two join us at Pierre Gagnaire at 9? Don't bring Matthew, I can only handle him in small doses."

"I'll look forward to it... just need to figure out how to get my secretary away from your brother!"

"Ha! Good luck with that, he is very fond of blondes. Keeps several 'secretaries' on call."

It was a high note for us to leave on, a good result. In our taxi back to the hotel Nikki was pleased with our performance.

"Much better than training."

"It's my natural environment. I'm more comfortable here."

"Don't say that on your first run, you'll live to regret it."

She could say what she liked, but my confidence was swelling. My training had given me the tools, but when back amongst my more regular surroundings I felt invincible. Back at the hotel I treated myself to a generous pour in my room and could hear Nikki still awake in the next room. Whether it was the rush from the evenings work, the drink, perhaps a bit of both and the feeling of unfinished business, I knocked on our adjoining door to see if she would care to join me.

"No. Go to sleep."

It brought me back to earth a little. I hadn't said anything. Ego slightly roughed up I sent a late message to Charlie.

"Have Pater call me secure in the morning."

"Will do. Bon nuit."

I was sure Capstan had already sent an email to David but it didn't worry me. I finished my drink and indeed got ready for bed. Nikki was still moving around in the next room, and I drifted off thinking it was an opportunity missed.

＊＊＊＊＊

"I want him pulled back,
it's getting out of control."

"Hold your nerve."

It was seven in the morning, six GMT, when my phone rang.

"Piscator, good morning. Are you alone?"

"Morning Pater, yes. Secure?"

"Yes. How was your evening?"

"From our perspective, promising. I think they could be useful assets for us in the long run and despite Capstan's efforts I may even be able to get BP across the line. We have been invited to dinner again tonight so I would like to extend our stay by an extra few days."

"Good work. Matthew didn't seem too happy with you yesterday. He called me at home to whinge at your behaviour, but from the sounds of it you played the right game."

"The elder brother suggested they had worked with us before? I didn't see any mention of that in the files."

"Your predecessor spent time in Africa, and the business world can be quite small in the desert."

It seemed a rational explanation. Paths crossed every day in the city, and the talent pool in emerging dictatorships was bound to be much smaller. I didn't think any more of it. The day was spent indulging my colleague. My advance had been rebuffed swiftly the night before, but it wouldn't be fair of me to take a lady to Paris and not show her the sights. As much as I hated the tourist trail it was quite enjoyable. There were awkward moments when the conversations would grind to a halt, only so much I could talk about before Nikki started shaking her head and changing the subject over fears of revealing too much about herself. Little morsels of realism started to shine through as afternoon turned into evening but I couldn't tell if they were part of her legend or the genuine article. I like to think it was the latter. She looked stunning when she came downstairs for dinner, and I would have been flattered to have her on my arm rather than walking dutifully behind me. I'll admit that under the laddish bravado that drew me to her door the night before, some saplings of affection were growing.

"Gosh, you clean up well, don't you?"

"Probably the most insulting compliment I've had, but at least you're trying."

We took a car the very short distance to the restaurant. It was easily nice enough to walk but I don't think Nikki's feet would have appreciated it. Gagnaire had received his third Michelin star a couple of years before and I was really looking forward to my first visit. On arrival we were ushered inside to a corner table where the brothers were sat, protected by walls on two sides and tables of security staff on the others. They stood to welcome us to the table, Saadi planting several lecherous kisses on Nikki's cheeks. Unlike the night before when we had focussed on soft topics, I was keen to pick up my conversation with Hannibal where we had left of. As I tucked into my delightful confit I decided to face the matter head on.

"I think it's all pretty obvious what it is we're looking for as far as SC goes, or BP for that matter. I'm sorry that I have neglected to ask what it is you're hoping for."

"We hope for many things, but for us right now our biggest concern is handling the anticipated increase in revenue. LAFICO is our sovereign wealth fund, but it has been limited by the unjust sanctions of the last twenty years."

"Our trading team are well versed at handling large scale institutional investment; it would be no problem for us to offer that service."

"We are not looking at the stock market. Perhaps government debt but not stocks and shares. Too risky. My father likes land, he says that it is good to have because they don't make it anymore."

"Open land? Commercial? Residential?"

"Everything. I've been looking in Paris, Saadi likes Italy, my older brother has been looking at London. We want to buy it, without buying it, if you understand what I mean."

I most certainly did. They needed shell companies set up, accounts, clean paths through the continent and a paper trail longer than the Nile. All totally legal but convoluted enough to prevent widespread knowledge of their ownership.

"I understand, don't want any undue attention while everyone is still being desensitized to Lockerbie."

"Exactly."

Of course, it was all bollocks. It was plain to the most middling individual that this wasn't about a low profile, it was about one family personally profiting from a national asset. Spreading funds around the world in a fashion that could be syphoned as they saw fit. Nonetheless, this was my way in and one with which I was comfortable. It would also be profitable for the bank and make us invaluable to the ruling family. If that wasn't enough to sway the decision in BPs favour, then I didn't know what would be. As dinner concluded we headed to the bars and clubs just north of the restaurant, Saadi desperate to get Nikki into a place with hard alcohol and dark corners.

The brothers liked attractive company and weren't shy about paying for it. We always had a roped-off area with only a select few allowed close to our table, but once there, they were showered with vintage champagne to their hearts' content; Cristal was the brothers' bottle of choice but I always preferred Krug. The drinks did enough to push their ideas up a notch and they decided to drive themselves to the next club. Nikki and I were riding shotgun with each brother and security following in a chase vehicle. We ripped round the Arc de Triomphe before racing down the Champs Elysee, the speedometer tipping 110 while Hannibal cackled louder than the exhaust. Inevitably the police were soon flashing their blue lights in our rear-view.

We pulled over, but before the police had a chance to get close to the vehicle the security team jumped between them. The arguments became heated and eventually their security chief came tapping at the window. Hannibal handed over his passport and put the window back up.

"Diplomatic immunity. They can't do anything but complain."

Laughing at his fortune, we mocked the futile efforts of the gendarmerie from behind our burly and bulletproof barriers. We cruised around the city in our immunized convoy at less abrasive speeds for another hour, talking fast cars and fantasies. If there is a universal truth aside from the natural human lust for money and power, it's that we are all more likely to do business with someone we 'like', perhaps even call a friend. It was fun, but also concerning to see the legal power afforded to dignitaries in comparison to mortals. When we eventually returned to the hotel in the early hours of the morning, Nikki made her excuses and went upstairs, having had enough of Saadi's advances for one night. I joined them for a nightcap in their suite but didn't want to overstay my welcome. We agreed to meet again later that week for more of the same. Hannibal knew plenty more clubs in Paris where he could visit and show his generosity to the locals, just as long as they were under thirty in age and waist. When I got to my room the "do not disturb" sign was hanging on the outside of my door. Perhaps I had put it there out of habit when we left earlier. I went inside and flicked on the lights which illuminated Nikki reclined on my bed with nothing but a glass of champagne and her necklace. It was a very pleasant case of déjà vu, but I was in a far better state than before.

"Is it weird that I don't even know your real name?"

"Does it really matter?"

In the moment it still mattered, but not enough to stand in my way.


She stared up at me with those deep hazel eyes and that mischievous post-coital grin. Her hair was ruffled in a quaint yet endearing manner, highlighting that rare quality of being one who looks better when least prepared. "Comfortable?" I asked, to which her only retort was hitting me with a pillow.

"Is this breaking some sort of rule?"

"Funnily enough, it's actively encouraged. Most places try to avoid a workplace fling, but in the service its seen as a way of avoiding the introduction of an outsider."

"Oh, so this is a 'workplace fling' now? You are filling the secretary role very well." She struck me with the pillow again and hopped out of bed, wrapping herself in a bedsheet. It cascaded round her hips like a classical sculpture as she went for the room service menu, ordering up some wine and cheese to be delivered to her room.

"Not staying?"

"I have to report to London, but I'll join you for breakfast." She came back over to the bed for one last embrace but when she attempted to pull away, I kept hold of her hand.

"Can I ask you something?"

"Now would seem as good a time as any."

"When I was being interrogated, who was the man opposite me?" Having slowly pieced together most of the faces I had met, it still bothered me who the faceless man was that I had cruelly brought near to emasculation.

"Nobody. Just some detainee we had in for questioning the same time as you."

"Your boss had suggested he was a threat to me personally. That he would have let me pull the trigger."

"Don't be silly. He just wanted to see your reaction. You think too much, get some rest."

"You're not the first person to tell me that. Night, 'Nikki'," I replied making cheeky quotation marks with my fingers.

She went to leave but hesitated in the doorway. "It's Penny," she said, smiling. The honesty of the disclosure had lifted a weight from her shoulders and I could see her face light up as she said it. No doubt, she saw the same reaction in me.

\* \* \* \* \*

"This makes me nervous."

"Don't be. We took care of it last time."

I woke to a knock at the door: breakfast delivered for two. The sun was shining through the curtains, beckoning me to pull them back and allow a beautiful Parisian morning into the moment. It was a good start. My half of our joining door was still ajar so I gave her side a light knock to let her know breakfast had arrived. No response came and I assumed she was in the bathroom so I decided to do the same. Afterwards, I tried her door again. Still no response but I could just about hear the water running in the room. Although I had just showered, I wouldn't have turned down the opportunity to join her should the situation arise. I slowly opened the door and crept into her room hoping to surprise her. As I neared the bathroom door I could feel the wet carpet beneath my feet, the water having spilled into the main room. I knocked on the bathroom door, knocking louder, and louder again until I was hammering it with my fist. The door was locked from the inside and she wasn't responding. I took a few steps back and ran at the door, lunging at it shoulder first. The lock burst through the frame and the door swung open, smacking the stainless steel towel rail behind with a clang.

The bloody liquid ran over the side of the bathtub and

covered the floor. Penny lay grey and lifeless below the surface, her hair dancing in the current while the tap flowed more and more water over her limp rippling face. She had long deep cuts along the length of her forearms and across her inner thighs, like flaws in the ruby waters. I instinctively grabbed her by the neck and pulled her face up towards mine, slapping at her cheeks in a hopeless effort to illicit some response. It didn't take long to accept that I was too late. Holding her forehead against my cheek, I reached behind and shut off the tap. I forced myself to let her go but as she sank below the surface again I couldn't help but stroke her hair back away from her face. I don't want to leave. She would have understood I was left with no choice.

I put the do not disturb tag on the outside of her door before returning to my room and locking the connecting doors. I tore open the emergency envelope and dialled the line for the Paris station.

"Good morning. Urgent message for station chief, Piscator Sierra Oscar Sierra."

"Code?"

"Zero, one, two, niner, one, six, seven, three, eight, six, zero."

"Location?"

"George V, room 431."

"Thank you. Remain in place."

I burned the instructions in my ashtray and rushed to gather my things. Whatever instructions would come from station I had no plans to remain in place longer than needed. I paced back and forth humming to myself like a pensive professor to fight against what I had just seen and held. It's one thing to see a photograph, another to feel it against your skin. Death is the sickliest thing in the flesh. At the time I couldn't care for the how or why, I just knew for my own immediate sake I had to get out of there. Within the hour I heard footsteps in the neighbouring room. Muffled voices seeped through the walls and whilst I was pondering whether I should interfere, there was a knock at my door. Peering through the peephole, I was relieved to see a tired-looking concierge, making one last call before the end of his shift. He was carrying a small envelope on a silver salver, which he dutifully presented as soon as I opened the door. I snatched it and immediately shut the door in his face. Inside was the receipt for our stay and a single ticket back to London on a train due to leave in a few hours. I would have rather sat in the station than stay at the hotel and did a final sweep of the room before leaving. The door was knocked once again. I furiously marched towards it, thinking concierge had the gall to ask for a tip. It wasn't him. Harry pushed his way into the room as soon as I turned the handle. He scanned the room and checked behind the curtains without even saying 'hello'. Next he tossed every drawer from the dresser, bureau and bedside table.

"What are you looking for?"

"Anything. Anything that might indicate you're compromised."

"Did you try next door? Might seem the obvious fucking choice right now!"

"Never mind about next door. Fuck! Nothing!" He was rattled, stripping sheets from the bed and flipping over what furniture remained untouched.

"Harry, I've got to get out of here. I need to get to the train."

"Leave your room key, I'll drop it off when I leave. There has to be something…"

"Harry."

"Yeah."

"I'm sorry."

"Me too, mate. Me too."

I was twenty yards down the hallway when Harry came jogging after me.

"Alex, one more thing. You haven't seen me, this never happened. You got your instructions and left, got me? Don't trust anybody."

"Understood."

I said that, but couldn't understand why Harry would make such a request. That said, I wasn't going to question it. If he had meant me any harm, he would have done it already. As I walked through the lobby to find a taxi I doubled back to reception and asked if they could deliver a note for me. Despite the personal cost and fragility of the venture, I didn't want to burn my bridges so scribbled a hasty note to my newfound friend.

"H, Personal issues have forced me to return to England urgently. Please let me know a convenient time to continue our conversations. Best, A"

I handed it to the front desk with my business card and the suite number for delivery. A taxi had just dropped off a fresh guest and I was able to hop into their still-warm seat. As I pulled away, it wasn't Penny or Hannibal that played on my mind, but Tom and Dick.

I had spotted them in the lobby when I was leaving, hunkered down in the high back chairs near the lift and peering round the edge to watch me.

\* \* \* \* \*

"Fuck! Fuck! What gives you the
bloody right?"

"You're not the only one to give orders."

*"I'm sorry."* Hamilton commented when I stopped to take a stock of myself. It was unpleasant to revisit those memories.

*"You've nothing to be sorry for."*

*"Still, it must have been hard."*

*"It was..."* I wasn't going to lie to the boy about it. *"First times are always hard, whatever the scenario, but the first death sticks with you. Especially under those circumstances. I can still smell it, the dirty copper smell from the blood mixing with the water and spilling out. The only way I can describe it is like counting 1 p and 2 p coins, the musty and metallic smell that sticks to your fingers and nostrils."*

*"Pennies?"*

*"I was trying not to describe it that way."*

*"Of course. I'm sorry, you must have cared for her very much."*

*"I think of her often. Sometimes fondly, other times more pragmatically that our situation was professional. What I will say is that I greatly regret what happened to her. I would have liked to know her better. That's as far as I'm willing to go."*

*"Right."* Hamilton made a quick note. *"You were on your way back to London?"*

28

As the Eurostar emerged into the English countryside and accelerated towards London, I received a message from Charlie: "Come straight to the office." P had the reports from Paris station and called an emergency meeting.

When I arrived at St. James they were already sitting inside, talking quietly amongst themselves. Without so much as a welcome or checking if I was alright, P opened the questioning. He wanted a breakdown of everything that happened since we left London, which I was happy to provide. Nobody interrupted, allowing me to run down the entire trip in one go. David made a few notes as I was talking but Charlie and P kept their eyes fixed on me throughout.

"What a very sorry state of affairs. She had so much potential," said P when I was finished.

"Who did this?" I asked.

"I think you are perhaps a bit shaken up, Piscator. Judging by what you have told me and my reports from station, the young lady took her own life. Such a tragedy." Charlie nodded in solidarity with P's sentiment.

"Bollocks! I refuse to believe she would do that to herself. She would have no reason to."

"How would you know? Were you close to her?" asked my friend opposite me.

"I suppose so. She was a good officer to work with."

"I mean outside of work my friend."

"We never met socially, no."

"You know that's not what I'm asking."

"Not that I see it as relevant to the conversation, but yes there was an incident of that nature."

"When?" P suddenly interjecting with a forceful tone.

"If you must know, last night."

"Sweet Christ! You didn't think to mention it?!" shouted P, leaning at me across the table, close enough for his spit to land on my face. "A psychopathic Arab takes a shining to my agent and you think the best way to deal with that is to fuck her? Do you know the kind of people we're talking about here? How low they would stoop out of jealously or spite?!" I wasn't going to back down to his accusations and stood up so quickly it took him off guard.

"Yes, I know the kind of people we're dealing with! I've been closer to them than you ever have!"

"How dare you, you jumped-up little shit!"

"Patruus!" roared David from the head of the table, the first word he'd said since I arrived. "Sit down! Both of you! This is not a time to be losing our heads."

"Pater, I cannot be dealing with this. I am not putting my people on the line for someone who, despite our initial thoughts, is clearly not ready for his post. I have the head of the Security Service and several ministers breathing down my neck over the bloody Irish, not to mention working on our new venture with Procurator. I never wanted him dealing with the Libyans in the first place, we both know what happened last time."

"Then don't deal with it! He has never been your charge, nor will he be. Consider this meeting over."

P didn't need a second invitation to leave, storming from his seat and flinging the door open with such anger that it ricocheted off the bars and nearly closed itself again. Charlie remained seated for a moment, just looking at his father, before he shook his head and left to follow P.

David got up, I assumed to leave, but instead he closed the door again and turned on the power. "Alex..." he began, forgoing our titles for the first time in the cage, "I am ashamed to admit that I was not as honest with you about Libya as you would have liked. In light of recent events, you deserve a more complete brief."

"David you're worrying me."

"When the Libyans spoke of dealing with us before, I do know what they are referring to. Your predecessor attended some meetings in Cairo with representatives from Tripoli. He was there with the British ambassador to assist in the negotiations over Lockerbie and advise on the state of frozen assets within the UK system."

"There's nothing in the file."

"There is nothing in the file because he never made it back." David sat back down and, digesting the gravity of his statement, I did the same. "Once his meetings were concluded he was due to come home. We had good communication, using the secure system at the embassy to touch base every few days. Then the day before he was due to fly, the vehicle he was travelling in was ambushed. We're told it was bandits in the Sinai. The burnt-out vehicle and its occupants were found a few days later."

"How could you let me walk into a situation like that without warning me?"

"We had no information to suggest there was anything untoward going on and I didn't want to worry you. P has a good network in North Africa left over from the Irish gun running in the 80's."

"Then why was P saying he never thought I should have gone to Paris?"

"He doesn't trust the Libyans and that clouds his judgement. With Cairo he was certain it was the Libyans despite the lack of evidence, and he's jumping to the same conclusion now. Whether we have interests in the oil or not, he believes the Libyans are using us."

"To be honest, I found them to be quite pleasant company. Welcoming and eager for business. Although different to what I'm used to."

"P is living in the past. We all expected the IRA attacks to stop after the Good Friday agreement, but it hasn't. Hammersmith, the BBC, the underground."

"Nobody has been hurt in those attacks. It's just some splintered individuals who refuse to accept the peace."

"I agree with you, but when they fire an RPG at Vauxhall Cross, P takes it very, very personally. It's dragging up old fears and prejudices for him at the moment."

"Do you believe what he said today?"

"I have no reason to doubt him, Alex, but he also lacks any evidence to back up his claim."

"David, I can categorically tell you it doesn't fit together."

"Why? What can you tell me that P hasn't said already? You said you found her like that."

"Yes, but the door was locked. If the Libyans killed her out of spite, why bother to try and stage a suicide? Why risk further negotiations over a woman?"

"Maybe it was a suicide."

"No. Absolutely not. I knew her, she wouldn't do it."

"You think you knew her. The truth is, no matter how much you don't want to hear it, you really didn't." I didn't like being told what I felt to be false. I stood up and began my habitual pacing around the table while David remained steadfast in his seat, as calm and collected as anyone could be during such a conversation. The pacing was becoming too much of a habit for me. A tell.

"The Russians! What about the Russians?" I blurted out, clinging to any explanation I could think of rather than accept the guilt being dropped at my doorstep. I was so close to revealing my encounter with Harry but I stopped myself. He wouldn't have come to me without good reason.

"We have no indications of them showing interest in our activities. If there was some external involvement in this, then the Libyans are most likely. In light of this situation I think we are going to have to pull out of BP. We can't get a clear picture and there's too much personal risk."

"David, please. Don't throw away what we've done so far."

"I don't see any choice, what if something were to happen to you or Charlie in the field? I couldn't live with myself."

"Just give it a bit more time."

"I'm sorry, I can't."

I followed the lead of my colleagues and stormed out of the office. I refused to believe any of it and was furious that David would pull the plug. When I finally got home, I called Charlie to try and talk to him about the situation and how he could have turned against me in such a blatant fashion. Yes, I wanted to vent at him, but I could also have done with some company. Strangely he took some persuading to stop by, but at least he bore gifts on his arrival: a very pleasant bottle of whisky with which to lubricate our conversations. He was disinterested in everything I raised, from Penny, to David's plan to dump our stock, or my own worries. All he wanted to talk about was the Libyan meetings.

"Why does it matter anymore? The old man wants to close out."

"Because, my friend, just because he wants to close out BP doesn't mean we can't keep tabs on crude and whoever else may get a bite at the cherry. Did you learn anything interesting?"

"No."

"Well tell me about the uninteresting stuff then?"

"Charlie, for fuck's sake why do you even care? I found my friend dead this morning!"

"I don't want to be Devil's advocate here, but she wasn't your friend. She was your handler. I think if you'd remembered that then maybe things would have been different."

"Wow, so your way of helping me through this is to continue telling me the same bullshit as everybody else?"

"You may not like it my friend, but the truth isn't always pleasant."

"You have no bloody idea what it's like to sit in my chair. Not a clue. You didn't have the balls for the job!"

"You're upset and I understand this is part and parcel of you coming to terms with this…"

"You bawled your eyes out like a pussy before even getting started, so don't dare try and tell me how to handle this situation! You don't know half of it!" I flung my glass across the room, shattering it against the wall. Charlie calmly stood up and grabbed a towel from the kitchen, kneeling to mop up the mess and gingerly pick up the shards of crystal from the floor. I held my head in my hands, taking deep breaths and apologizing profusely for my uncharacteristic outburst.

"I'm sorry, Charlie, that was uncalled for."

"I think you need some rest, my friend, it's been a long day for you."

Charlie gathered his things and headed to the door. He stopped as he reached for the handle.

"Maybe you should take some time away. Level yourself out, you know?"

"I'll be fine, thank you."

"If you say so. For what it's worth, I'm sorry."

"Thanks."

He closed the door behind him. I stood listening to his footsteps fade down the corridor before I locked the door and put the deadlock across. Maybe he was right, I should've looked at getting away for a while. I thought about what Harry had said in Paris about not trusting anyone, and flashed back to Julian's advice to have a plan to disappear for a while. I couldn't bend my head around the situation and some time away could bring me the clarity I needed. I retrieved my case from Derek the doorman, counting out stacks of currency on the coffee table. I decided to deposit some in my regular account but keep most as cash, both with me and stashed downstairs. It was a difficult night at home, as although Penny had spent limited time there it still reminded me of her. It was a strange situation; even then I knew we weren't an 'item' at all, more like colleagues wrapped up in Parisian charm and hormones, but that didn't make it any less painful.

I didn't rush into the office the next day, but when I arrived things were already in full swing. David had started passing the instructions to Stephen to close out all our positions in BP, I just shook my head as I walked past and overheard him giving the orders. I didn't believe it was the right decision for us to be making, but it was out of my hands. It would take Stephen weeks to unload the stock and despite a solid capital gain I thought we were running away from the opportunity. I had an email arrive overnight from an unfamiliar address, but a familiar name.

"A, Sorry to hear of your troubles at home. Please come for a visit to continue discussions. H"

It wasn't the most eloquent invitation I had received, but I wanted to accept. Not because of the financial upside, we were haemorrhaging stock from every permissible orifice. I wanted to find the truth, however dark it may be. Rather than respond to Hannibal's invitation immediately I was compelled to ask David's opinion.

"Absolutely not!" I argued the case to David: the financial rewards from our current holdings and the security benefits for the service of potentially digging out the Irish connection. He wasn't having any of it. "Alex, after what we discussed I cannot allow it. If P is right, then it's simply too dangerous. If you were a faceless asset I would agree with you, but you are not. I appreciate you as a colleague, I know your family well and… and…well, let's just say, Pactum will need you here when the day comes that I can't be." The gravity of what he was implying didn't sink in at the time. I carried on.

"You once told me the feeling in my gut was my subconscious responding to things I may have missed. It's screaming at me to go."

"You are a grown man, I can't stop you. I am asking you, please, stay here. I'm closing all our positions, whatever the potential upside may be. The risk is too high."

I debated with myself the rest of the morning, flipping back and forth over what I should do. Eventually, my decision was made: I needed some time away and that was what I was going to do. I made a few phone calls and the arrangements were made. I didn't bother with the files, they contained nothing more of use to me, but I wanted to leave a message for David.

I wrote a simple note on a piece of paper and stuck it to my office door with a drawing pin. All it said was, "Gone fishing."

\* \* \* \* \*

"Bravo Tango Niner, prepare for intercept."

"Confirmed, nearing Tobruk."

Tripoli wasn't a popular tourist destination for obvious reasons, but the chance to do some business and perhaps visit Leptis Magna were an enticing prospect. I pulled onto the tarmac at Stansted airport where a Bombardier jet was waiting for me, skipped up the steps and was met by some crew and the same head of security I'd met in Paris. I wasn't sure if he was there for my protection or as a minder, but he proved a useful translator between myself and the cabin crew. It was my first experience of long-distance private aviation and despite the implied luxury you would expect, I found it terribly unpleasant. The shrunken stature of the aircraft made me feel far less secure in flight and the size of the cabin with even our small number of people was like being trapped in a hotel room with a group of strangers. Yet, as we burst through the clouds over the south coast of England I felt a sense of freedom. Free from suspicion, expectation and judgement.

The flight was trouble-free but I wished it had the same bar service as British Airways. Fruit juice and bottled water didn't really cut it for any flight longer than an hour. That being said, the journey itself was just a few hours and we landed in Tripoli in the early evening.

The airport was quiet, a few short haul services, but with them only now emerging from the international wilderness it wasn't buzzing with activity. There was a large motorcade waiting for us as we pulled towards a secluded area away from the main terminal. The door opened and the warm African air rushed in. The climate wasn't as harsh as I was expecting, similar to the rest of the Mediterranean but with more distrust and economic disparity in the air. Stepping down, Hannibal was waiting for me with open arms to welcome me to his little corner of Africa.

"There he is! Welcome to Tripoli!"

"Thank you for the invitation and the lift! Good to see you."

Among the police vehicles and military presence were two regular cars. One BMW 7 series and a Mercedes S class, popular with unelected and 'elected' officials across the continent. The S Class was just to carry luggage and smuggled wine cases. Hannibal and I sat in the back of the BMW together, cruising the few miles down the airport highway at a much slower pace than our previous journey. To say the city wasn't what I expected would be a bit misleading, as I had no idea what to expect. There was a mix of stunning Arabic architecture and flat featureless buildings similar to those you see in the western world, architecture from the decades that taste forgot. The roads were not the dust tracks of hearsay, showing at least some effort from the ruling family to put oil revenues to good use. We turned into a military compound that was fortified to a level that made Monkswood look like a scout camp. The vehicles deliberately slowed down as we passed a strikingly ugly yet poignant sculpture in front of a derelict-looking building. A giant golden fist crushed a poor imitation of a US fighter jet, something to commemorate the failed US bombings from fifteen years earlier. The compound had been occupied by both the Italians and the British during its tumultuous history, as well as the King, and when Hannibal's father came to power he too chose to base himself there, building several government buildings within easy reach of the complex. It had expanded over the years as a private compound but was still home to several military units. Specifically, those in which his sons had served with (or rather, commanded) during their brief time in the military.

There were several private residences inside the walls, and we pulled up outside the largest, but obviously not the most modern. I could see a tent fluttering in the gardens, and Hannibal told me his father had taken to living there when he could but still enjoyed the various facilities of the house. Unlike the giant men the brothers had surrounded themselves with in Paris, the security at the residence was almost entirely female. Another surprise was the décor. It was a peculiar mix of low-cost construction and extravagant detailing, attempting to disprove the long-held belief that you can't make a purse out of a sow's ear. Hannibal seemed quite proud of the house and I wasn't going to offend him with my honesty. My room had a covered balcony, part of a surrounding veranda that echoed some of the more historical designs of the region. From there I could see the compound and take in its enormity and absurdity. My initial thoughts were that if Michael Jackson ran a country, he would have commissioned similar facilities. A zoo, fun fair rides, football pitch…all things necessary for governance.

"Quite the set up you have here."

"I'm glad you like it. I will see you for dinner shortly." As the sun began to set over the horizon, denied its final flourish by the imposing walls, the call to prayer rang across the ancient city. Despite what you imagine as an idyllic scene it sent shivers down my spine. The pitch of the Azan rang through my bones with the same resonance as the aural onslaught I was supposed to have been desensitized to. On top of which, it was the most obvious indication I could get as to just how far away from home I actually was.

Dinner a short time later was a stranger experience still; I didn't realize how large the family was or how two-faced it could be. Hannibal's father was with us for only a brief time, but during that period the entire atmosphere stepped back a century. We drank nothing but water and they spoke nothing but Arabic despite my presence. I started to recognize a few familiar words, those that lacked an obvious Arabic equivalent. 'Striker' and 'goalkeeper', for example. I bullishly offered a misguided opinion to Hannibal in a failed attempt to include myself.

"I hope that your national team will soon enjoy the same inclusion in football that you seek politically."

"Nobody asked for you to speak!" I didn't know Hannibal's father, Muamar, even spoke English. He stared me down with piercing brown eyes, cutting through the darkened lenses of his glasses like knots in timber. There was no emotion, no blinking or looking away. I could now understand why he was called the Mad Dog. It was a relief to all of us when Muamar left, drawn away by the allure of his personal guard. However, it wasn't until the eldest brother, Saif, left that things became much more familiar. Hannibal called for the proper drinks to be brought out, offering me a glass of red wine. I declined instead, requesting a gin and tonic. Let this be a lesson to all of us: when you're in a country where alcohol is largely prohibited, if your host offers you red wine it means that is all he has. Hannibal was initially embarrassed at being unable to accommodate my request, but he forgot the incident by the end of the next bottle. In all walks of life, it amazes me how quickly a situation can change, from intimidation to camaraderie in less than half a case. I made it through the night with my morals intact, despite the offer of a personal security detail to accompany me upstairs.

I was woken by the dawn call to prayer, a very Libyan equivalent to the morning radio burst I used to enjoy at home. As such it was almost autopilot that guided me outside for a morning smoke on the balcony. The view had no equivalence to London, not in the geography nor the hive of activity already underway in the distance. Yes, there were those attending prayer, but also those readying for drill at the nearby barracks and an audible scuffle breaking out nearby. I walked to the edge of the veranda to try and discover its source, having to lean over the railing at stomach height to catch a glimpse of what was happening.

I spotted a three-axle military truck with a canvas back, the puffs of black smoke from its exhaust sitting thick in the air. A group of five or six men were wrestling another from the back under muffled objections. I immediately pulled myself back out of view; it wasn't my business nor was it my place. A gentle knock came to my door, quietly repeating until I finally heard it when I returned inside. It was my breakfast, a stunning collection of pastries that wouldn't be out of place at the finest Parisian patisserie. I initially assumed a decadent dictator had flown them in for his own pleasure, but as I was to find out, they were in fact local. The city had a huge number of bakers, plying their craft on almost every corner from the early hours of the morning. The scent of nuts and honey was flowing down every alley of the old town until lunch time and later that day I cracked the window in my corner of the BMW to snatch another sniff.

Despite the ugly buildings I had seen the previous day and

the embryonic modern architecture I passed on my way from the compound, far more beautiful to my eye were the ancient structures of the old city. Carved doors like those in Morocco, Italianesque villas remaining true to their Islamic history and future. Even the flaking paintwork held its own charm. I wished those walls above many others could talk. The repeated cycle from Rome to Islam had left an inheritance that could prompt envy in any of the ancient capitals. Hannibal had brought me to the old town for one reason, for him to celebrate the history of his country and for me to lay my eyes on the Marcus Aurelius Gate. I had seen the structure in books when I was younger but I doubted I would ever have the chance to see it myself. Sat between the residential and quasi-commercial edge of the souk, it was much smaller than I was expecting. I had pictured it as a forebear to the Arc de Triomphe: in reality it was closer to a clay model but no less impressive, in some respects more so. Its tanned sandstone leapt from its low level to a background of whitewashed buildings and lush green lawns. The military had closed the thoroughfares, giving me unprecedented access to an underappreciated wonder of the ancient world. I wandered through all four arches under the umbrella of privilege, running my hands over the soft curves and blunted edges of its engravings. It was truly and honestly staggering, even the cracks and lost imagery carried an innate nobility. To think my hands were stroking an area carved 1800 years ago was humbling.

"Politics aside, your country remains beautiful. What a priceless inheritance you received."

"We hope to be able to share it with the world, from our great cities of the future to those of the ancients."

"I hope so, there isn't a man alive who wouldn't appreciate such things." We walked together around the structure,

Hannibal voicing his hopes for the future while I only had eyes for the past.

"To share this with the world, we need the world to first accept us. My father, he is not one to welcome this without incentive. When Saif called on him to welcome private enterprise, it took years for him to agree. The bakers you saw, the metal workers in the souk, all were underground from the late sixties to the late eighties. They are small steps, but positive steps."

"Hannibal, if I can be brutally honest with you. You do realize that with each step you take towards the western style of governance; your own position becomes more threatened?"

"No, no. No! You don't understand the difference we have made to the people. We are loved by all."

He couldn't possibly be farther from the truth; not even the most celebrated democracies in the world could hope for that level of support. Like many similar families over the course of the twentieth century he had come to believe his own propaganda. When we returned to the car, I tried to bring up the oil rights and our hopes to get involved. He ignored my query, instead turning my attention to other city sights which he hoped would become major tourist attractions in the future. The historic red castle by green square. The more modern structures like the football stadium. He was selling the country, not the oil rights. I should've recognized this side effect the previous night when Saadi boasted that he would be playing professionally in Malta the coming season, much to the delight of his relatives. He was predictably becoming the pride of the national team despite the skills at his feet.

When I got back to my room for a break from the latest pitch from Tourism Tripoli, I was beginning to regret my journey. My efforts to further my understanding of the business situation had fallen on deaf ears and, as of yet, I had no inclination as to the true happenings in Paris, what had P flustered, or how any of it could be linked to my predecessor. That was about to change.

\* \* \* \* \*

"Do you know how many have died because of them? Almost three thousand so of course it's worth it!"

I was dreading dinner as soon as I heard Muamar's voice echo up the stairs. I thought it would be another very quiet time for me but it turned out to be the total opposite. I was being asked questions from all sides, nothing uncomfortable or probing but genuinely pleasant conversation like one may have at a dinner party, the ratio of Arabic to English now skewed politely in my favour. They were keen to know my thoughts on the city and were eager to hear where I thought things may be improved. Muamar was still colder towards me than the others, but better than before, even stifling a laugh when I made a joke at the expense of the US President. He stayed longer than before but when he decided to leave, he walked along the table and stopped. I was surprised to realize he was stood by my shoulder looking down at me, only prompted by the looks of others to turn around. I went to get up, thinking he was waiting for my thanks, but before I could he gently put his hand on the side of my face. Rubbing my cheek with his thumb and giving me a look that left me unable to decide if he wanted to fight me or fuck me. He smiled broadly and started to laugh, not helping my indecisiveness.

"Hungry Caterpillar. I like it, very funny."

He proceeded to pat me on the cheek like an ageing aunt before he left the room. Strange man. The family began to dissipate to their own houses in the residence and wings within the main house, until eventually only Hannibal and I were left. He invited me to join him in the garden for a drink. Although my initial inclination should have been to wish him good night, I was feeling more positive after dinner. Good moods lead to good conversations, though I was still wary that I may be dragged into another debate over hotel locations in the city. While he waxed lyrical over the wine he provided, I was biding my time to give him one more push on BP. I was quite taken aback when, sat under the canopy of an African sky, Hannibal was the one to bring it up. Like a shot from nowhere he jumped straight into what they needed from my side.

"We are interested in working with the British, but we have conditions. As we discussed in Paris, we need help organizing our investments overseas, but there's more. My father. He wants the Prime Minister to come to Libya. Be seen talking with us, working with us." That explained the change at dinner; his father had offered his blessing and conditions.

"I'm not involved in politics. I can't even think how I would start to enquire about that. Let's focus on what I know we can do with your investment ambitions."

"Alex, that is what has to happen for us to start working with British companies again. Right now Italy, a country with which we had a far worse history than yours, accounts for 41% of our exports. Almost all our oil revenue is coming from just across the sea. For us to turn away from them, even slightly, must carry a major incentive. The warnings from them and Malta allowed our family survive the bombings in '86. We owe them a lot."

"I understand that, but politics isn't my game."

"Don't kid with me. You're being a kidder, aren't you? The last man from your bank was in the politics game. Why aren't you?"

"Who are you talking about?"

"Jayms. Peter, good man."

"Ah, yes. We called him Jimmy in the office. It was tragic what happened to him."

"If you say so."

"Do you say differently?"

"We look after our friends. I've told you this before. Come with me."

I followed Hannibal back inside the house, weaving through service corridors behind the kitchen to an unkempt back room. The area was decorated differently to the rest of the house, like a forgotten storeroom that didn't need to impress anyone. The familiar yet anonymous head of security sat at the base of a rickety metal staircase on a chair that could barely hold his own weight. With a nod from his employer, he bent down and slid a giant stone circle across the floor to reveal another level of the building where a similar spiralling metal staircase disappeared into the darkness. As I looked over the edge a horrendous smell came up that forced me to clasp a hand over my nose and mouth.

"It's okay, keep going," sproddedHannibal from behind me. He yanked a switch box to turn on the basement lights and I could see down the short flight of stairs to an area cloaked in cream tiles on all sides. I slowly made my way down, waiting for Hannibal at the bottom. As we walked down the corridor the smell became almost unbearable. We reached a reinforced steel door and Hannibal pulled a giant key from his pocket, turning it like a motor crank before opening the door. Inside was what looked like a surgical slab. A naked man lay strapped down, shuddering randomly with blood spattered over his body and still dripping from his limbs to the tiled floor. Traumatized stubs took the place of certain fingers and toes, while other where barely recognizable with nails completely absent. His face showed little life, with his cheeks and lips collapsing into the gap where his teeth once sat. One eye socket was gaping like a bloody well and the other eye dangled down towards his ear.

"Do you recognize him?" asked Hannibal.

"I'm…" I started to reply.

"I wasn't talking to you," he interrupted with worrying calm. Hannibal walked over to his captive and picked his eye up between his thumb and forefinger, rotating it towards me. His capture spat blood out of his toothless mouth and writhed against his ties.

"Alex! Please! Jesus! Fuck!"

I knew the voice despite his disabled enunciation: it was Tom, or at least what was left of him.

"Hannibal, what are you doing!" I made towards them but was stopped by the outstretched arm from his head of security.

"I told you, we look after our friends. This one, he is not your friend like us." He now grabbed Tom's eyeball in his fist and crushed it like a piece of fruit. He opened his hand to admire it, waited… then pulled it straight from his skull, the nerves and vessels snapping like bundled guitar strings. I turned away trying not to vomit. Tom screamed like a child as he was left in permanent darkness. He was trained to handle the worst any man could throw at him, but these were the actions of an animal. "Why don't you tell him what you told me earlier? Huh? You may not have much left to lose, but it can get much worse. Why are you in my country?" Tom whimpered to himself, trying to remain silent, but Hannibal dug his finger into his eye socket until he rediscovered his ability to talk.

"To kill him! Argh! To kill him!" My sympathy for the man evaporated with those few words.

"Why would you want to do that to my friend?"

"Because those are my orders! Argh!" Hannibal pulled his finger out and wiped it on Tom's hair.

"Paris? What happened in Paris?!" I shouted across the room. Tom began to cry and stray tears so red they looked almost black pooled in his empty eyes.

"I killed her," he said softly.

"Why?! What did she ever fucking do to you?!"

"Nothing! I was just following orders!" he pleaded.

"And who else had to die because of your goddamn orders?" Tom bit his lip with his gums, still trying to keep face despite an untenable position. Hannibal loosened his tongue by simply stroking his forehead with a finger.

"Kirkman! Bobby Kirkman!"

"His name was Bertie, you heartless cunt!"

"I'm sorry Alex, I'm so sorry. You've got to believe me!"

I turned to Hannibal. "I'm done here."

"So are we," he replied, pulling a solid gold Italian-issue Beretta from his hip.

"No!" I shouted lunging my hand towards him, to the alarm of security. "I'll do it."

"No need for you to do this, consider it a gift. One less rabid dog in the world."

"But it's a dog that belongs to me."

He thought for a moment before handing over the pistol. As I stood over Tom, I pushed the muzzle into his sternum.

"Alex, please, I'm begging you mate. I'm just a man doing a job."

"That makes two of us." I replied, hardly a second before

pulling the trigger. His lips went limp and sunk back into his mouth. His neck relaxed to let his head fall to the side and he lay motionless apart from a few twitching muscles that hadn't got the message yet. A few wisps of smoke rose from the hot muzzle still pressed to the wound in his chest. I pulled the pistol back, dropped the magazine and ejected the loaded round. Finally, I locked the slide to the rear and turned to hand it back to Hannibal. He was staring at Tom's fading corpse with glassy wonder, smiling broadly and rubbing his thumb and forefinger together, feeling the last drops blood and ocular fluid lubricate his fingertips.

"Would you mind if we went somewhere more comfortable?" I asked with the air of a man who had killed before, holding out his gleaming yet soiled sidearm. When we returned upstairs my ears were still ringing from the shot, yet despite this I felt no sadness over what happened. I wasn't singing hymns in my head or pretending I was somewhere else. I remembered what Harry had said about the first time he killed a man, how in that moment he was just a pigeon. I wouldn't go that far in saying I thought of Tom as anything other than a man, but I was satisfied I had not only done what was needed but had also given Tom a far better ending than he really deserved.

A woman approached with a tray of warm towels, and Hannibal passed one over to clean up my shirt and wipe the splatter marks from my right-hand side. Another woman appeared carrying a device similar in size to a laptop and handed it to Hannibal. I followed him back outside to the contrasting calm. He placed the device on the table and opened it to reveal a handset and antenna. It was a satellite phone, albeit a very outdated model. He lifted the receiver and started dialling a number, and when it answered started talking animatedly in

Arabic to whomever was on the other side before handing the phone over to me.

"Good evening," I said, hoping whoever it was spoke English. Thankfully, they did.

"Mr. Hope. How nice for us to finally connect."

"I'm sorry, who is this."

"My name is Peter Jayms. It would seem we have a few matters to discuss."

Not the name I was expecting, and it took a moment to digest. "Back from the dead?"

"Only visiting."

Hannibal sat patiently puffing on a cigar and enjoying the warming glow of a lapsed Muslim while Peter explained the circumstances surrounding his disappearance. As part of the negotiations, the Libyans had offered intelligence they deemed of value to the UK and her allies. He reported back to London but within twenty-four hours was tipped off that he was to be forcibly removed from the equation. With no idea where else to turn, he went back to the source: Tripoli. A hasty deal was arranged for someone to take his place, and in return he would offer guidance and counsel to the Gaddafi family for the price of a new life.

"So, you're in Libya?"

"Afraid not, but I'll see you tomorrow and we can discuss further."

The line went dead and Hannibal closed the clunky plastic case, handing me my drink with a smile.

"So you will help us, yes?"

"Of course, more than happy to help with what I can. I can't promise how soon I can get the ball rolling, things have become a bit more complicated."

"For you, yes. I just want to know that you will be there when I need you and work on the politics. We look after our friends, you see that now."

"I do."

"I'm glad. My plane will take you to meet Mr. Jayms tomorrow."

"And where might that be?"

"Same place as most of our exports, Italy."

\* \* \* \* \*

"We've got him heading north over the Mediterranean."

"This could be an opportunity for us."

"How?"

"Alienate. Isolate. Control."

It was just before noon when we arrived at the airport. My bags had gone ahead of me, along with a parting gift from Hannibal: the geriatric satellite phone we had used the night before.

"Turn it on at 4 o'clock local time. He will call you."

It was too large to fit in my briefcase, so became one unto itself. I wondered if people felt the same frustration at the dawn of the mobile phone and realized my office issue Nokia wasn't that awful. I thanked Hannibal for his hospitality and he reiterated his hopes to be hearing from me soon to start our work, a sentiment I mirrored ardently. As he stood on the runway with his entourage and the jet began to pull away there was one thing I was certain of: I had no intention back then of ever returning. I had seen enough and could barely imagine what they might do to me should any arrangement turn sour.

Feeling more at ease, physically speaking, than my first flight, my mind turned to two glaring questions: why did Tom kill the others and come after me next? Why was I so eager to hop on a plane to meet a man I had, until less than twenty-four hours before, assumed to be dead? The answer to the second question was simple, it was my need to answer the first. Tom was not a pleasant man, no doubt, but he was a soldier. A loyal and committed weapon at the disposal of his commanders. He was not a gun for hire, he simply did what he was told. His orders had to be coming from inside the service. I wanted to rule out the Russians based on Tom's loyalty, but he had the necessary language skills to make it feasible. Could it really be possible that a foreign power or a rogue officer was working inside the service? Someone high enough to be aware of Pactum and my role. If so, then what had I done to make me such a threat? My mind was twisting possibilities and as I rolled theories around, I began to lose sight of which were possible and those I could deem plausible.

As we flew over the southern tip of Italy and continued north towards Rome the landscape grew greener, something I was looking forward to after the dust of North Africa. Coming in to land at Ciampino Airport there was just one small dilemma: I had no idea where I was going or what to do. Having been hurried through a small customs post I sought a taxi for the short ride to the Hassler. There were better hotels available I'm sure, but the Hassler held an ace up its sleeve: like many well-aged hotels of its class, it always had rooms available and would always accept cash, no questions asked. Just as long as you have enough of it. The rule probably wouldn't apply to a South American drug lord arriving in his flip flops with a bouquet of prostitutes, but a cut glass English accent and Saville Row suit would be absolutely fine. I had stayed at the hotel with Charlie and David a decade before when we took a trip to Rome for the World Cup, a handful of gentlemen in an army of hooligans. Some of those fond memories came back to me as little had changed at the hotel. When I opened the door to my room the windows were open, a Roman breeze creating a slow dance with the flowing white curtains. I had a wonderful view across the Tiber towards St. Peter's and the faint bustle of tourists traffic tinkled through from the outside. Far from being able to admire the situation I felt suddenly nauseated. I plucked a chilled bottle of water from the bar but, before I could open it, I was forced to rush into the bathroom. The situation in Tripoli had caught up with me. Some people suffer physical or emotional reactions after their first time. While I felt fine within myself, my constitution was lagging behind the curve. I dabbed my mouth dry and splashed some water on my face, struggling with the awful adrenal shaking that comes afterwards.

As it got closer to 4 o'clock I fired up the old phone and made a second attempt at the water bottle. With some time to kill I was struck by a promise I had made to an old friend, and dialled her number into the hotel phone.

"Pronto?" she answered.

"Miss Smyth-Cummin, that's quite the accent you've acquired."

"Alex? Why are you calling me from an Italian number?"

"Funnily enough I'm in Italy for a few days and remembered someone offered to show me around."

"What on earth are you doing in Italy? Dad didn't mention it."

"Mostly blondes but I'm willing to make exceptions."

"Ha ha ha! Behave yourself! Where are you?"

"Rome, thought we could grab a bite or something."

"I'm a good few hours north, but I could make it down on Friday for lunch?" The satellite phone started to ring and I rushed to get off the phone.

"Perfect, shoot me a message when you have a plan."

"But Alex, why are you…"

I cut Amelia off but couldn't risk missing the other call. As I dropped one receiver, I picked up the other.

"I'm here."

"Church of Domine Quo Vadis, 6 o'clock."

\* \* \* \* \*

"Still no check in from Alpha 3 sir."

"Activate Beta."

"Yes sir."

*Hamilton stopped taking notes before my tale had left Libya.*

*"You okay over there, young man?"*

*"Sorry…ummm…so it was the Libyans that changed you, they're the ones who made you want to come out?"*

*"God no. Deeply flawed and violent in many ways, but not rare in that."*

*"Did you provide information to the Hague during the trial?"*

*"No. They had enough without my input. It wouldn't matter for Hannibal anyway, he's retired to Muscat. Saw him a few months ago funnily enough. He's doing rather well."*

*The dark side of my confessions didn't sit well with Hamilton. It wasn't what he expected from a story of market manipulation.*

*"And did you ever face prosecution for your crimes?"*

*"My crimes? Does a soldier get put on trial for war? Do we arrest people for self-defence? Your liberal sensitivities need to take*

*a back seat, young man, that is not how this world works. It's never been the buttercups and picnics you see on the surface. It's hell. Hell with a varnish and three spoonful's of sugar so people like you find it easier to swallow between charitable donations and Christmas sweaters. If that's not something you're willing to accept, then I am talking to the wrong person."* I hoped the risk of losing the story would pull him back in to line. I was right.

*"I understand."* He flipped his notepad to a fresh page and prepared to carry on.

*"You think less of me, don't you?"*

*"No, but differently."*

*"You've met far worse people than me. Sometimes good people need to do bad things in order for right to prevail. Remember that."*

Rush hour traffic was not on my side. It dragged a half hour journey out to a full hour but luckily I still arrived at the old church at a quarter to six. It wasn't a large church, but quite pretty on the outside with its yellow paint and white stucco features. At the centre of the church was a pair of footprints impressed into the floor. Folklore says they were those of Christ himself, but to be honest I had seen more convincing efforts in whimsical Bigfoot articles. I sat and admired the arches and pious declarations of subordinates for a few minutes. Some of it reminded me of Leadenhall, though I wouldn't dare tell the local clergy that. Checking my watch, I wandered back outside to wait. The sun was shining straight through the doorway and as I reached for my sunglasses, I caught sight of a man as I crossed under the mantle. Like a reflex I spun around and put my hand up just in time to stop his, then realizing who it was, let out a sigh of relief and let go.

"Calm down, mate, I was just giving you a wave."

"Sorry Harry, you scared the crap out of me. Good to see you again."

"At least you're still kicking. Come on, he's meeting us down here."

"You're meeting Jimmy too? I didn't know you knew him."

"He'll explain, mate."

We walked towards a fork in the road, taking the left hand onto the Via Appia, and followed it for a few minutes until a taxi stopped maybe a hundred yards in front of us. Out stepped a very tall man with white hair combed into a side parting. He began walking towards us with a lumbering gait, flat-footed and tired. As we got closer, I recognized him. I had only met him once or twice in my younger years, but the now older face was still familiar. He was dressed like a man attempting Italian style but in a very British manner, wearing a linen shirt with jeans and a navy jacket, yet with old brown brogues on his feet. Harry hung back a few steps, allowing us to greet each other privately.

"Mr Jayms, good to see you, or should that be Jimmy?"

"Yes, and still in one piece thankfully. No, please call me Peter."

"I thought everyone called you Jimmy?"

"Gosh no, that was only because Peter and Pater were so similar. David started doing it and it spread to the city. I always hated it."

"Peter it is."

We ambled together down the pavement at a pace Peter was comfortable with. Harry jogged ahead and put a twenty-yard buffer between us, keeping a vigilant eye on our path. The road began to degrade from its 20th century cladding back to its stone roots when Harry stopped at a rough wooden door. He held it open for Peter and me to walk inside before closing it behind us and standing guard. We were in a quaint but overgrown garden, its feral nature providing shade from the sun and prying eyes. There was a grunt from Peter as he tried to gingerly lower himself down to the floor, instead making a bit of a thump and almost rolling backwards.

"Alex, I'm really sorry you have gotten dragged into this mess. I had hoped you could have skirted the edges, but as soon as you went to Paris I knew this day would come, and the sooner it could happen the better it was for you."

"What exactly have I been dragged into? All I know so far is that you were given some intelligence by the Libyans and now people, people I cared about, have been killed and I'm sitting on a shabby lawn with a dead man."

"We need to go back to before Cairo. P had sources on the ground in the former Soviet bloc and they came to him with solid intelligence. They told him of a plan for Chechen terrorists to bomb three locations in Russia: Moscow, Volgodonsk and Buynaksk."

"Volgodonsk, the Russian mentioned that name in London."

"I'm sure he did. P naturally went to the Russians and traded them that intelligence for information on the Irish."

"So where did the money come into it?"

"As the date approached P was still getting reports that the attacks were going ahead, so he went back to the Russians. They didn't care. They wanted to attacks to happen, needing an excuse to enter Chechnya and lay a path for Putin's succession over Yeltsin. With that knowledge it was like a switch was tripped in his head: can this information still be useful to us? Can we profit from it? He came to me asking about the impact of the attacks on the stock market. I told him I didn't see how it would damage our positions, thinking that was the reason behind his query."

"Well no, any major impact would be limited to Russia."

"Exactly, but that wasn't why he was asking. He thought maybe Pactum could use the information to trade Russian GDR's for gain. In the end he went back to the Russians with a new angle, totally without my knowledge."

"What did he do?"

"He went for straight old-fashioned blackmail. Pay up, or the information is leaked to the press and local forces. In the end they settled on 300 million sterling of Gazprom stock for us to look the other way and keep our mouths shut."

"He allowed people to die for profit, with no benefit to our national interests or some higher purpose?" I asked, incredulous to the suggestion.

"In his eyes it was in our national interest, funding the service."

"How could David let that happen? We're supposed to hold ourselves to a higher standard."

"Pater didn't know about it. Neither did I until it was too late. I confronted him about it, threatening that should he ever act that way again then I would go to Pater or perhaps higher."

"How did he respond to that?"

"He never really did. In short order Pater had me involved in the Lockerbie negotiations. I was in Cairo and it was going extremely well. As well as the agreements for the bombing suspects, the Libyans offered to hand over those responsible for the Fletcher shooting and much more. Then Hannibal comes to me with this intel they pulled from Sudan, that a group of Islamic terrorists were planning an attack against the West. The information was sketchy at best. We knew the mastermind was referred to as 'The Sheikh' and that he was planning a mass casualty event to target infrastructure and civilians. I did some more digging and the same name kept coming up: Abu Shaytan. Shiekh Abu Shaytan."

"What did you do?"

"I'd come across that level of humint before and reacted same as I always had, reporting directly to P so he could validate the information. I was sat in Cairo waiting to hear back from P about my next step, when Harry turns up at my hotel in a panic. London had claimed I was posing a threat to national security and issued orders to nullify the situation. He and I rushed to put a ploy together to make sure the plan appeared successful. I wasn't left with many options so I called Tripoli and made a deal. Hannibal provided the staff and stage for the dramatics and Harry made sure it went off without a hitch. As luck would have it, he led the team from London. That brings me here, bouncing back and forth between Rome and Tripoli to help the family in return for my life."

"Do you have proof that P was behind this?"

"Not proof, but nobody else fits the situation. Any activity from The Incident Team has to come from his office. He has control over what is referred to as 'the list', a list of all current targets for the incident team. Every name that goes on the list must come with approval from P's office or the minister."

"And what does Pater know of this? Does he even know you're still alive?"

"He mustn't, it's too dangerous for him. You're yet to know what the man is truly capable of."

"I held her and found out what he's capable of," I replied in short order, wringing my hands together.

"Did you really? Do you know how your friend Bertie died? Harry told me what happened, how P tried to get you to shoot him yourself without knowing it. He was furious with your reaction, so they made arrangements for the bombing. Sending messages from your phone to build the backstory before stuffing that poor man in the back of an old Volvo with plastic explosives and bags of bolts strapped to his chest."

"Bertie was the bomb?"

"Can you imagine how he felt, bound and helpless in the dark waiting to die?" It was almost too much for me to think of my friend in such a situation and the anger was building in me like a storm.

"I'll bring him down myself as soon as I get back to London." I said through gritted teeth.

"How do you intend to do that, Alex? Think about it for a minute. Far more capable people than you have taken pot shots at the service over the years, where did it get them? Nowhere. If you want to stop this, we first need to understand it. Otherwise we're boxing under a blindfold. We need to find out what information P is willing to kill for and what he plans to do with it."

"So, what have you found out so far?"

"No much I'm afraid, I'm limited by my age and my anonymity. I get bits of information from Harry, but that tends to be on the moves back home rather than the root cause. That said, there is someone who could help us. My late sister's son, Daniel. He works for the service in the Middle East."

"Why do you think you can trust someone in the service?"

"Because blood is thicker than water and he hasn't given me up yet."

"And oil is thicker than blood."

"Not with my diet. I would like you to do what I can't. Go and find out the truth. Not just for our own sakes, or that of Pactum, but for those that have been lost along the way."

"Where's your nephew?"

"Dubai."

"How do I contact him?"

"You don't. I'll make sure he gets hold of you."

I could hardly return to the UK with the knowledge that

my name was on the list, especially when P hears about Tom. My farewell to Peter was as unorthodox and cautious as our meeting. We staggered our departure with Harry and Peter leaving ten minutes before me, heading in opposite directions. There was no reason to stay in Rome any longer than necessary and the further I was from London the better.

I sent Amelia a message to see if she would mind just meeting for coffee instead. I had to 'rush back for work' and she was very understanding, suggesting she meet me at Café Greco before my flight. I had never tried booking a plane ticket using cash, but thankfully it was still possible via a travel agent and first thing the next morning I was able to book myself onto an Emirates flight later the same day.

I sat in the Café Greco for hours, but Amelia never showed up. My waiter became concerned as most customers only stop for a few minutes to shoot down an espresso and I had already had several. I tried to call her phone but it just rang off to voicemail repeatedly. Under normal circumstances it would be worrisome, but not overly so. In this world it was much more concerning. I stayed as long as I could and still hadn't heard from her when I reached the Emirates desk at Da Vinci Airport. I came close to calling Charlie to ask if he had heard from her but stopped myself short. What if Charlie let slip to P where I was? I couldn't risk it. Finally, when it was time to board, I got a message from Amelia.

"I'm sorry. Something came up."

"God you had me worried! Maybe next time, take care. A"

# Pactum

"We need to keep him in the dark for as long
as possible. Those two are very close."

The heat and humidity were stifling. It hit me like a wall the second I stepped off the aircraft under the Arabian night. I had expected it to be hotter than Tripoli, but the humidity seemed to work against the stereotype I had in mind. The Mediterranean was like Brighton in contrast. I am usually desperate to depart a plane after a flight but I was half-tempted to turn back for a few more minutes in the air conditioning.

When you start to stretch the distances you travel, there is another change that is as obvious as the climate: the smell. As soon as I entered the terminal the air was filled with a combination of Oud and tobacco. Despite nearing midnight, the terminal was heaving and it took an arduous hour to finally clear immigration and gather my things. I once again battled the temperature to hail a taxi, sweat running down my face and seeping through my shirt. I removed my jacket, my tie, and my cufflinks (to roll up my sleeves), essentially removing as many items as I could without causing a public display, and finally made it to the front of the queue. Leaping into the back of the car, I pleaded with my driver to turn up the air conditioning. He graciously obliged, and as the temperature fell to a level I was more comfortable with, he reached across the passenger seat for a sweater.

While we cruised through the city night towards my hotel, I marvelled at the contrast between the older buildings and the new skyscrapers starting to sprout on either side of Sheikh Zayed Road, an artery running almost the entire coastline of the Emirates. I could imagine this was what Hannibal was hoping to create in Libya. Turning onto more relaxed roads, we approached the hotel, highly illuminated and intentionally visible from quite a distance. The Emir was proud of his horses, but his heir was the builder in the family. The taxi glided past security and up the bridge to the entrance. I must admit the Burj Al Arab was very impressive, a giant sail sprouting from the Gulf, but the décor was not to my taste. That being said, I could still appreciate the service and the effort to impress and amaze to a certain point. Climbing above the foyer in the lift, I was certainly not rising above the absurd; the gold and bright colours on every feasible surface would have made Liberace blush. When I reached the room I had to shoo away the bellboy who was trying to teach me how to use every possible function of the suite. At my age I was confident in my ability to use a television and frankly couldn't give two shits how to adjust the brightness of the lighting. I wanted sleep, and the few hours I managed made the world of difference.

Fresh and focused I descended the next morning for breakfast, digested the morning paper with my yogurt and mixed fruits, and gazed over the sapphire seas from behind climate-controlled glass. I was interrupted every few minutes by the overly attentive waiter but then a new figure came to my table: fair hair, fully suited, dagger-straight back and a strong chin, carrying a slender scarlet briefcase and a crisp English accent.

"Do you mind if I join you?"

I nodded and conducted a glancing appraisal, immediately

narrowing my choices of who he could be. He was certainly service and I wasn't going to be a shrinking violet in my dealings with him.

"What have I done to deserve breakfast with DXB station within eight hours of landing?" The comment caught him by surprise but I just continued to read my paper.

"Well, this is the first time we've had The Fisherman on our turf and to be honest, we are wondering…why?" I ignored the question, seeing how far the desk jockey was willing to push me. "You London types don't understand how things work in this part of the world, and frankly having you here could cause some issues for us."

I calmly folded my paper and laid it on the table. "Let me put this simply: whether I am here on holiday or otherwise is no concern of yours. You have been here several years judging by your complexion and ability to withstand the weather. Therefore, I would guarantee every asset both local and foreign has a file on you two inches thick… and you think it's appropriate to just turn up and interrupt my breakfast? I might as well be staying with the fucking Ambassador." He looked down sheepishly at having his blatant error explained to him.

"My apologies, you know where we are if needed." He stood up and buttoned his jacket. "Enjoy your stay." I gave him a hollow thank-you as he left, returning to my paper and breakfast. I began running some potential scenarios for switching hotels to avoid further undue attention, but it was too soon to do so without arousing suspicion. When it came time to settle up, I realized my morning visitor had left his briefcase under the table. It was a dead drop, but I couldn't know from whom or for what purpose.

I retired upstairs with the briefcase, setting it on the desk in my room. Nothing particularly special about it, a simple red leather case with brass fittings and three-digit combinations on each clasp. I pushed the catch to the side but the case was predictably locked. "Great. Just perfect," I said to myself. Either I didn't know the code that I was supposed to, or the man at breakfast had genuinely left his case behind by accident. If it was the latter, then it was his problem. I wasn't going to walk up to the embassy and offer it to lost and found. If it was indeed meant for me, then the code must be something I knew. I tried my birthday, no. I tried my room number, no. All zeros, again nothing. 123456? No. I wondered, could the six digits equate to six letters? It couldn't be that simple, could it? It wouldn't work with double-digit letters but I could drop the second digit for each letter. 1-1-3-2-2-1. Click, and the case opened. Quite clever really, the numbers in the alphabet corresponding to Pactum, something so simple as long as you knew what you're dealing with. Inside was some currency, a map, a mobile phone with charger and a sealed envelope. As I lifted the envelope it revealed something else in the case: a fully loaded Glock 17. I hadn't seen one since the fort and wasn't very happy about what its presence implied. The envelope contained a very simple message: "Turn on phone. Call Daniel." I grabbed the phone, plugged the charger in and turned it on. Navigating my way through the menu I found the phonebook and saw only one contact in the memory. I dialled and it was answered immediately.

"That took longer than I was expecting."

"I had to finish breakfast first."

"I see, well sorry for interrupting that."

"So, why have I travelled halfway round the world to see you?"

"You haven't, I'm just here to facilitate. Keep the phone on and she will contact you."

"She? Daniel is a bit of a strange name for a woman."

"I'm Daniel, but she's who you need to be talking to. Keep the phone on."

With that he hung up. The battery was low. I wasn't going to be leaving the room while I waited for the call.

Despite what Peter had told me in Rome, I wanted to contact David. Not to reveal all that had happened or my intentions, but just to touch base. I pulled the sat phone out and set up operations close to the window. I knew the glass was going to distort the signal but I wasn't going to set it up on the terrace below or use one of the mobiles. It was only seven o'clock in London but I was confident David would be in.

"Piscator for Pater secure," was all I said when Joan answered. The next voice I heard was David's.

"Pater secure. Alex, thank goodness. Where are you?"

"Middle East, I'm following a lead from Tripoli. I don't know where it's going to take me but I have a feeling it's big."

"I need you back here. I hardly see Patruus, who is totally preoccupied with the Irish. Procurator is engrossed in America and we still have billions of pounds exposed to oil. Unless your efforts help those situations, I need you home."

"I'm not buying the Irish story. Yes, there have been three attacks this year, but not a single fatality. It's vandalism now, not terrorism. I thought you had dumped the oil?"

"We are but the price is going against us, Stephen is close to a coronary trying to get us out of it by himself. No matter your opinion on the Irish, or Patruus's, I still need you here. Have you thought that maybe you're being led on a wild goose chase by the Libyans? What if you come home with nothing?"

"I'm in the Middle East. Everything here is to do with oil so I can guarantee I'll come home with something. I need you to check the files for me."

"Only once Alex, just this once. You have seventy-two hours on the ground to feed your paranoia then I want you back in the office, is that clear?"

"Crystal."

"Right, name?"

"Sheikh Abu Shaytan."

"Spelling?"

"I can't be certain, use your better judgement."

"My better judgement tells me to toss it in the bin."

"Mine says you'll find something." I hung up and immediately powered down the phone. I felt like a petulant child refusing to do his chores and wasn't comfortable ignoring David's initial instruction. He must have felt something, or he wouldn't have given me time. The deeper I got the more I felt I had to keep going, and if I had to work in seventy-two hours so be it. If it took longer, I would apologize when needed. Time was the least of my worries. I sat in the room for a further two hours waiting for a phone call that didn't come. I grew concerned. Then inpatient. Before I eventually decided to visit the pool before the devil made work for idle hands.

I stood out as the obvious European business traveller. Surrounded by the tanned and toned clientele, I looked like a golf ball as I floated on my back under the blazing sky. The only thing that would have made it worse would have been the addition of a speedo. I put a shirt back on for the sake of the bystanders before flopping on a sun lounger with a fresh gin. Still no phone call. The battery logo was already flashing at me, pleading for more juice, but I couldn't stand all the hanging around. After the urgency with which I was summoned to Rome, the change of pace made me think of what David said. Maybe this was a wild goose chase from the Libyans or some conspiracy of a disgruntled pensioner. Just as I was about to give up and turn my full efforts to the bar, the phone finally rang.

"Yes, hello, hi, how…"

"Well, that's quite a way to answer the phone," came an assertive lady down the phone with a distinctly British accent muddled with something more local.

"Sorry, I think the phone is about to die and the charger isn't at hand. I'm just trying to rush upstairs."

"Don't bother. Al Nafoorah, Emirates Towers. Nine o'clock. The reservation is under your name."

She hung up. Quite rude really, but something I was getting used to and had done so myself. Par for the course, I thought. It was only three o'clock so I had time to unwind, another gin or three and a fresh lacquering of SPF 30 sunscreen to see out the afternoon. I was supposed to be on holiday after all.

$$\star\,\star\,\star\,\star\,\star$$

"That was not your decision to make!
He's my man, not yours!"


"You can thank me later."


"We'll have to bring in our friends,
I don't have the personnel to go that far."

I had never had Lebanese food before and wasn't sure what to expect of the food or the company. I gave my name to the maître d' who informed me that my colleague had already arrived. It was lucky he escorted me to our table; left to my own devices, I couldn't have picked 'my colleague' from a line-up. As a chair was pulled back for my convenience, she looked up at me quite sternly. I adopted a safe and silent position, although I was dining with a stranger it seemed only appropriate to allow the lady to speak first.

"So how are you enjoying our city?"

"I've only seen the airport, my hotel, and this restaurant. All very pleasant. They warn you about building a house on sand, but when there's oil beneath it I suppose anything is possible."

"Don't suppose anything, most of the oil is down the road in Abu Dhabi."

"Fair enough, then rather than make small talk would you like to tell me why I'm here?"

She was about to answer when the waiter arrived with our menus, handing them to either side and placing the wine list to my side of the table. My colleague turned to the waiter and gave him instruction in flawless Arabic before reaching across the table to take the wine list from me. The waiters initial shock gave way to reverence and calm conversation, no doubt enquiring how this white woman learned the language. She flicked through the wine list and finally spoke some words I could understand: "pinot noir". I wasn't going to object to her choice.

"That's quite impressive."

"For you."

"Well, I wouldn't comment on anyone else's perception."

"You would do well not to comment on anything." I try to maintain a level of decorum in all situations, but times like these have always tested me.

"You would do well, madam, to remember that Peter called me. I am more than happy to get on a plane tomorrow and bid you farewell tonight. I suggest you start explaining why exactly I travelled to the sand pit of the world, put my career in jeopardy and am sat at dinner with a woman who seems as intent to offend me as she does to compensate for a long-standing chip on her shoulder." I sat there with my eyebrows raised and arms crossed waiting for her to answer. Meanwhile, she stared me down from across the table, obviously appreciating neither my choice of words nor the insinuation she needed me in anyway. She sat back in her chair with the certainty this was a battle of wits she could win.

"What makes you think I'm compensating for anything?"

"Well, you are overly assertive in both your manner and attitude towards male company. You may have a British accent, but your heavy-handed attitude towards makeup and jewellery, coupled with the modest dress sense and language skills, say you have spent most, if not all, of your formative years in this part of the world or under its influence. You're not married and you are certainly not Muslim in your beliefs…"

"And now what makes you say that?"

"Despite the small fortune ordaining your hands and wrists, nothing on that one finger. Plus, if your husband would allow you to meet a strange man for dinner he would be more secure in himself than any man I had known. As for the Muslim comment, you are taking dinner with a young man in public view without family and you just ordered wine."

"Maybe I ordered it for you."

"I can order my own drink."

"I do not have a chip on my shoulder."

"You're a female professional, if you didn't have a chip on your shoulder you wouldn't be doing yourself justice. I'm Alex, by the way, and you are?" She was Zahra, and my God had I met my match. As arrogant as it sounds, there weren't many conversations I had been in where I was left so conscious of my own abilities.

She was born and raised in the area despite going to school back in England. To call Arabic her second language wasn't fair; she had two first languages. It was funny how she would sometimes use Arabic grammatical structures or terminology when speaking English. I wasn't brave enough to point out the occurrences. Although obviously defensive at first, she opened up quite quickly. It certainly wasn't because of my charm or anything so naïve. Clearly, she had been holding back this information for so long that it was a relief to finally reach someone to discuss it with. Zahra had previously worked at the Embassy in Dubai alongside Daniel, who it transpired was her brother, before moving out to the private sector in banking. With all the money flowing in and out of the Middle East there was a strong market for anyone with a Western education but a full grasp of the local dialect. The rewards were more than tempting enough to lure people away from a civil service salary. While we continued to indulge in small talk and graze over dinner the other guests slowly started to filter out of our area of the restaurant, providing enough privacy to begin talking business proper.

"It has taken some time to find the right person," Zahra began. "I talked to Peter about the whispers I was hearing but he said he couldn't act on them now. They aren't whispers anymore, they're being shouted from the rooftops in certain areas. We're all hoping that someone will listen to you."

"What are they shouting?"

"They are building up to something big."

"Sorry, you will have to start at the beginning. Who is building up to something big?"

"The Sheikh and his people."

I was coming in fresh, Zahra needed to take it back a few steps. "Again, slow it down. Are we talking Mujahedeen? I thought they were only useful for Hollywood story lines and frustrating the Russians."

"Far from it. It started in 1992 with the Yemen hotel bombings and the failed attempt to topple the north tower of the World Trade Center in 1993."

"I remember that, truck bomb wasn't it?"

"That's the one. Well, things quietened down and after the Oklahoma City bombings in '95 and people forgot about foreign threats, they had bigger problems, but the threat never went away."

I nodded. We were almost on the same page. "There were the embassy bombings a few years ago in Kenya and Tanzania but from what I remember that threat was dealt with locally."

Zahra shook her head, still a few pages ahead. "You're missing the big picture. These have always been targeted at Americans but they never had the resources to take them head on. Last year there were two attacks on US ships in the Gulf, USS Cole and USS Sullivan."

"I only heard of one, the Cole."

"The Sullivan failed, think of it as a practice run for the Cole."

"Okay, so they're getting feisty."

"You need to take this seriously! Something big really is coming, not just big for them but bigger than anyone else has done before."

"Isn't this something you should be telling the Americans about?"

"I don't trust them, not the ones here anyway. I trust Uncle Peter and he sent me you. Was he wrong?" He wasn't. I wished he was.

"No."

"Good. I have a client in Dubai this week. There's a meeting tomorrow. I would like you to come with me and see for yourself."

"Who is he?"

"He is 'he'. Saudi, just arrived here from Pakistan for some medical treatment. Been moving a lot of funds through our accounts. I can bring you along as a potential UK channel. Maybe it'll change your mind."

The waiter came to clear away our plates, bringing the conversation to an abrupt halt as we clumsily transitioned into mindless chit chat about the weather. Sun. Hot. Sun. Not much variety.

I was struggling to build credibility in my mind for what Zahra was telling me. I couldn't do anything with chatter from her clients. As the waiter handed me the bill Zahra leaned across the table in an attempt to snatch it, but I pulled my hand back out of reach. She gave me a look like she was about to reach across the table and scar my cheeks with her jewellery. Negotiations were intense and we finally reached an agreement that I could pay for dinner if I allowed her to pay for lunch tomorrow. She gave me a lift back to my hotel with a guided tour of the city on the way, pointing out the older parts of town and commenting how much things had changed over the years. The transformation was amazing with the old and new divided around the creek. We agreed we would meet at the hotel at midday before heading to the hospital. It was approaching midnight when I reached the hotel and the foyer was still busy with a fresh group of visitors. I considered a nightcap at the bar, but having seen it teeming with Americans celebrating their independence I decided to call it a night. The phone Daniel gave me was now fully charged and out of habit I checked it before readying myself for bed. No messages, no surprise, but while I was in the bathroom I heard it beep from next door. Toothbrush still in hand, I went to check. It was a simple message from Daniel: "See you for breakfast at 8". I hadn't invited him, but at least he was giving me some notice this time.

\* \* \* \* \*

"I want to know who she is, what she knows, who her friends are, who her family are, and I want to know it yesterday!"

When I entered the restaurant for breakfast the following morning Daniel was already there, sat in a private corner table with papers around him, an untouched bowl of fruit to his side. I went and sat opposite him, ordering a cup of coffee and perusing the menu while he organized his papers into various piles and folders.

"Your sister seems nice."

"What?" He stopped his papers and looked at me in shock.

"Very pleasant."

"What's that supposed to mean?"

"Nothing at all, just being polite. Christ, what is it about men and their sisters."

"Oh, right. You don't have to be polite, I know she's not the most welcoming person at first. Okay, you two are going to be at the American Hospital for two o'clock, but she'll pick you up at twelve so you can prep. You will be meeting this man." He handed me a brown paper file with an alphanumeric code stamped on the front, similar to the files back in my office. "The Sheikh, Sheikh Abu Shaytan, SAS, Saif-ullah…"

"…Saif-ullah?"

"The sword of god."

"Seems dramatic. Do we have a real name or just the list of aliases?"

"That's what we have. The man is a ghost. Every time Zahra's dealt with him it's been under a different name or company. What we do know is he was a Mujahedeen fighter in Afghanistan, Saudi national, wealthy family and has the kind of contact book we could only dream of. He is head of a growing global terror network. That's who gives him these names, they think of him as a prophet for the new millennium."

I studied the very few photographs we had in the file, some of him shaking hands with individuals more familiar to my Western eyes. Amazing how swiftly someone can shift from ally to enemy. Yet in every picture his face was either covered or turned away.

"You couldn't manage one good picture?"

"You've no idea what it took just to get these. Now, he's receiving treatment for his kidneys at the American Hospital over the next few days, travelling with a personal security team of four, his own nurse, and his own doctor." Daniel handed over photographs of the team from their arrival in Dubai. They were much clearer to identify. Far from being a group of muscle-bound goons, they appeared totally normal, a sign that his security team hadn't been selected for their perceptions but for their loyalty.

"Sounds like he either has some trust issues or is extremely paranoid."

"Both. He was visited by family yesterday and some local friends, which makes me think today will be more business. Zahra has been handling funds for his family for a while, but this will be the first time she will meet him personally. They may not allow you in the room, but hopefully the cover fits and Zahra's can get you in. Your cover is standard: you're a British banker specializing in international investment hedged against foreign exchange risk, and in this case you're going to help Zahra flush and invest the funds he has coming out of Saudi, Switzerland and Bosnia."

"Bosnia?"

"The group was active there in the early nineties, he actually held a Bosnian passport at one point. The Saudi High Commission for Relief in Bosnia and Herzegovina acts like a cross account to avoid too many questions. You can gather as much information as you like, but only from that standpoint, investment suggestions and such. Don't start interrogating him or asking personal and direct questions or he may get spooked."

"Pretty straightforward. Who else is on this?"

"Nobody, this is totally off the books. Even as far as DXB station is concerned, this never happened."

"Good, that's the same on my side."

"We have kept a distant eye on him as a person of interest, but nothing more. Any time things got hot on our side someone would quickly cool it down, and that normally means he's an asset. This will only go to London if you take it there. Speaking of which, I need to return those files to the office after breakfast. Absorb whatever you can."

There was a floor plan of the hospital showing the location of his room, photographs of the staff arriving and even a diagram to show the positioning of the patient's bed. Daniel had certainly been busy with what he could be. The financial information contained several blanks during the time line. There was inherited wealth and interests mainly in Saudi, with transactions being run through relatives. There was a $3 billion sum held in a miscellaneous column from decades ago, but no trail to show where it went or what became of it. I could see in the profile some bullet points on his activities in Afghanistan and a short list of what his education may be. I ran my finger down the page looking for any mention of language skills, not wanting to be caught out like I was in Tripoli.

"How's his English?"

"Officially, we are not sure. Unofficially, anybody with his wealthy background would have a decent grasp of the language, possibly even fluent. Don't assume you can speak freely at any time during the visit."

"And what's the risk profile?"

"Minimal, as long as you maintain cover. The worst that can happen is you're not allowed in or asked to leave. Believe me that while I wouldn't have any issues pushing you into a high-risk meeting, I'm far more cautious with my sister."

I continued to absorb as much as I could, from obscure facts to useful indications of the man's character. He was described as gentle, intelligent and softly spoken. Sounded more like a lonely heart column than a threat. Daniel reached under the table to retrieve a plastic bag, handing it across the table to me and suggesting I should take it with me as a hospital gift. There was an Arsenal football shirt and a biography of Field Marshall Montgomery.

"He's a football fan. Supposedly spent a year in London and got a taste for the gunners."

"Looks more like a Chelsea fan."

"No. He's spoken to Zahra about it on the phone. He's also a history buff so I thought that biography would be another appropriate gift. These are all things you could have learned from Zahra, so it won't risk your cover. Should help break the ice."

It seemed such a silly concept amid an ultimately serious

situation, pandering to his football fantasy. Before I had a chance to finish the file, my time was up. Daniel was due at the embassy and had to return the files before arousing suspicion. He packed his things and wished me luck before leaving. I could feel the butterflies start to flutter in my stomach already and they got worse over the next few hours. I prepped for my cover putting together a rudimentary investment plan, looking at a balanced portfolio across several sectors. Medium Risk and a selection of bearer bond recommendations. Surely a man in his situation would appreciate the anonymity and lack of traceability involved with bearer instruments, if he didn't hold a number already. Suited and booted with my best banker's foot forward, I went to the foyer at 11:55 AM. Zahra was ready and waiting.

We headed across town towards the creek with Zahra demonstrating a driving style that I assumed was familiar to locals but left me pressing my foot into an imaginary brake pedal. I made her aware of the details from breakfast with Daniel and what was discussed. She already knew but I wanted to make doubly sure we were on the same page. We were going to the Iranian Club for lunch, only a short distance from the hospital. Zahra insisted this was because of the available parking and good food, but I thought she chose it as the least likely place to run into any Americans. She certainly didn't trust the company officers, American intelligence, in the area and I wanted to find out why. Once we were seated and the food was ordered (not by me), I jumped into it. She was hesitant at first and I had to reassure her I was asking because it was important regarding how I handle the situation going forward.

"Before I moved into finance, I worked at the Embassy with Daniel. I had been there for a few years working on the consular side of things when I was asked to move across to...uh...you know. It wasn't like people were queuing up in London to learn Arabic and move to the desert. We were a small group, very close-knit, but relied on the Americans for all our signals intelligence and any human intelligence from the smaller emirates. None of us liked being the junior partner but we didn't have a choice. Any spare personnel in MENA were focussed on Libya, still probing Lockerbie or the Irish weapons routes. As the junior it was my job to look at all the incoming information from our ally and prepare the briefs for the team. Naturally, they weren't giving us everything and we wouldn't give them everything we had either, but I noticed that over time the holes in the data were getting bigger and bigger. It reached a point where there were more black lines on the page than words and I started asking questions. I complained to my superiors, despite Daniel telling me leave it alone, but nothing changed. The next time I talked to the company men I asked them directly. Things got a bit heated over the phone and I said some things I shouldn't have. You might describe them as accusations, but they weren't meant that way. Anyway, I was terminated a few days later. Daniel said it was cost-cutting but I know it was pressure from the other side. So that was the full scope of my career at the service, a few months behind a desk."

"Sounds like you hold grudges. I'll have to be careful."

"I don't forget."

"You're like an elephant…" If looks could kill I would have died before finishing the sentence. I have a habit of prompting that sort of response from the fairer sex. "…not in that way, obviously, not in the slightest. Quite the opposite really."

"I'll remember that comment," she said jokingly as our food arrived. It was becoming an easy habit to slip into casual conversation when we were together, and we had to make a conscious effort to turn the subject back to business. We were already on the same page regarding the market and what would be appropriate investment advice for her client. However, I needed her to bring me up to speed with the current portfolio and the client's objectives. He was receiving dividends from the family construction company in Saudi via relatives as well as contributions from other sources that she wasn't familiar with. The current portfolio was spread over several foreign currency deposits with minimal investments: some ETFs, physical gold and the bearer bonds I had predicted. Zahra explained the client didn't have a specific risk profile or objective, mostly concerned with easy access and liquidity.

"I have a few bonds to recommend and a balanced collection of equities. Blue chip, nice and easy to dump if he wants to. I know of a few physical gold ETFs out of Switzerland that could be a nice option. Where are the accounts?"

"We have some based in Switzerland, most under a brother-in-law's name, and a few we are running out of shell companies in Lichtenstein and the Cayman Islands."

"Ok, the usual suspects. It should be a pretty straightforward pitch. If you know it's a brother-in-law, why can't we get a fix on the Sheikh's identity?"

"Saudi families can be massive, and just because I'm told it's a brother-in-law I can't prove that. The service isn't putting manpower on this. It's just us. I just hope he agrees to speak with you. This is the first time I'm meeting with him face to face, so I can't just waltz in with you on my arm."

"So, how do you want to play it?"

"You can wait in the corridor, hopefully only for a minute, while I explain."

"And if he says no?"

"We can cross that bridge if we come to it."

With lunch over and the time approaching, we rehearsed some final details: how did we know each other and for how long, etcetera. She was starting to get nervous, flicking at her hair every few moments. Thinking back to her limited time and role in the service this was probably her first time in the field, even if it wasn't her first client meeting.

Once we reached the hospital we sat in the car for a few minutes, she took several deep breaths and I straightened my tie. As a result of my hateful training I became calmer the closer we got to the hospital door, like I was putting on a mask. I took the pistol from my case and stowed it under the passenger seat. Nothing could blow my cover quicker than a banker carrying a 9mm. We walked straight past the front desk to the lifts and headed up to the third floor. As the doors opened and the bell chimed our arrival, Zahra took one last deep breath before we stepped out.

\* \* \* \* \*

"They saw him today;
I've given our approval."

"Did you give them the GPS data?

Turning down the corridor, his room was obvious; two men stood either side of the door with several more sat on chairs along the wall. Some I recognized from the pictures Tim gave me of the entourage. Others were new. The door opened and two men came out and walked towards us. Zahra gasped and looked at floor, allowing her hair to fall forward and obscure her face as we passed. I could tell who they were without her telling me: blue shirt with a dark suit is always a giveaway. I assumed all American diplomats used the same tailor.

As we got closer two security guards rose from their chairs and blocked our path. I was patted down and had to show every object that caused a lump in my clothes: cigarettes, wallet, phone. We handed over our bags to be thoroughly examined. A more vocal man appeared to be in charge and wasn't happy about something. Zahra discussed things with him and relayed to me that he wasn't pleased with my unplanned attendance. We each handed over a business card which he took inside for our host to evaluate. It was an uncomfortable delay, standing in the corridor with distrust coming at us from all angles. When the security guard re-emerged, he was accompanied by another man in traditional Saudi dress. I didn't recognize him from the file and Zahra didn't react to seeing him. He was now in possession of our cards and discussing matters intensely with the security guards who held our belongings. Zahra piped up an opinion which was enough to settle the discussions. The Saudi man put our cards in his pocket, turned back towards the open door and bid farewell to its occupant before leaving. The collection of unrecognized men around us got to their feet and quietly joined him.

Finally, we were invited to enter the room.

It was a large well-lit room with a comfortable feel. There were flowers on the window ledge and a generous selection of foods on the table. A nurse came forward to offer us dates and coffee while her patient chose to nurse a bottle of Nesquik. To one side of him a dialysis machine was spinning its magic while on the other side were chairs for him to receive his guests. He was a very tall man, using every inch of available space in the bed, but looked slightly frail and discoloured with the first specks of grey starting to appear in his beard. Hardly what you consider from his reputation and nom de guerre.

He greeted Zahra warmly and she seemed much happier to have heard his voice, its familiarity a welcome change from the tension in the corridor. It was like she was meeting a friend but with the respect normally reserved for senior relatives. The security guard brought in our papers and gifts from the corridor, leaving our bags and personal items outside. Zahra gave her reason for my presence, which he seemed perfectly content with. When the guard handed him the book and football shirt, he laughed and came across as genuinely grateful. In my experience there aren't a huge number of pleasantries which are universal around the world, but football is definitely one of them. The only other example I have found is ice cream.

He and Zahra talked for some time between themselves while I organized my papers. I was trying to listen for words I might recognize from the conversation as I had in Tripoli, but only picked up a few place names and currency designations. Nothing I could use. I was eventually invited to speak, with Zahra acting as translator. My suggestions for bond investments in Europe received little response, just a few nods and the odd word between the two Arabic speakers. I then broached the subject of equities, with Zahra translating as I spoke.

"I think we need to have an equity element in the portfolio. Nothing risky, large caps in a few sectors: financials, pharmaceutical, oil, mining. We can hold it under the companies you have or establish some new ones, I'm happy to assist in setting those up should you wish, perhaps Gibraltar would be another location you could use." He lay in the bed nodding along with the suggestions but remaining attentive. "I would like to spread some of the FX risk for you by building a portfolio of blue chips in the US as well, build some holding in banks…" Before I could finish he stopped me.

"No!"

This surprised Zahra, who had no idea he could speak English, but I was relieved that he lived up to the expectation Daniel and I had discussed. I could then actually be involved in the discussions.

"I'm sorry, sir, but can I ask why? With your international holdings, it's sensible to have an inflation hedge against the dollar."

"Have you been to America, Mr. Hope?"

"Yes, a few times."

"What did you think of it?"

"It has its charms, similar to anywhere else. I admire their temperament, a very positive people."

"Maybe for you. I too have been to America. I visited Indiana and California, very different places. The land is very beautiful and is filled with variety but the people were not positive towards me or my wife. We were stared at like a freak show everywhere from the airport to the shops."

"With all due respect, sir, I like to think times are changing…"

"They are. I have friends in the West, followers in America as we speak. It's the dreams of men like that which will change the world. Flying higher than we ever thought. We put hands across the desert and the Sheikh Abu Shaytan, praise be to God, was ready to walk with us." I didn't blink. If the near-invalid before me was speaking of Abu Shaytan, then who was I talking to? I tested the water.

"Abu Shaytan…Zahra, is this another client of yours?" Zahra didn't have any way to answer that. The Sheikh answered for her.

"He is not a client of anyone. He is an angel, one who has fought for peace for decades. He helps us. We help him. He helps the world. If we are a sword, then he is the shield. One is nothing without the other."

"I think we can all hope that the next generation will have little need for either."

"They will always need both, but they will succeed where I have failed, aim higher than I ever could."

"A bit like Arsene Wenger?" I suggested, naming the successful manager at Arsenal football club.

"Ha! Yes! Exactly! I am hoping that we can get another double like we did a few years ago."

We all laughed and defused a situation which had cut a bit close to the bone, but our host had one final thing to say on the subject.

"But being serious, I do not want anything invested in America. You would be sensible to avoid doing so yourself, bad idea. Trust me."

I took it more as discriminatory comment than anything else and we continued with our planning. There were moments during the conversations when he would revert to speaking Arabic with Zahra, and I couldn't wait to get out of the hospital to learn exactly what he had been saying. We planned to establish new companies to handle his UK investments and would arrange the paperwork to be signed by relatives in the country who could handle his assets. There were some potential stumbling blocks with moving funds, but as long as they passed through one or two companies or the High Commission on the way over I couldn't see any problems. The discussions and our brief visit were drawing towards a natural close. He said he planned to remain in Dubai for another week to continue treatment and tests, so he requested to meet again to finalize the plans. It makes my skin crawl to describe him this way, but my one meeting with The Sheikh left me with the impression he was nothing special. He didn't leave me with a sense of impending dread. Instead I felt like I had wasted a lot of my time chasing a hollow theory.

As we walked back to the car I was moving at quite a pace, desperate to get back into the air conditioning but also out of frustration. All I had learned from the meeting was that this man had a lot of money, didn't like Americans, had one strict parameter around his portfolio, and was not the 'he' I was promised. Just another whisper of the mysterious Abu Shaytan.

The most I could take back to Peter with me was that this one-time American ally from Afghan War was knee-deep in money laundering and had also heard of the ghost. That was it. I swung open the car door, retrieved my gun and put it back in my briefcase, hurriedly yanking my seatbelt into place and sulking for the first few minutes of the journey.

"So what do you think?" Zahra said, breaking the silence.

"Honestly? Not a lot." I snidely replied. She didn't appreciate my response at first but rather than cowing down she responded in typical fiery fashion.

"Well you didn't ask the right questions."

"The right questions? If I had asked the questions I wanted, then both of us would be in trouble. There is only so much you can do in this cover."

"Wrong. You could have played it as a sympathizer, taken an anti-Semite route to try and gain trust and find more information. Go deeper."

"Oh, I'm sorry! The woman who sat behind a desk for a matter of months is telling me how to do my job?"

"The *woman?* Nice, can't stand having your mistakes highlighted by a woman, can you?"

The bickering continued most of the way back to the hotel until I felt I had to apologize. Whatever my opinion, she had meant well. My apology fell on deaf ears. As we reached the main entrance I thanked Zahra for her help during my visit and hoped to part on good terms. She could still prove to be a useful contact. She ignored me and kept looking straight ahead. As the car door closed she raced away, and, as best I could tell, out of my world. I planned on arranging to return to Rome as soon as possible and deliver the bad news to Peter: it was a dead end. I also had to rush back to London and face the ramifications of my actions in Libya. It had been the wrong decision, chasing ghosts and red herrings across EMEA. As I crossed the foyer, I stopped by the front desk to check for messages. They had a package for me. I opened the envelope as soon as I got upstairs, which transpired to be from Daniel. It held a photograph of the man who'd left with our business cards, with a post-it note stuck to the front:

"Prince Turki Al Faisal, Head of Saudi Intelligence"

This changed everything. The head of Saudi Intelligence, American diplomats, and a known terrorist meeting together in a hospital room, and one of them already confirming the existence of Abu Shaytan. It had to be something they could only discuss in person and in private. I frantically called Zahra, hoping she would answer. I had to call three times before she finally answered.

"What?"

"Things have changed. I think you're right, this is something. Dinner?"

"Maybe."

"I'll be there tonight, same as before. I hope to see you there."

"I said maybe."

"Then I'll take a maybe."

It would have to do. I had to touch base with David and see if he had found something, anything that could piece the different strands together and give us a clear picture. It was still late morning in London and David, to my surprise, was pleased to hear from me.

"Secure?"

"Secure. I've got something for you, Alex, but not from where we were thinking. Abu Shaytan loosely translates as 'son of the devil'. Our files came up blank, and P hasn't come back with any info from the service as yet, but I spoke to Jules. He says Abu Shaytan was a legend employed by the service from the late seventies until the early nineties. A name used for two reasons: to spread unrest in the region, and to channel arms everywhere from Afghanistan to Morocco. It would be used to spread propaganda, disrupt weapons traffic to those we opposed, and bolster whatever faction served the nations interest at the time."

"So who is he?"

"He wasn't anyone. Literally a ghost story used to scare the locals or hide our support for groups with a less than savoury image. He's just a cover. It's nothing."

"It's more than that, David, I have known groups on the ground claiming to be working with him even today."

"Not possible I'm afraid. It's just an old war story."

"It's the perfect cover. Any investigations that led back to the man would eventually be written off as fiction. It's like that film Charlie made us watch, the greatest trick the devil ever pulled was convincing the world he didn't exist."

"Do you have any proof such a man exists?"

"I have proof that the Americans think he exists, the Saudis, and the head of a major terror network who swears he's working with him and has done for decades."

"It's circumstantial, but it's something. I'll extend that seventy-two hours to a week. Let me know what more comes across your desk and I'll pressure P for the service files."

"Thank you, Pater."

"And be careful, if what you say is true then it's too much for you to handle alone." I hoped he was right in the first sense, and crossed my fingers he wasn't in the second. Time would tell. That evening at the same restaurant and the same table, I waited, and waited some more. Almost one bottle of wine deep and on my second plate of kebbeh, Zahra arrived.

"You could've waited."

"I didn't think you were coming."

"I very nearly didn't."

"Well, I'm glad you did." After Zahra had ordered I filled her glass and explained the photograph Daniel left for me at the hotel, and my fears for its implications.

"I think there is something coming, soon, an attack on the US mainland. The Sheikh and Abu Shaytan working together, a two-pronged attack. It fits with what Peter told me about a Russian incident and the different countries we have in play. I'm thinking it's an infrastructure or stock market play, hence his protests today. It's not about the fact it's investing in America, it's about losing money. If he was just anti-American he would never have accepted their help against the Soviets. Don't get me wrong, I think the attack is ideological, but that's not why he's avoiding the investment. Their attack is going to shift the market."

"I told you there was something."

"I know, I know. I've already apologized and I'm not going to keep doing it. Now, I need to know about those Americans we saw at the hospital. Where you know them from and what they're doing there?"

"They were doing the same thing as you, that's the station chief and number two from out here: Robert Whistler and Michael Strieler."

"Station chiefs don't visit assets or gather intel, they shuffle paperwork and have cocktails with the ambassador. It doesn't add up." Things were coming together to form a miserable picture. Intelligence services converging on one man, and that man partnering with a ghost story from the back catalogue of British Intelligence. All I could think was that Abu Shaytan was still being used as a cover from the service. I would need to speak to Charlie. Somehow get a line of communication across the pond, outside of Pactum but still a secure channel. The US and British interest wasn't my biggest worry at the time though: the Saudis were. While every service would step outside international law from time to time, the Saudis never stepped inside. "I think you need to get away for a while. It will only be a matter of time before Saudi Intel figure out enough to raise suspicion, which could put you in danger."

"Alex, this is my home and I've done nothing wrong. Why would I leave?"

"You don't want to take that risk, not with these people. Choose anywhere."

"No. This isn't my fight."

"I didn't think it was mine either until a few weeks ago."

Before I could push the subject any further, the waiter approached our table and pulled out the seat beside Zahra. I didn't know we were expecting company.

* * * * *

"They have everything they need;
he won't get back to London."

"Accidents happen."

Zahra's face glowed as she flung her arms around Peter.

"What on earth are you doing here? What a wonderful surprise!"

"I'm sorry to interrupt but I had to see the two of you, thankfully your brother keeps close tabs on you taking dinner with strange men. What have you found out?"

"We have more pieces in play than you originally thought. The Sheikh and Abu Shaytan are separate people working together. I was about to explain to Zahra what I learnt from London that Abu Shaytan was a cover story used by the service in the past. I believe someone kept it going, off the books, for personal gain in the present."

"P?"

"After what you said, that's where I'm leaning. I'm sure there is going to be an attack on the US mainland in the very near future. Russia all over again," I replied.

"Do you know when or where?"

"Not yet, but I think we're talking weeks or months. No longer than that judging by the Sheikhs reaction."

Peter turned his attention back to family with rekindled concern etched across his eyes. "I think you should take some time off, sweetie, you're too involved already."

"That's exactly what I've been trying to tell her."

"I think you both need to stop telling me what to do!" shouted Zahra, who inadvertently aroused the attention of anyone in earshot.

"I am just concerned for you," said Peter softly, to calm the situation.

"I don't need your concern and I certainly didn't ask for it!" Still irate, Zahra immediately rushed away from the table. I stood up to follow her.

"Leave her, Alex. I still need to talk to you," said Peter, stopping me in my tracks. "The only secure way I could think of doing this was in person. Harry is back in London but he faxed me an update to the list." He pulled a photograph from his case and slid it across the table to me.

"I don't need to see any reminders of what happened in Paris, London or anywhere else."

"I know you don't, this isn't a reminder."

I flipped the picture and was shocked by what I saw. It was Amelia walking the Via Condotti in Rome, the same street where I had coffee at Café Greco.

"How old is this picture?"

"Few days, maybe more."

"I spoke to her when I first got to Rome, we were supposed to meet on there the next day but she never showed. Where is she now?"

"I'm afraid I don't know. Neither Harry nor myself have had any luck in trying to find her. I never thought he would have the audacity to attack so close to home, one of David's children."

"Does David know?"

"I don't know. There's more." He pulled an envelope from his case and put Amelia's picture inside.

"How many pictures do you have?" I asked, hoping for a low number.

"Just one. The target has been issued but I no action has been taken as yet."

"Is it Charlie?"

"No." Peter slid the envelope to me across the table and grasped my wrist in hope it would bring my attention. "They're burning you, Alex. Anyone you've talked to. Anyone who can vouch for you…and that includes my niece."

I snatched the envelope from the table and bolted from the restaurant, hoping to catch Zahra at the valet. She was already getting in the car. I shouted for her but she didn't stop. Instead I flung myself onto the bonnet of the car, clinging to the windscreen wipers to prevent myself sliding over the opposite side.

"Can I get a lift?"

She begrudgingly agreed. Rather than trying to justify my earlier advice, I took a deep breath and laid out all that I had seen and heard in the previous moments. She didn't say anything but I could feel her fear build in the car, the whites of her knuckles visible against the steering wheel as she drove far slower than before. I was sure it was the first time in her life she had heard such stories and felt a genuine concern for her own wellbeing. I did only what I thought was right in the situation, to try and offer some comfort and assurance. I placed my hand on hers and promised her it was going to be okay. Her initial reaction was to sharply pull away. Then she surprised both of us by slowly replacing her hand under mine.

"I think you should stay with me tonight," I nervously

suggested. She didn't refuse, just kept on driving. It was like she knew it was the sensible option but not something she wanted to admit. It was a risky suggestion for both of us, especially for her. As we parked the car, I realized the previously steadfast confidence had faded from those deep blue eyes. They no longer challenged me, instead giving up a combination of anxiety and innocence, looking to me for comfort. It's funny what aspects of a woman truly capture a man's heart, ironically often the idiosyncrasies and perceived flaws a woman may try to hide: the way she laughs, the minute creases at the corner of her mouth when she offers a genuine smile, those accidental moments of candidness or social awkwardness when her guard is down and you glimpse the individual behind it all. For me it was that look when she placed her life in my hands.

Thankfully the sight of a European couple at a hotel raised little suspicion, but we still felt nervous and kept our distance until reaching the refuge of my suite. We stood separate in the lift and she stood several yards behind me while I slid the card to open my door. I held the door as she walked slowly and somewhat awkwardly inside. This was a new territory for me to try and navigate, as I had always perceived these situations in a shallow and usually inebriated manner.

"Coffee?"

"Yes, please."

I set the machine and stepped towards her, pausing for a second as I ran my fingers through her hair and leant towards her.

"Sorry, but would you mind...uh...brushing your teeth first? I don't smoke."

I naturally obliged and as I came to the corner of the bedroom on my return, could see her shoes on the floor. She was fast asleep, still fully clothed atop the bed. There was that moment of disappointment natural to any red-blooded male, but it faded so quickly. Instead, I took the blanket and softly laid it over her to avoid the chill of a Westerner's taste in air conditioning.

I sat on the chaise longue and just admired her. As far as it was from my usual persona, I could then recognise those few who have been lucky enough to encounter an individual who affected them in such a way. They will likely understand the feeling I am failing miserably to describe.

I hoped she was comfortable. I was able to admire her silhouette and the innocence with which she crossed her feet while sleeping. Wrapped in awe, I lay down on the chaise, still fully clothed (with fresh breath I might add) and slowly fell asleep, fighting the fatigue until the last second just to savour one more glimpse of trust.

*****

"It's not him."

"Are they sure?"

I woke the next day to the sun slowly cooking my back. The bed lay vacant with no sign of its previous occupant. I picked up my briefcase and went to see if she was getting breakfast, but again, there was no trace. While I was downstairs, I decided to stop at reception to ask if any messages had been left and to request the use of their shredder to destroy my meeting documents. As I stood calmly at the desk I could feel the growing presence of undesirable interference behind me. The normally smiling face at reception turned sour and frightened. As they came closer, I could see their chiselled reflections in the countertop and made sure to leave the documents safely in my case. They announced their presence with that predictable American twang and textbook request: "Sir, would you mind coming with us?"

The cliché was blissfully interrupted by screeching tires outside, a battered old land cruiser upsetting the otherwise polished parade of vehicles. A familiar face sat behind the wheel and his urgent arrival was the only invitation I needed to run for the door. I leapt into the rear passenger seat and before I could say a word we were on the move.

"I have to say, Daniel, this time I actually appreciate you interrupting my morning."

Daniel didn't even glance back, jabbing numbers into his phone with his thumb while the other hand stopped us from cantering into the Arabian Gulf.

"I have him. We'll take the low road. Extraction route beta," he said before flinging the phone from the window into the sea. The chase had begun, with two giant American SUVs hot on our tail. Thankfully as we passed the security gate the guard raised the barriers behind us, putting some distance between us in the early moments of the pursuit. It was nice to know we still had some friends in the area. Treating the red lights more as a guideline than a rule, Daniel raced through town while I anxiously kept watch out of the rear window.

"Who knew you were here?"

"Just Peter. Nobody else had a fixed location."

"I know Peter did, he turned up at my flat last night but someone's bloody talking. We had Yanks blowing up the phones all night and this morning raising hell over your hospital visit. I've heard murmurs of discomfort from London and Washington too. Keep your head down!"

I lay flat on the back seat, only peering up when we came to a stop. We had reached the creek in the old town and pulled into the British Embassy. Daniel jumped out and returned moments later, throwing me a dishdash and keffiyeh with a plastic bag and some sandals.

"Get changed. Drop everything you can."

I kept only my underwear, briefcase, and watch while stuffing everything else into the plastic bag. Daniel returned dressed in similar garb. He grabbed the bag from me and handed it to the security guard at the front of the car park while two other locals switched our number plates at pit stop pace. We were back on the road again.

"Where's Zahra? Is she okay?"

"She's fine, I told you her safety was a far greater priority to me than yours."

We rushed east into thinning development and shrinking skylines. I would like to say we were weaving in and out of traffic in a dramatic fashion, but the locals had such disregard for the speed limits that we just ran with the bulls. As the traffic faded away, we reached the limits of Dubai and the monotony of the desert became the norm. There's little vehicular traffic so our biggest concern quickly became camels and sand drifts. The day was fading and the colours around us began to morph with the changing light.

Suddenly, the familiar shape of our pursuers reappeared in Daniel's rear-view mirror as the sun began to set over the sand. He yanked the wheel sharply to the side and we bounced off the tarmac into the rolling dunes of the empty quarter. We could feel the vehicle immediately slow and labour its way over the changed surface and reached the peak of the first dune. We had to stop.

"Where in the hell did they come from?! We need to let air out of the tyres, I'll do this side and you do the other."

The searing heat of the sand burnt my toes as I bent down to the tyres. The Americans had been closing fast and were already on the straight where we left the road. I hoped we would be lucky enough for them to fly past but they stopped exactly where we exited. One man got out of the front passenger door of the lead vehicle and lined us up with his binoculars. Daniel and I were both on our second tyre when he lowered the binoculars and raised something far more serious. Three cracks echoed up the sandbank.

"Fuck! The fuckers fucking shooting at us! Shit! Shit! Shit!"

The flying sand left by my running feet was only bettered by those left by our tires as Daniel stamped on the accelerator. We bounced over the edge of the dune and plummeted down the valley.

"Do you still have that gun in your case?" asked my unusually calm companion as I nodded. "Then get ready to fucking use it."

We meandered down the valley while I retrieved the Glock from my briefcase. The lumbering SUVs crested the dune behind us, the first vehicle catching air and heading nose first into the downslope. The second vehicle beached itself at the peak and took up a firing position. The gunshots were drowned out by the sound of our heaving engine, but the pings of bullets hitting our bodywork rang clear.

"Shoot back, for God's sake!"

I took aim behind us and let ring my first shot. Our rear window immediately shattered into a thousand pieces as I shot clean through it. I saw the puff of sand where I struck; it was woefully far from my intended target but this was a far greater range than I had practiced on. I tried again and hit the windscreen of the beached vehicle, enough to pause the offensive fire for a moment and put more distance between us.

"Go for the one that's following us, take his lights out."

Despite emptying the rest of my magazine, his headlights were still bright in our eyes. Daniel reached across to open the glove box, revealing two loaded magazines. A few more rounds and a brief pause as we turned up the next dune allowed me a better platform and I took out his left headlight.

"Good, keep going! He can't follow us if he can't see!"

As we neared the top of the next dune, he came perfectly in line with us. One good shot would be enough to leave them blind in the desert. Thankfully, though more through luck than judgement, I hit the target.

As we dipped over the top Daniel killed our own lights,

relying only on the feel of the wheels to keep us upright. We hit the deck and headed off into the night as quickly as the terrain would allow, leaving our disgruntled colonial cousins shouting and waving flashlights in our dust. We drove on until they were out of sight, then stopped and killed the engine to see if we could still hear them.

It was quiet, eerily so. Daniel got out and opened the boot, brushing the bullet casings and sand aside to reach his backpack from under a blanket. Returning to the driver's seat he turned on the interior light and handed me a bottle of water. The condensation caused it to slip through my fingers at first but after a sip I offer it to Daniel, who in the meantime had unfolded a map and pulled out a compass.

"Is this kind of thing normal round here?"

"More often than you'd think."

I would have happily swapped places with anyone back in London. I missed the days when my biggest debate on a Friday night was which bar to head to next, not who was trying to kill me. The cloak and dagger stuff was good fun, but this was the first time the dagger had fired back. It was unnerving to say the least. Daniel pulled a cell phone from his bag, far more compact than the antique I had been lugging around the place.

"Slight change of plan, we had to take the high road. If I cross north of Al Ain I can get him to the Al Buraimi pass between routes 5 and 7, can you pick up there? I'll have him there by two. Copy, confirm." The dialogue cleared, Daniel continued to busy himself with the map. Whether I was punch drunk from gunfire or dumbstruck by the location, I don't know, but I took time to admire my rare yet troublesome surroundings.

I appreciated the night sky, but rarely had the chance to see it that clearly. London shines so brightly that it's often a struggle to see anything besides the moon. The prehistoric darkness of the desert was as beautiful as it was humbling, allowing a myriad of stars of all sizes and colours to be displayed in their unabridged number, pricks of light against a canvas of blended purples, blues and blacks. Stood in the sand facing the astrological reminder of my insignificance, only one thing then crossed my mind. I wondered where Zahra was and hoped she was able to enjoy a similar view.

We continued our way across the sand at a steady pace but didn't see another soul. As we became more secure in our solitude, we had a chance to talk.

"I'll be honest with you, Daniel. I feel like I've fallen into more than I can really handle on my own."

"What were you expecting?"

"I wasn't totally sure. All I was doing was following a lead, a lead that I assumed to be important to just one man. The man who forced Peter and I together. I didn't expect to find myself caught in some conspiracy between ghost and governments."

"A conspiracy? We have just been chased from the city by a team who are supposed to be on our side! Trust me, nobody pulls a trigger over a conspiracy."

A pop followed by repetitive tapping erupted from the engine, the only sound less welcome than gunfire in our current predicament. The strain from hours of sand had pushed our engine to its limit. Quite possibly the first time a Toyota had ever been beat. We were finishing our long journey on foot. It's no wonder militaries like to train their people on sand; it sapped energy from us like it did the engine of the Toyota. We were both nervous, ducking or crouching at the sound of any vehicle no matter how distant it sounded. Daniel would check his compass periodically and change our course when required.

As we stood atop a dune, we could make out the distant lights of Al Ain and Al Buraimi far off. We had to cross several roads on the route, the few yards of concrete giving us a chance to empty the sand from our sandals and stretch our tired muscles. Eventually we reached another road and Daniel stopped.

"This is it. This is where you want to be."

We'd crossed the border into Oman without knowing it, something that's impossible nowadays. He put out his arm and pointed to our right.

"You just head in this direction and keep walking. Someone will pick you up within the next hour or so."

"Someone? That doesn't sound very reassuring."

"I don't know whose handling you tonight, Alex, but I trust the people organizing it. I know it's not much for you to be working with, but it's all you've got."

"If in doubt, I can always trade my watch for a friendly camel and head off into the desert. Lawrence of Arabia did alright in the end." Daniel's memory was jogged by my quip. He unbuckled his watch and held it in his hand, obviously uncomfortable with what he was about to suggest.

"You know the history of us Brits in Oman?"

"Nothing, I'm afraid."

"In 1970, the British helped bring the Sultan to power in Oman, largely thanks to one of my father's friends, who had known the Sultan since his days in Sandhurst. My father was part of the SAS group who helped cement the Sultan's position and defend the state later that decade. He gave this, amongst other things, to my father as a token of thanks for his help and friendship. I want you to take it with you."

"Daniel, I can't accept something like that."

"Oh, this isn't a gift. It's a trade, and we'll switch back next time I see you. I just want you to have it tonight, because if you get stopped by police or military before pickup, this watch may just save your life."

He handed me an old Rolex submariner, stainless steel with the Omani logo on the face. I could barely make it out in the darkness, but the light from the moon was just enough that we could make the swap without dropping each other's items. They held great meaning for both of us and I was sure they would be returned in the future. We wished each other well and set off in our respective directions, at least I could walk on solid ground rather than facing another godawful trek over the sand.

The landscape was noticeably different in Oman. More jagged and undulating. I could see the silhouettes of the landscape against the night sky as the road cut its path into the valley. It was past three in the morning when I heard a vehicle coming up behind me. When it was close enough to capture me in its lights, it sped up, and I stepped off the road and set myself back a few yards from the tarmac. The vehicle, a saloon, slammed on the brakes and pulled in front of me. Two men jumped from the rear seats and started shouting at me.

"Yallah! Yallah!" I didn't know if that was my cue to smile or run.

"Let's go! Let's go!" came a thankfully translated follow-up from one of the men. I gave them a wave as I walked closer to greet them. Rather than grabbing my hand to shake it, they grabbed me by the arms and rushed me towards the car. My sandals slid across the tarmac as I tried to gather my footing. Another man got out of the front of the car and popped open the boot for the others to dump me in there like sack of potatoes.

"I'm sorry, there must be some mistake. Look, I have this very nice watch..."

"British?"

"Yes, but you see a friend of mine."

"Fisherman?"

"…of sorts, yes."

"No mistake."

He threw a bottle of water on top of me and slammed the lid of the boot. I had been demoted from a passenger with Daniel to cargo for whomever had control of me now.

\* \* \* \* \*

"If you want a job doing right…"

I could hear the group talking in the car. Every once in a while, someone would bang on the rear seat and shout "Okay?" I doubt they even heard my response, a garbled request for more information and a more comfortable seat. As the sun started to come up, light would cut through the cracks around the boot lid. Unfortunately, it also signalled the rising temperature, which for a man of my origins was already uncomfortable. I stopped trying to wipe the perspiration from my face when I realized my sleeves were sopping wet already, and instead of keeping the sweat from my eyes it just rubbed it around and made it worse. The sounds of other vehicles had me hoping we were nearing my journey's end, but having spent a few days experiencing local driving I was also terrified that should we be rear-ended by another vehicle then I would essentially form part of the vehicles crumple zone.

I guessed we were in a city judging by the noise, but soon the vehicle found itself on quieter streets and at a mercifully slower speed. Shortly afterwards it stopped all together and the engine turned off. I resisted the urge to start banging on the lid for my release because for all I knew we might just be getting petrol. When the lid opened the light was blinding, but the fresh air washed over me like a blessing. As I managed to focus my eyes, I saw my escorts looking down on me in a kindly manner.

"Ahlan wasahlan."

"What?"

"Welcome. Welcome to Muscat."

They helped me out with much more delicacy than when they had entombed me. I was standing outside a beautiful Arabian villa, whitewashed walls shining in the morning sun. One of the men kept hold of my arm as I walked to the door, my legs still unsteady from the journey. One offered to carry my briefcase, but I wasn't letting it out of my hand. A small Indian gentleman opened the front door and came out to greet us. He thanked my handlers and handed them a hefty envelope.

"Welcome sir, please. Please, this way." We headed upstairs with the bannister offering much needed support as I tried to keep up with my guide. He opened a door and gestured me inside. Some fresh clothes lay on a bed in front of me.

"Please sir, make yourself at home. Please. Please."

I thanked him with a look that spoke a thousand mercies as he graciously left me alone. After cleaning myself up I rested on the bed before waking up to the midday call to prayer. My initial aversion to it had mellowed over time, and I was beginning to appreciate quite how beautiful it could sound. I heard some voices downstairs and decided to investigate further, at least introduce myself to whomever had provided me sanctuary. I could hear two male voices and two females. After making my way down the main stairs I followed the voices down one or two further steps to a large reception room. It had sofas going all the way round the outside and several other seats inside, dividing the room into different areas. The small Indian man I had encountered earlier was stood next to a group of people and noticed me sheepishly peer into the room. He was one of the voices.

"Ah, welcome sir. Welcome. Please." Seemingly his favourite words, and he waved for me to join them. The group stopped talking amongst themselves and all three turned to look at me, standing up as I approached. A tall Arab gentleman spoke first.

"Sanjeev, please get Mr. Hope something to drink before lunch," came a crisp British accent, not what I was expecting from his olive-toned and white-bearded exterior.

"Welcome to my home, Mr. Hope, I trust your journey wasn't too uncomfortable."

"Thank you, sir. Under the circumstances I was more concerned with its success than its comfort."

"Please call me Rashid, and this is my wife Fatima. I believe you already know my goddaughter."

It was Zahra. It was such a relief to see her that I almost failed to acknowledge Fatima. She looked radiant but very different from how she had been in Dubai, wearing an intricate woven blue and gold ensemble. It suited her, and whether it was the company or the new location, she seemed much more comfortable. In turn I was able to relax and speak more freely than I had before.

"It's good to see you." She blushed and nodded in reply.

"Come, sit with us. I understand you have been having some trouble," said Rashid. Sanjeev returned with some mint and lemon juice as I took a seat next to my host.

"It's been a shocking few days to say the least. I dread to think where I would be if it hadn't been for Zahra and Daniel's help."

"Yes. It's a very messy business. These are troubling times in this part of the world, resentment is building in some areas while comfort consumes others. Things are being twisted to suit agendas. In the old days we could quash it, not so anymore. What do you intend to do?"

"At the moment, nothing. We need more information and a better idea of where to take it."

"You are welcome to stay here as long as you like, I would encourage you to keep a low profile for a while."

"Thank you, sir, that's very kind."

"Good. That's settled then. I have some friends who are retrieving your items from Dubai, they should be with us tomorrow."

Thinking back, that was the first time since joining Pactum that I wasn't working. No phone was going to ring, no leads to follow or people to meet. It was strange that in the midst of the chaos I was finding peace. Recalibrating myself on a new zero. Thinking. Even when I shouldn't be.

The spices mixed with the frankincense in the air over lunch, with so many foods to choose from I didn't know where to begin, or what many even were. It was incredibly relaxed, sitting on the floor against cushions and taking time to spread the meal over several hours, enjoying the company as much as the cuisine. The only addition I would have made would have been a nice bottle of wine, but by then I knew better than to enquire about alcohol unless it was offered.

As the afternoon wore on and the lunch came to a natural close, people tended to themselves. Zahra retired to the garden with a book to sit under a canopy and after an appropriate period of time I decided to follow. The breeze blowing through the garden made the temperature tolerable and I enquired if she would mind me joining her, to which she offered no objection.

"Have you spoken to Daniel?"

"No, he'll be keeping quiet for a few days I'm sure. Is that really what you wanted to ask me?" she answered bluntly.

"No, but I wasn't sure how to broach the subject of the other night."

"Is there anything to discuss?"

"I just wanted to say how much I enjoyed your company. Simply that I enjoyed spending time with you. I was initially confused when you weren't there in the morning, of course I now understand."

"You need to be careful how you word things like that, people will make assumptions." The stern face I had first known in Dubai was back in play, even if only momentarily. I didn't know where that emotional guard came from, and frankly I didn't think it my place to ask. She continued, "I appreciated your restraint. It was a strange day for both of us and I was feeling very insecure, but it could have caused a lot of trouble. You were a gentleman, despite my original perceptions of you."

"One does try," I responded sarcastically, feeling quite plush at being described as a gentleman rather than an arse.

"Seriously? You just had to ruin it." Eyes like organ stops and mouth open in semi-disbelief.

"I'm kidding!" I replied as she playfully pushed my shoulder a few times. "I trust your escape was less eventful than mine?"

"Danny messaged me at about 4 a.m. telling me he was coming to see me. He wasn't very happy when I told him where I was." We both laughed at the thought of Daniel jumping into protective brother mode yet again. "He had already picked up some things from my flat and drove me to the airport in Abu Dhabi. I got the dawn flight out to Muscat and Rashid met me at the airport. Pretty easy really. I didn't understand how serious things were until I got here and they told me the plan for you."

I could see the cheerfulness starting to drain from her face, as if she felt responsible for the way things escalated. It was a feeling I knew only too well. There would be time to dissect matters later and it would probably be better to tackle them one at a time. I had an idea to lighten the mood.

"Do you want to get out, just see the city? It's my first time here and I would love to be nothing more than a tourist right now. Pretend like I'm actually on holiday at for a few days." She didn't answer immediately, but then gave me the answer I was hoping for.

"I'd like that."

Muscat is a beautiful city. While so many areas of the Middle East are trying to mimic the skylines and success of the west, Muscat remains true to its heritage and aesthetic. Since 1992, the Sultan decreed buildings couldn't be taller than ten stories and must be finished in the traditional whitewash. It may sound archaic to our western ears, but the results are truly beautiful. One of Muscat's greatest assets is the natural beauty it has nestled itself within for centuries, the deep blue gulf and the mountains surrounding it. The policy allows the area to blend the traditional and modern in a delicate and respectful manner. We were able to walk along the corniche, stopping for drinks when appropriate and, for the first time since we met, truly be ourselves without the weighty presence of business hanging in the background. Every conversation was a chance to know more about one another. Over the coming week we spent most of our time together during the day, still dining with our hosts each evening. Sadly, as I should have expected, the happiness was to be short-lived and our little bubble was cruelly burst.

I came down one morning to see Zahra bawling over the newspaper. I asked what the matter was and she simply handed me the paper before rushing from the room. The headline read, BRITISH DIPLOMAT DIES IN ROBBERY. Reading on the article painted a story of a robbery in the desert, but one which bore the familiar twisted hallmarks of the intelligence community. A lone man exploring the dunes only to be gunned down and robbed, according to the article. My immediate observation was when a man is gunned down, you don't require two sheets several feet apart to cover his remains. We had been cruelly rushed back to reality. Daniel had never made it home that night in the desert.

\* \* \* \* \*

"Has he tried to contact you?"

"Why the hell would he do that?!"

Rashid had heard the door slam to Zahra's room and came to investigate the commotion. I simply handed him the paper as it had been handed to me.

"This was no accident," was all I could coldly add to his understanding. I went to see if I could comfort Zahra when Rashid put his arm out to stop me.

"Have you ever lost someone so close?" he asked, tears visible in his eyes.

"Yes, but not like this."

"It's not the same. Please, let her be. She needs to be alone."

I heeded his advice, instead choosing to retreat outside and contemplate the ramifications and circumstances surrounding the situation. I was still wearing Daniel's watch and rubbed its face with my thumb. I regretted our first meeting and how I had spoken to him with such arrogance before. I felt guilt about the great service he had done for me and how it was now impossible to repay that kindness. That night in my room I could hear Zahra, her stuttered cries drifting for her window to my own. It only made it worse. She didn't emerge until the follow afternoon, quietly creeping downstairs to grab something from the kitchen. I was there when she entered but didn't talk, just put my hands on her shoulders hoping it would remind her she wasn't alone. She spun around like a top, wrapping her arms around my chest so tightly I imagined she'd fall if she let go. When she pulled away, I removed Daniel's watch from my wrist and pressed it into Zahra's hand.

"This was going back to him, instead it's right that it goes to you." She pushed back against the suggestion.

"He gave it to you for a reason, whatever it was. Keep it."

I think she could tell that I was realizing there was only one way I could make Daniel's sacrifice worthwhile and she didn't like the implications.

"Don't go. Please just stay here."

"I will, I promise." It was a blatant lie, but one she needed to be told at the time. She needed to be held and assured that someone was there for her. The mood in the house had plummeted from pleasant to miserable, everyone could feel it. Zahra rarely joined the others at meals, spending a lot of time either by herself in her room or cocooned silently by my side. I didn't know what I could say or do to make things better, instead trying to make pointless small talk with take her mind off things. After a few days I couldn't handle the rudderless path anymore. I had to address the elephant in the room: we needed to ascertain what was happening and what we could do about it.

I gingerly knocked on Zahra's bedroom door before opening it. She was lying on the bed staring out of the window. I asked how she was doing, knowing full well the answer would be "fine" even though she was a wreck. I approached the bed, sitting next to her and rubbing her back, trying to tread the fine line between comfort and intimacy.

"I think we need to talk about what's happened."

"I don't want to…"

"It will do you some…"

"I can't! Okay! I just can't!" she cried, slamming her face into the pillows and bursting into a fit of emotion. Every time her back jolted with her cries I wanted to grab her and squeeze her tightly. I couldn't endure seeing her torn apart in such a way. I tried to say something but struggled to even get the words out. I tapped her gently on the back and held my hand there before walking away. When I left her room, Rashid was stood on the landing waiting for me.

"It is still not time."

"I hoped it was. We have some much to discuss."

"It can wait."

"I don't think it can wait anymore."

"Come. Let's walk the gardens and you and I talk."

"I truly appreciate the offer, but the fewer people we drag into this mess the better."

"You have been staying at my house for almost two weeks. Whether you like it or not, I am in this mess."

He was right, and as we walked the gardens I told him the story I've been telling you. I divulged every detail, forgoing the promises I made and commitments I'd signed. We walked and talked in a slow circle around the gardens for hours. Rashid listened intently, letting me unload the questions and frustrations bouncing around my head. I told him how I wished I could simply make it all go away and stay in Muscat like I had promised. He waited patiently for me to finish before inviting me to sit down beneath the same floral canopy Zahra had been fond of reading under.

"I cannot tell you what you should do or answer the questions you have, but I would like to tell you a story. Many centuries ago there was a man. He had a great life: a loving wife, many beautiful daughters, and a successful business. Despite all this he felt like something was missing from his life, that there was something he needed to do. He didn't know what it was, but it began to eat at him on the inside. He began taking long walks up the mountains and asking himself out loud, what should I do? One day he was sat in a cave and he heard a voice. It said, 'Read!' and he replied that he was not one of those who read. Again the voice told him to read and he replied that he could not. The voice came a third time, 'Read!' and he finally said, 'What should I read?' Like you he was struggling with what to do. When he finally got his answer, it was telling him to do the one thing he thought he could not do. He didn't let this stop him and even though it would initially cost him his home, countless friends and family. He persevered."

"Rashid, I'm sorry, but I don't understand what you're suggesting."

"Sometimes we have to do what we think we cannot in order to do what is needed. I believe you will figure it out, you just need to aim higher."

He left me to contemplate his words by myself as his final phrase repeated over and over in my head, taking me back to the hospital and remembering the smile from the Sheikh as he said the very same words. I had been too busy trying to make football jokes and endear myself to notice, but he had the arrogance to tease me with it. I began to connect the dots together in my head: friends in America, flying higher than before, the failed attempt in 1993…of course he was going to aim higher. The truck bomb had failed, so he was going to take the North Tower of the World Trade Center down from the top. Probably a light aircraft. If successful, it would impact stocks from banks to arms manufacturers, foreign exchange to tourism. That's why he wanted to keep his money outside of the US. That's what Abu Shaytan would exploit. I jumped to my feet and raced after Rashid.

"I know what's going to happen!"

"I thought you already did? That still leaves the question of what you're going to do about it."

If I wanted any chance of stopping the attack, I had to take a leap of faith. I knew I couldn't trust P or the local embassies. The only people I could trust and knew how to contact were Charlie and David, so I ran upstairs and dug out the satellite phone.

"Piscator for Pater, secure."

"I'm sorry sir, he is not available, I will transfer you to Procurator." The phone went quiet for moment before Charlie came on the line.

"What the fuck, Alex? Where are you? What is happening?"

"It's a long story. I've got something big, very big."

"What are we talking about?"

"There is a terrorist attack brewing in the US. Massive. I believe they are planning to crash a plane into the World Trade Center in New York. Like the truck attack of 1993 but from the air, some form of aircraft laden with explosives."

"Do you have proof?"

"I have enough, but this is far bigger and darker than I thought. This needs to stay between you and me until I can speak to Pater. Patruus is compromised."

"What?! No, that's not possible."

"I don't like it any more than you do, but it's true. He has known about this attack since before I joined. That's why he was so supportive of us expanding into the US."

"This has to go to the cage and across the pond. Gerry has our office set up in Chicago and Pater is checking another one for NYSE. How soon can you get to London? The old man is leaving soon."

"A few days at most, just keep it to yourself until I get back and we put a plan together."

"I'll do what I can. Where are you?"

"Tripoli. Thanks Charlie."

It's a sad state of affairs when you question giving information to your oldest friend, but I couldn't trust whether P had kept track of the in-house lines at Pactum and whether Joan could be trusted to keep the lines secure. It might have put Charlie at risk to tell him, but I could get back soon enough. I began to pack my things when I saw Zahra stood at the door. She didn't say anything, just shook her head and waited for me to speak first. I didn't have anything to say. I wasn't happy about it, but it was what had to be done.

"I heard you and Rashid talking outside."

"And?" It wasn't the right way to answer her. I regretted it, like I was knocking her when she was already down.

"You promised you would stay," she reminded me.

"I would if I could. I don't want to go but how could I live with myself if I stayed?"

"Happily. You could live happily." I was selling my reasoning but she was selling hers better. A battle of equals negotiating each other's arguments and fleeting between frustration and forgiveness.

"Selfishly, and I've been that before without even knowing it. Others have paid the price."

"If there is nothing I can say to make you stay, can I say something that will bring you back?"

"If you are here, then I will come back. You don't need to say anything more."

We stood apart from each other in silence as we realized the gravity of that sentence. A new experience for me and she looked to be in the same boat. She gave me that same stare she had in Dubai, but not over fear for herself: it was a fear of losing what we had. What I would have done for us to meet under better circumstances! At that time, I knew I had to keep my distance, that what had started as a contact had quickly become my greatest weakness. I couldn't risk having my feelings lead to her harm.

"I still need a passport but don't think I can risk the embassy."

"I can help with that," came Rashid's voice from behind Zahra. He had been skulking by the door like a chaperone. "I just need some things from you."

"Anything."

"A passport photograph and the watch you're wearing."

Rashid fixed up an improvised photo booth in the hallway and Sanjeev was sent to the shops to get me a suit and tie. It was probably the worst-fitting suit I had ever worn but would have to suffice. After a few shots and some trimming we had what could pass as an acceptable passport photo. It would have probably been rejected by the passport office back home, but thankfully other parts of the world weren't quite as selective. When Rashid was ready, I slipped the watch from my wrist and handed it to him. The already-bulky timepiece seemed heavier than before, the weight of expectation now resting on its bezel. I crossed my fingers that its value to the locals had not be overestimated.

I was determined not to waste my remaining time with Zahra and insisted we take a walk downtown like we did before things came tumbling down. We walked slower that time and sat on the corniche with the sea lapping at the shore and the call to prayer echoing from minaret to mountain wall. When we finally returned to the villa we could see Rashid's car had already returned, and Zahra sought out and squeezed my hand. I don't know what she was more afraid of: the realization that it was already time for me to leave or whether Rashid's ploy hadn't worked. I know which one I feared more.

As we entered the house Rashid was talking with Sanjeev, who was taking notes. Both stopped when they saw us with Rashid obviously unimpressed at the sight of us holding hands, no matter how briefly. Rashid beckoned me over as Sanjeev was dispatched elsewhere.

"You leave in the early hours of tomorrow morning." He handed me a passport under the name of Daniel Landon and a ticket to London. "The British Airways flight stops in Abu Dhabi but only to refuel so you should be fine."

"Thank you for everything."

"You are very welcome. You are a good man and I am happy to help you do the right thing. We are having a traditional farewell dinner for you tonight, for luck. You two better get ready."

Upstairs, my things had finished being packed aside from some travel clothes, my briefcase and wash things. Laying on the bed was a dishdash and massar that I could only begin to assemble myself. Sanjeev came to knock on my door and could see my confusion, kindly helping me with the massar. As I came down the stairs, I could see the rest of the family all dressed in their finery. Zahra looked stunning and Rashid was beaming alongside her. Behind them were some men I had last seen in a bleary heat-exhausted state, the morning they dropped me at the house. Far from the simple peasants they had appeared that dark desert night they were now dressed in full mess dress, greeting me respectfully with their hands over their chests. It felt grossly over-the-top but was the essence of Omani grace and hospitality. Rashid made the introductions: they had served under him during his career in the military where he first became close to Zahra's father. The men had brought their families with them and the evening had a joyful atmosphere despite what it signified. When it came time to eat the men and women ate in separate rooms, which struck me as a little strange but had its perks. One of the guests was not as devout as the others and cheekily offered me a sneaky sip from his flask.

As the night progressed, I became increasingly anxious of how much time I had left and who I was spending it with. After the meal the groups remained separated until Sanjeev came and tapped on my shoulder. It was time to head to the airport. I toured the room with my thanks and farewells, keeping Rashid until last and struggling to convey how much his hospitality and help had meant to me. He gave me Daniel's watch, something I was relieved to have back on my wrist knowing it had done its job and it was now my responsibility to see it through. I tried to venture to the other side of the house but it was not possible, instead being assured my thanks would be passed on to the ladies. I changed into more regular clothes and loitered on the stairs hoping to see a Zahra one last time, but time was running tight. I headed to the car feeling deflated, robbed of the goodbye I wanted above all. Imagine my relief when Sanjeev opened the back door and Zahra was sat in the other passenger seat.

I didn't know what to say. I spent most of the journey staring at the foot well and nervously ringing my hands together. In a reversal of positions, she placed her hand on mine to calm my nerves. As the car pulled up to the airport, Zahra and I got out while Sanjeev pulled my luggage from the boot. I thanked him for his efforts during my stay before turning to Zahra. She gave me a hearty hug that I would cherish going forward, something so small but was still so valuable. I began to regretfully walk towards the terminal when I heard Sanjeev say, "I won't tell anybody." I turned to see what he was talking about when Zahra nearly knocked me off my feet, leaping into my arms and kissing me like I had wished she would since Dubai. I couldn't help but grin as she pulled my neck downward and our noses brushed against one another.

"You promise to come back," she asked for reassurance.

"I already did. *Dictum meum pactum.*"

"I don't speak dead languages."

"'My word is my bond.' It's the motto of the London Stock Exchange."

She kept holding my hand as we started to go our separate ways, stretching out those final seconds of contact until our fingertips eventually parted. I didn't look back again as I walked into the terminal. It was time to put that part of my life to the back of my mind. I had a plane to catch and a job to do.

\* \* \* \* \*

"Start going short, I want the trades complete before he gets here."

I had no trouble at the airport and flew through departures, the passport working just as intended. Safely cocooned in my seat, I was able to request some homework and a long overdue gin. G&T in my right hand, copies of the Financial Times and Wall Street Journal in my left, I brought myself back up to speed with our portfolio. Scanning the tickers, I could see why David was so frustrated when I called from Dubai. BP had quickly receded back to the mid 400's. The best thing about the stock market is also the worst: things are always evolving, like a living organism. It was like catching up with an old friend after an extended absence and noticing how much they had changed in a way someone less familiar would barely notice. Looking over the historic data for the index, I saw a dip from my time in Dubai and dug up an article towards the back of the paper which indicated why. There had been another IRA bombing in London, this time in Ealing, and this time there were casualties. Why now? After several attacks with no loss of life, why now did we suddenly have fatalities? I wondered if it was like the bombing that killed Bertie, a cover rather than an attack and something to sow worry at home. I couldn't find the answers to that until I got back to London. By the time we had picked up some fuel and stragglers in Abu Dhabi and were flying high over the Arabian desert, I decided to tuck away my papers and force myself to get some shut eye before descending into the drizzly reality of Heathrow.

True to form, a damp and cloudy September morning bumped and slid us along the tarmacked welcome mat. I had the new experience of filling in a visitor's landing card, reminding myself several times of "my name" during the process. The border officer who greeted me gave me an easy ride, swallowing up my story of dual national who was yet to replenish his British papers. I took a taxi straight home, noticing a news board by the side of the road announcing the football results from the night before. Arsenal had been doing well and I knew at least one person would be pleased at that. Arriving at my flat I got the expected cockney welcome from Derek at the front desk.

"Look what the cat dragged in! I was starting to wonder if you would ever be coming back."

I trundled upstairs with a bag full of post that had built up since I was away. It was a strange feeling coming back to the flat, familiar but uneasy. My answering machine was full, as to be expected from an extended absence. I began to play over the messages and learned two things: television companies don't appreciate you forgetting their bill and mothers appreciate uninformed extended absences even less so. I ambled to the kitchen. I knew I would need to pop to the shops for some provisions but thought I had left some water in the fridge. When I opened the door, I was surprised to see fresh milk and juice sat in the door, and the hairs stood up on the back of my neck when I realized that someone else had been there before me.

The bedroom door was closed and I crept towards it. I kicked the door open but there was nobody there. Sat on the bed was a little box wrapped in a bow and a small typed note.

"Welcome home."

I unravelled the bow and popped open the box. Sat in a pristine box, sand-spattered and scratched, was my watch. I slammed the box shut like I had seen a ghost.

I frantically regathered my bag. I don't even remember if I shut the door when I left. As I got downstairs Derek was surprised to see me again so soon.

"Not off again are you?"

"Afraid so. Do you have that package I asked you to hold for me?"

"Certainly do. Been sat in the office ever since you gave it to me. I wondered if you had forgotten about it actually, was tempted to take a peek if I'd known the combination." He reached around the office door and pulled that dusty case from behind a cabinet.

"Fantastic." I scrolled in the combination and popped it open at the front desk, unzipped my bag and started stuffing the cash inside. Derek's eyes widened with shock. I doubt he had ever seen that much hard currency.

"Is this something I should pretend I never saw?"

"Not at all, it's all above board. Just can't trust banks as much these days." I took a few stacks of notes and handed them to him.

"Hush money, is it?"

"No, just think of it as your custodial fees. Take the wife away somewhere nice."

"Wow, well she's always wanted to go to America."

"Too cold this time of year, try the Bahamas."

I left the old case for Derek to dispose of and jumped into

Betsy. She had missed me. I embarked on a tour of London's seedier pseudo-financial institutions. The important thing was that they were happy to provide me with a deposit box without asking too many questions and willing to open up for me on a Sunday. With a bit of persuading I managed to open eight boxes in total, fifty thousand cash in each. I kept one lump in my possession and pulled up to my final destination in Eaton Gardens, the only place in London I could feel safe. Charlie answered the door and I pushed my way past him.

"Sorry Charlie, I need to speak to the old man."

"What are you doing here, Alex?"

"I can't stay home, Charlie, is David here?"

"Jesus. You've gotten yourself into a right fucking mess, haven't you? The old man is on his way to the states, signing new contracts. Now that we're face to face, are you going to tell me what the hell has been going on?"

"Can I stay here?"

"Always. You know which room to use."

I left my things at the door and we sat down at the kitchen table. I told him how things started in Libya, my meeting in Rome, Abu Shaytan, and the trail to Dubai. The Sheikh at the hospital and the chase which followed. I asked if he was aware of any American situations via his role as Procurator, which he denied. His best explanation was that they were pursuing me as a man who had been seen fraternizing with a known extremist. I broke the news to him about the list, watching as his eyes welled up thinking of Bertie and how all the colour drained from his face when I told him in as delicate a way as I could that his sister was missing.

"I just had an email from her a few days ago…"

"But have you seen or spoken to her? It could easily be part of the cover. Similar to how they used my phone to lure Bertie in. I hate to say it, Charlie, but I really think something could have happened. P is rotting Pactum from the inside, anyone who gets close to learning the truth is taken out."

"What could Amelia have known?"

"I don't know, maybe it was simply her connection to the three of us. We need to get hold of David as soon as possible, I can try to speak with Julian. See if there is anything we can do to get above P and put a stop to this. Do you think you can get a message stateside, alert the authorities?"

While I was trying to keep us focussed on the bigger picture, Charlie just stared over my shoulder at a picture of him and Amelia on the kitchen wall. Eventually, I stopped talking and just gave him a hug. It turned into a late night. I don't think we had a true heart to heart for a very long time, Charlie was more likely to plaster over his emotions with humour. So was I, for that matter.

Charlie shook me awake early the next morning, already dressed and far smarter than usual. I followed him downstairs where my coffee was already waiting. I was sure one day he would make someone a very good wife.

"Right, my friend, here's the plan. I've called a Pactum meeting for eight o'clock this morning, you're obviously persona non grata right now so I will meet with P alone. I will try and get a timeframe for this thing and will meet you in the club at eleven."

"Then what?"

"Get the information to the old man and crucify the cunt."

"Are you doing alright?"

"Of course."

"It's hard, Charlie, but you have to try and keep your

personal feelings out of this. We both have scores to settle but we can't lose our heads, nothing we do can change the past."

"I know that. Don't worry about me."

Before leaving the house I tried to reach Julian at his Parliamentary office but he was yet to return from summer break, running a few days behind schedule. I found a small phone book in a kitchen drawer and flicked over the pages searching for Dawes. I was sure David would have Julian's London number or mobile. Thankfully he had both and Julian was in town.

"Good morning."

"Julian, Alex Hope calling."

"Ah, hello young man. How are you?"

"Spot of bother I'm afraid, hoping you may be able to help."

"If I can, of course."

"Could you meet me at the club at 11:30?"

"Well, I have a meeting in Whitehall at eleven…"

"Pactum is compromised."

"I'll be there."

Perfect, Julian would give us the upper hand. I grabbed my case and jumped in Betsy. Time to head east. Charlie and Julian were bringing me ahead of the game. Finally.

\* \* \* \* \*

"Everything is in place."

"Good. Just follow our plan
and this all ends soon."

I was stood in the club checking Daniel's watch every few moments. At 11:15 I was starting to really worry about Charlie. I couldn't wait anymore. I retrieved my case from the front and hurried down the steps of the club, taking the sharp left turn to the office. The door was cracked open and as I jogged down the corridor the lift was waiting for me. When I reached upstairs there was no Joan behind the desk, her bank of phones lay strewn over the floor amongst scattered paperwork, the beeping of dead phone lines emanating from unhinged handsets. The hairs stood up on the back on my neck and I wished I was armed with more than my wits. The big double doors were ajar and I could hear voices from within. As I went closer, they became clearer: Charlie and P were in heated discussions with a third party. I opened the doors further and looked upon the cage.

Charlie and P stood around the table, analysing charts and dictating instruction to a speaker phone.

"Okay, Stephen, these are going to trade on CBOE, Chicago, we'll confirm on the floor. Puts for AMR and UAL."

"Should probably short the financials, too: Morgan's, Merrill's and B of A," added Charlie.

"Definitely. Stephen, we also want to go long on Raytheon

and Treasuries. That can all be done in New York. No rush."

"Alright. The boss approved these?"

"Of course. The old man asked me to call it in for him because of the time difference."

I edged closer to the cage, listening to the pending trades pile up for the US open. P's head snapped towards me like a startled cat. He cut the line to Stephen and leapt to the cage door, slamming it shut before pushing the bolt across. Charlie flicked the switch by his father's seat and the cage crackled to life.

"Piscator, so glad you could join us. You've been a busy boy."

"Not as busy as you, Patruus, or should that be Abu Shaytan?"

He stood defiant but nervous against me. He had grown to fear someone he had trained for compliance rather than conflict.

"You are confused, Alex. Think rationally, this is something we need to happen."

"Why? What can possibly justify this?"

"Do you know the story of Pearl Harbour?"

"I'm getting bored with history lessons."

"Well you're getting this one. We were being hammered by the Luftwaffe, our ships sunk by U-Boats and still the Americans wouldn't join the war. For two years we fought our corner begging for help. Begging! But all they sent were boats of supplies, knowing full well how many would end up at the bottom of the ocean."

"And you think that is a good enough reason to allow an attack against our closest ally?"

"Let me finish! Then one day we had actionable intelligence that the Japanese were going to bomb Pearl Harbour, and the decision was made not to warn the Americans. We knew it would drag them into the war with the weight of public opinion behind the President."

"How can you even compare that to this? We're not at war with anyone!"

"Open your eyes, Alex! The biggest problem we faced with the IRA was funding, the millions of dollars flowing in from America. Shaytan was born out of the necessity to stop the arms reaching them from Africa and the Middle East. Abu Shaytan, the son of the devil. The ghost that kept on giving and could evolve and change to suit the changing worlds and needs of foreign policy. You think I could let that die? I had hoped the Good Friday agreement would put an end to all the troubles. Abu Shaytan kept quiet, but in touch. You understand hedging, and that's exactly what this is: a little something up our sleeve just in case. If America learns what it's like to face terrorism, then maybe they will finally stop paying for it."

"There is peace in Northern Ireland!"

"Really? Then please explain Hammersmith Bridge, Hendon, the BBC, Ealing or having a rocket fired at my bloody office! All since they signed that damned agreement! We act in the best interests of the British people, and in this instance the best action is none."

"What about Russia? What about the hush money they paid you for the apartment bombings? What purpose did that serve in defence of Queen and country?"

"That was different. We went to them with the information and they ignored it. There was nothing we could do about it, so why shouldn't we profit from that situation?"

"People died! Innocent people died and you just walked away with your grubby pockets bursting with blood money! And now, with this, you find your own justification to do the same again. Taking your thirty pieces of silver in trade for morality." I was ashamed of my colleagues and the way they betrayed what the institution stood for.

"I don't expect you to understand it, but I do expect you to accept it. When current events are long forgotten and our people stop living in fear, maybe then you will understand."

"He's right, my friend," intervened Charlie. "It's not a pleasant calculation to make, but it's one that needs to be made. As for us, we should view it no different to any other investment opportunity." He came alongside P at the front of the cage. "There are times when no matter how unsavoury it may seem, the end does justify the means." He came closer to the bars and passed a small folded piece of paper between them. I quietly took it in my hand. He winked at me before making his play.

"Get to Pater!"

He grabbed P by the wrist with one hand and grabbed the bars of the cage with the other. The bars started to spark and whine as the two of them convulsed between each burst of current. Bolts of electricity shot from one side of the cage to the other and the lights around the room shattered one by one. I could see every muscle and sinew in Charlie tighten to the point of bursting and his teeth begin to crack under the pressure. Smoke was coming from his fingers and his eyes clenched tightly closed. Like boys playing with an electric fence, it was the one at the end of the line who received the biggest jolt. In this instance, it was P. He was stiff as a statue and slowly turning black, smoke gushing from his collar and mouth as flames began to ignite around the metal of his cufflinks. With a mighty bang the table at the centre jumped a good two foot in the air as the fuses in the switch finally blew. The table itself began to smoulder but the cage murmured back down as its power drained.

P fell forward, tense, blistered and lifeless, smelling like the forgotten fat at the bottom of a hot oven. Charlie, on the other hand, collapsed in a pile by the bars, his fingers red raw and welded in place. He was kneeling but limp with the full curve of his spine visible and his head almost touching the floor. I reached through the bars to touch him as he slowly raised his head, taking the deepest breath he could and squeezing out one word.

"…Pater…"

With that he wilted, to the floor again. I opened the little piece of paper he gave me and saw the address of a Chicago office. I looked across at P's corpse with absolute disdain, I still felt that death was too good for him, but looked on it as the end of his deception. Abu Shaytan had truly become a ghost. I closed my eyes for a second and nodded my head in solidarity with Charlie before running to the door. If we were shorting stock now, the attack had to be imminent; there was no time to spare. I needed to get to David in Chicago, pull the plug and warn the US authorities. I considered going straight to New York, but without the evidence from Chicago I would have faced certain arrest before they'd listen. The meeting with the Sheikh had cast a long shadow. I ran full speed out of the door towards my car. A shout came over my right shoulder as I pushed the key fob to unlock the doors.

"Alex!"

It was Julian stood on the steps of the club. Before I could answer him I was blown back against the wall by a blinding explosion, smashing my head against the stonework. The last thing I remember seeing was the black smoke billowing into the London sky before I briefly lost consciousness.

I came to with a paramedic standing over me and could feel the various cuts to my front from the glass. I was lucky: running my hands down myself I couldn't find any serious shrapnel wounds. My ears were ringing and painful, and putting my hands up, I felt blood oozing from the left one. Behind the paramedic I could see what was left of my car, a cindered shell surrounded by strangers in fluorescent jackets. I couldn't make out the words the paramedic was saying but I could see Julian talking with police and tried to get his attention. He ran to my side and shooed the paramedic away. I was shaking my head to clear my ears and grimacing as I clambered to my feet. Julian kept repeating the same question until I could finally understand what he was saying.

"Where's David? Where's David? Alex, can you hear me?"

"I've got to get to him," I gasped. "I need to get to the airport."

"What the hell happened, where are the others?" I pointed at the office door, shook my head and ran a finger across my throat.

"Jesus Christ," was all Julian could say. I grabbed his shoulders to pull his attention back to me and almost lost my footing. I gave him I simple and short message.

"Find Peter Jayms. Call the Libyan Embassy in Knightsbridge and tell them to call Hannibal Gaddafi. Just say Alex Hope told you to call Peter. He can tell you everything." I handed him the crumpled note Charlie had given me and turned to leave.

"Where the hell are you going? We need to get you to a hospital!"

"Chicago! I have to get to Pater!" I staggered down the street, slowly getting my legs under control and building into a jog. This time, they weren't going to fail me. I ran into the nearest pharmacy and bought some baby wipes and the strongest painkillers I could get without prescription, not that they would do much more than take the edge off. My shock and adrenaline were keeping the pain at bay, but I knew it couldn't last. I was looked up and down several times by the lady at terminal 3. I could tell by her concerned look she was wondering why I needed a first-class ticket to Chicago with no bags to check and blood stains down my shirt. Rather than probing me too closely she simply asked, "Are you okay, sir?" I replied with the best excuse I could come with at the time. "Yes, just fell off my bicycle." Thankfully, apart from stronger medication, duty free in the terminal was able to provide everything else I needed.

\* \* \* \* \*

"Jet on standby sir."

"Thank you, have the car waiting and get me a secure line."

As the seatbelt light flashed on and its informative tone sounded around the cabin, I woke to the extreme soreness I had been expecting. I pounded a handful of paracetamol and washed them down with a viciously negotiated collection of miniature whisky bottles. It was late on Monday night in Chicago and I was wishing Charlie could have given me the hotel address for David rather than the office. It was an easy address for me to remember: 311 South Wacker, Office 37-1. It was a long shot, but I went to see if David was still at the office, or maybe they could tell me where to find him. I got out of my taxi and strained my neck looking up at what was then the Sears Tower opposite. The Board of Trade was a short distance east at the end of La Salle and I looked forward to seeing it in person when all was done. I hadn't lived the open outcry era in London and envied the American situation with an active pit still being used and broadcast round the world. I think most of us in the mile longed for the romance of those days, now only found at the metals exchange.

I went to enter the office building, but the front door was locked. A plump and sleepy-looking security guard was perched nearby and seemed devastated at the prospect of walking a full twenty yards to see what I wanted. He opened the door just a crack to check my enquiry. I explained I was from the London office of SC Securities and wanted to see if Mr. Smyth-Cummin was still at the office. "Office 37-1," I added, holding out a business card for his reference. He took the card and closed the door, walking back to his little podium and picking up the phone. After talking on the phone for a few minutes he came back to me and opened the door.

"They can see you."

Surprised that David was still in the office, but equally relieved, I walked across to the lift with and hit the button for the 37th floor. When the doors opened I was facing a small foyer. The lights were so dim I could hardly make out any features beyond where the lights from the lift could reach. Black foam covered the walls and a single ominous door faced me. As I stepped onto the floor the lights slowly became brighter and a tall man came to greet me. He looked to be a similar age to myself, but had typically American hair and the colonial habit of wearing a pocketed shirt with suit trousers.

"Mr. Hope, welcome to Chicago. I'm JJ." He led me through the door to what I initially thought was a trading floor. Rather than stock tickers there were maps, clear glass projections with movements of personnel and TVs showing rolling news from around the world. This wasn't a trading floor; it was a command centre. I followed JJ round the periphery into a small white out room. There were cameras in the top corners, a mirrored wall and some sparse furnishing: a toilet sat against one wall and a stainless steel table and chairs were bolted to the floor in the middle. We sat at the table and JJ spoke out in his southern twang.

"Roll tape. Alex Hope, British national and person of

interest. JJ Angle conducting the interview. 2100 hours. September 10th 2001."

"I'm sorry, but I think there has been some sort of misunderstanding, I was asked to come here to meet Mr. Smyth-Cummin."

"He will be here in the morning, sir, but I just have a few questions for you. What can you tell me about your relationship with 'The Sheikh'?"

"I met the man once."

"Where was that sir?"

"You already know that…" There was a knock at the door and another American entered the interview, one I was already familiar with. It was the station chief I had seen at the hospital in Dubai, only now he was on home turf.

"Sorry JJ, can I join this one?"

"Sure thing, Mike."

"Thanks. Hi."

"Hello again," I replied.

"Stop tape," he said as he glanced towards the mirrored wall. "Why are you here?"

"I came here to meet a colleague of mine. I am trying to prevent what I believe to be a plot to attack the United States."

"Go on."

"There has been a deliberate attempt by the now-former head of the Secret Intelligence Service to not report the attack to the CIA. I believe a group led by The Sheikh plans to fly a small aircraft loaded with explosives into the North Tower of the World Trade Center in New York. An extension of the truck attack in 1993."

"What are you basing this information on?"

"The actions of my native service and my conversation

with The Sheikh in Dubai. You were there, surely we're on the same page?"

He shook his head and sighed, pulled a supressed 1911 from inside his jacket and sent a single 45 calibre hollow point into the back of JJ's head, passing through with perfect expansion before bedding itself in the metal table top. JJ's head rocked back and he slid off his chair to the floor.

"You couldn't just mind your own goddamn business, could you? You just couldn't leave it alone. Hope you're happy, another one to add to your body count."

"I'm sure it's nothing compared to yours."

"True. I'd be happy to add one more, but the banker wants to see you in the morning. Hope you're comfortable."

"I've stayed in worse."

"Oh, then you won't be needing anything from me, right?"

"Bottle of scotch, a pillow, some blankets…something to read would be nice, help pass the time."

"You're kidding me?"

"I never joke about scotch or literature." As you can imagine, he didn't appreciate the snarky comment. I was provided with none of those things. All my personal items were taken from me, but in a stroke of luck JJ had a pack of Marlboros and some matches in his pocket. The night was long, but the jet lag was working in my favour. The parallels between the Russian play and the current situation were stacking up: the timing of a new presidency, the foreign policy ambition and those on either side who were happy to let it happen. P's fingerprints were all over it, only this time he had the luxury of domestic market access thanks to Charlie's project.

Come the morning, Mike came back and escorted me to a different office on the same floor. He didn't manhandle me in any way, but he didn't need to. I was led into a plush room with a view out across to the Sears Tower and back up Wacker, the early morning sun shimmering off the glass megastructures in front of me. David's office within the CIA command centre could only mean one thing: I had wasted my time. He had been building himself a nice nest after turning to the other side. If it wasn't for the view, I could easily imagine we were back in London. There was even an old school picture of Charlie and me on the wall and one of the siblings on a ski trip.

"Take a seat, Mr Smyth-Cummin will be here soon."

Mike left me on the sofa for a few moments and returned later with the man he had previously called 'the banker'.

"Good morning, my friend, welcome to my Chicago digs. Good trip?"

Charlie was half the man he used to be. His front teeth now missing, giant red bags under his eyes joined the black and yellow bruising round his jaw and neck. Bandages were wrapped around both hands, leaving just his red raw fingers visible at the tips of the cloth. He limped into the room and across to his desk. I sat dumbfounded, heartbroken and speechless. He pulled my briefcase out from underneath and slammed it on the desk.

"What's the code, Alex?" I didn't answer. "Hmmm, could it be..." he scrolled in a combination "...ah, yes. P-A-C-T-U-M. Didn't even bother to change it. What do we have here, my friend, wow! Would you look at this: fraudulent travel documents, notes from a meeting when you offered to launder money for a known terrorist...you know you're not permitted to bring more than $10,000 of hard currency into the United States, don't you?"

"Why, Charlie? What in God's name are you thinking?"

311

"Thinking? No, my friend, you're the thinker, remember? I'm the one who just does his job."

I stood up and walked slowly and calmly towards his desk, hoping to bring some reason into his scope.

"The people. Jesus Charlie, the people who have died. The people who are going to die. Think of Bertie. Think of Penny. Think. Of. Your. Sister."

"The people, ah yes. Thank you for reminding me." He heaved himself out of his seat and gingerly made his way to the bookshelves where three televisions had been sat idle. Holding onto one shelf, for support he flicked them on. One had CNN, the other Bloomberg, and the final one a CCTV stream. "Come along, you don't want to miss the big show now." I reluctantly pandered to his request and went to his side. We both stood there and just stared. Waiting. He knew exactly what for and I had a sinking inclination I was outfoxed and out of time. "Just here. Watch now." He tapped on the black and white CCTV screen that showed a solitary man waking an empty office.

"Aha! There she goes! Ha ha ha! Right on schedule!" He was practically hopping with excitement as the boom bounced out of the television and the image shook furiously. Static started to strain the image and the subject ran to the window and looked down. The feed from CNN switched to an accident, then Bloomberg. Biblical images of destruction took over the airwaves as flames erupted from the side of the North Tower. I could barely believe my eyes nor his reaction. Charlie held his arms in the air in triumph turning to me as if he expected my congratulations. Mike was smiling in agreement with Charlie's jubilance.

"My god. How much explosive did they pack in that plane?"

"What are you talking about? There aren't any explosives. Just twenty thousand gallons of jet fuel between them." I didn't understand his calculation; there was no way that would fit in a smaller aircraft. "They're jet liners, Alex. That was the American Airlines flight to Los Angeles. This next one is United 175, again for Los Angeles." I remember thinking The Sheikh must have had a worse time in California than Indiana judging by his flight choice.

"Next one?" As I asked the question, the next jet smashed into the South Tower with even greater speed and devastation than the first. The news readers on television looked as terrified as I was and the CCTV feed blurred with smoke filling the room.

"How could you? How could you Charlie! Hundreds of people are dying!"

"It's not like it's my fault, my friend. It's not my plan, and I was never in a position to stop it either. If either of us has blood on our hands, it's you. We never asked you to tell Bertie about the Lovegood meeting, we never forced you to compromise Penny's position. You did that all by yourself."

"I never would have done any of it had I known the implications! What the fuck happened to you?!"

"I found my place, Alex, and an opportunity landed on my side of the table. I grabbed it with both hands and have watched you chase your tail ever since. P had no idea how to monetize this, he didn't even consider that we would have allies in this country who were just as eager as us to see it through." Charlie pulled a blue-covered book from the shelf above the televisions, holding it up inches from my face. "*Rebuilding America's Defenses from The Project for the New American Century*! I quote, 'the process for transformation, even if it brings revolutionary change, is likely to be a long one, absent some catastrophic and catalyzing event – like a new Pearl Harbor'. A new Pearl Harbour, Alex! As soon as I saw this, I knew I could find allies on this side. It didn't come cheap, though. Takes a lot of shares to buy your own CIA agents and set up an office, but your ADR idea made it much simpler." Charlie was beginning to hobble round the room and preach his justifications to me. "Everybody wins here: funding stops for the IRA, the American people are united and galvanized behind a new administration, the US has an excuse to begin campaigns in the Middle East, securing the oil supply they need for the next fifty years. In the middle sits Pactum, making an absolute killing. We never could have stopped this, so why shouldn't we at least profit from it? We are going to need more funding in the future than ever before, with technology moving quicker than we ever thought possible and us lagging decades behind. Someday, our successors will look back and say I was the one who brought Pactum forward into the 21st century."

"You are so far from what Pactum stands for, Charlie. Your father told me that with every action we hold ourselves to the highest moral standards, weighing every action as to whether or not it is right and in the best interests of the people."

"Exactly! The best interests of the *British* people. This fits that criteria and you are still arguing over it."

"If Pater were here Charlie, he would be ashamed of you."

"Oh, he is here my friend; he was always going to be. How's he getting along?"

Charlie was gesturing to the CCTV feed, which I approached heatedly. I looked closer. The smoke had cleared when the windows broke. I began to lean in. My knees and waist creaked in careful unison as I brought myself inches from the screen. I pulled away to rub my eyes, hoping to find both clarity and relief. Having secured neither, I calmed myself and attempted to digest what was playing out in front of me. A familiar figure, caught in silhouette against a cascade of fire, mayhem all around him and yet there he stood; stock still.

*Breathe…just breathe…,* I silently told myself in tempered repetition.

The man checked his watch, took a deep breath and tapped its face. His time was up. All I could think was that I mustn't react, but my hands and the foundations of that distant city began to quake. I fought back against myself, but despite all the training behind me, I broke. While he started his inevitable descent and the feed turned black, I began my own. Clinging to the shelving for support, my knees buckled beneath me. The outpouring of emotion erupted like a spasm in my chest, my stunted breathing firing out of my lungs every few seconds.

As the dust and screaming rose toward the skyline on the global news, I fell firmly to the floor and wept: partly in grief, mostly in guilt and blindly hoping for forgiveness from whatever higher power may be watching the moment in silent disgust.

"Your father should have labelled you Proditor rather than Procurator," I said between breaths.

"Traitor, how quaint and still so pompous. That's rich coming from the one who turned his back to the cage!"

"This isn't the fucking zoo, Charlie! That was your father!"

"Yes, and he would agree with me. He always put the job before his family."

"There is a big difference between absent parents and murder! I don't even know who you are anymore!"

"Don't be so fucking dramatic. There is no way Pactum could survive into the future while Pater kept it trapped in the dark ages."

"Whether it survived or not, at least it did so with a clear conscience."

"I'm sorry my friend, we could argue like this until the cows come home but I have business to attend to. Now is that crucial moment when you must decide who you are. Are you the fisherman or just another wet fish?"

"I'm neither. I'm not like you. This is not what I signed up for."

"Choose your words carefully, Alex. You are not in a position to negotiate." Mike came up to me, still knelt on the floor, and pointed his 1911 between my eyes.

I was faced with little choice. I looked away from the muzzle of the pistol and towards the televisions. Running over the cost to myself and that of humanity.

"Sorry to push you, my friend, but you don't have long to make your mind up here. You should consider yourself lucky to even be given the chance."

I turned to my old friend bleary-eyed and despondent, tears running down my face in ultimate defeat. We looked at each other for a moment and I opened my mouth to speak.

"Charlie, I..." I stopped. My attention was drawn to something on the floor. Something minute but massive in its implications. A red dot that walked its way across the floor and up Mike's leg, finally stopping at his chest.

"Charlie, I must regretfully decline," I said, rubbing my eyes and clearing my throat.

"Are you sure?"

"Absolutely."

"I am sorry to hear that. Very sorry. Funny to think that we couldn't get you in Libya or London. Mike came close in Dubai, but again you slipped away. Lucky for him, he gets another bite of the cherry. Who needs the Incident Team when you have the Americans right?"

"I do."

The glass behind me puckered and split as the round passed overhead and hit Mike centre mass. He dropped his gun and clutched at his chest, stumbling back a few paces before falling into Charlie's desk. It was Charlie's turn to look shocked as I got to my feet and straightened my tie. I picked up Mike's sidearm, checking the chamber for brass as the phone rang on Charlie's desk.

"You should probably answer that."

He pushed the speaker button. "Yes?"

"Good morning, Charlie. How are you?"

"Jules?"

"Yes. Small favour to ask, my boy, would you mind awfully if I borrowed Alex for a moment?" Charlie remained tight-lipped and looked at me with hateful eyes as he weighed up the situation. He waited too long and another round zipped across the room, hitting Charlie in the shoulder. It knocked him over his chair and left him sprawled over the floor.

"Fuck...fuck!"

"Charlie, language please," commented Julian over the speaker. "Come along, Alex, I don't think there's any reason to hang about up there."

"Will do." I killed the call, then crouched down over Charlie while he bit his lip and pushed down hard on the shoulder wound with his other hand.

"You know what I have to do now?"

"You don't have the balls."

"Unlike you, I have done this before..." I put the pistol to his chest, just like I had with Tom, "...and you deserve this far more than he did." Unlike Tom though, he didn't react. No pleading, no effort to move whatsoever. Didn't even close his eyes, just looked straight into mine and dared me to pull the trigger. I wanted to do it, but couldn't. He hand been found out and found lacking. The ghost was dead, the game was up. There was no reason to add any more bloodshed to a day that had more than it could possibly deserve. I gathered my things and went to leave, Charlie still laying there.

"Do you know what people with money and power want, my friend? It's always been the same, whatever the generation and no matter the country," he asked as I approached the door.

"What's that, Charlie?"

"More. You're the same, always wanting to push ahead academically or professionally. Wanting more recognition, more control and greater reward. We were like family, yet you side with them."

"I don't side with anyone. Just with what I believe to be right. Despite what you believe, I've simply had enough of all of those things."

I left him where he was and walked out to the command hub. It was manic after the events of the morning. Phones ringing, people shouting across the room and papers being flung between desks by some, while others ran into conference calls. Maybe it was like a trading floor after all.

The lobby downstairs was busy with people huddled round televisions or desperately contacting friends and colleagues in New York. Deafening screams and panicked tears echoed off the marble cladding as they came to terms with the shock and magnitude of what was happening to their country. It was under attack. They were now at war.

Immediately outside the door was an ambulance, tinted windows on all sides and the lights turned off. Once I reached the pavement the driver's side window went down and I saw

Harry in the seat, pointing to the back with his thumb. I opened the back doors and stepped inside, Harry fired up the lights and sirens to cut us the cleanest route out of the city. Peter was sat in the jump seat and Julian on the stretcher. I took a seat next to Julian and shook hands with them both. We were all very sombre, feeling for the people of New York. We had failed them. Julian handed me a letter written in that old green ink.

"You can't win them all. It's yours now. David" It tugged on a nerve as its true meaning sunk in.

"Where do you want to go?" asked Julian.

"What are our choices?"

"Well, all flights are grounded. Not sure for how long," Peter added.

"How far to Washington?" I wondered.

"No-go, I'm afraid. They had another jet hit the Pentagon and it would take too long to drive there."

"Shit…any other ideas?" With no answer coming from the old guard I leant forwards and yelled towards the front of the vehicle.

"Harry, know anywhere we can go?"

"Old pal of mine from Desert Storm lives in Milwaukee."

"Seems as good an idea as any, Milwaukee it is."

"Right you are, Pater."


\* \* \* \* \*


"He got away."

"I saw."

"What now?"

"This doesn't change anything, proceed as planned."

"Yes, Mater."

*Hamilton sat quietly that late afternoon, no longer requiring clarification on why I had come to him. As the bar started to fill with guests eager for pre-dinner drinks, it was time to bring our meeting to a close.*

*"I'm sure you have some questions?" I asked.*

*"I, I don't know where to start. The cost, the human cost of it all…"*

*"17,241.39 USD per unit at our last valuation. Civilians are a strikingly volatile commodity; supply seems to keep on growing, but demand is only revealed in hindsight."*

*"You have an exact number?"*

*"It's just one of the many reasons I'd had enough."*

*"I have so many questions."*

*"I had a feeling this would take more than one meeting before you're ready to print. I've taken the liberty of getting you a suite upstairs, that way we can continue our discussions tomorrow."*

*"No, I'm good. Got an Airbnb across town but I can come back tomorrow."*

*I stood from our table, finished my glass of wine, and checked around the room. I'd kept a man close by and he confirmed the coast was clear.*

*"I don't know who you're trying to impress with the struggling journalist routine…" I tapped a photograph on a newspaper I'd*

*brought with me before tucking it under my arm "…but I'm sure the Secretary of State would prefer you stay somewhere more secure. Parents worry about stuff like that and this city can be harsh on the inexperienced."*

*Hamilton smirked. "I should've known you'd do your homework. You got kids?"*

*"There's a nobility in creating your own path. I can respect that."*

*"You didn't answer my question."*

*"I know. Tomorrow perhaps."*

*"Sure." I shook Hamilton's hand and went on my way. Hamilton shrugged and gathered his things together in a fashionably tatty satchel before catching up with me as I signed for my bill at the bar. "So that was the 'him' that brought you to me? Abu Shaytan was what stopped you?"*

*"Yes."*

*"But you said he died." I put my older and more experienced hand on his naive shoulder, as David had done with me all those years before.*

*"Ghosts don't die, young man. They can't. Have a good evening."*

THE END

CPSIA information can be obtained
at www.ICGtesting.com
Printed in the USA
BVHW041744250719
554236BV00041B/1042/P